GOD'S COUNTRY
AND THE WOMAN

James Oliver Curwood

1st WORLD
LIBRARY
Literary Society

God's Country - And the Woman

James Oliver Curwood

© 1st World Library – Literary Society, 2006
PO Box 2211
Fairfield, IA 52556
www.1stworldlibrary.org
First Edition

LCCN: 2006905714

Softcover ISBN: 1-4218-2143-5
Hardcover ISBN: 1-4218-2043-9
eBook ISBN: 1-4218-2243-1

Purchase *"God's Country - And the Woman"*
as a traditional bound book at:
www.1stWorldLibrary.org/purchase.asp?ISBN=1-4218-2143-5

1st World Library Literary Society is a nonprofit
organization dedicated to promoting literacy by:

- Creating a free internet library accessible from any
  computer worldwide.
- Hosting writing competitions and offering book
  publishing scholarships.

**Readers interested in supporting literacy
through sponsorship, donations or
membership please contact:
literacy@1stworldlibrary.org
Check us out at: www.1stworldlibrary.ORG
and start downloading free ebooks today.**

CHAPTER ONE

Philip Weyman's buoyancy of heart was in face of the fact that he had but recently looked upon Radisson's unpleasant death, and that he was still in a country where the water flowed north. He laughed and he sang. His heart bubbled over with cheer. He talked to himself frankly and without embarrassment, asked himself questions, answered them, discussed the beauties of nature and the possibilities of storm as if there were three or four of him instead of one.

At the top end of the world a man becomes a multiple being - if he is white. Two years along the rim of the Arctic had taught Philip the science by which a man may become acquainted with himself, and in moments like the present, when both his mental and physical spirits overflowed, he even went so far as to attempt poor Radisson's "La Belle Marie" in the Frenchman's heavy basso, something between a dog's sullen growl and the low rumble of distant thunder. It made him cough. And then he laughed again, scanning the narrowing sweep of the lake ahead of him.

He felt like a boy, and he chuckled as he thought of the definite reason for it. For twenty-three months he had been like a piece of rubber stretched to a tension - sometimes almost to the snapping point. Now had come the reaction, and he was going HOME. Home! It was that one word that caused a shadow to flit over his face, and only once or twice had he forgotten and let it slip between his lips. At least he was returning to civilization - getting AWAY from the everlasting drone of breaking ice and the clack-clack tongue of the Eskimo.

With the stub of a pencil Philip had figured out on a bit of paper about where he was that morning. The whalebone hut of his last Arctic camp was eight hundred miles due north. Fort Churchill, over on Hudson's Bay, was four hundred miles to the east, and Fort Resolution, on the Great Slave, was four hundred miles to the west. On his map he had drawn a heavy circle about Prince Albert, six hundred miles to the south. That was the nearest line of rail. Six days back Radisson had died after a mouth's struggle with that terrible thing they called "le mort rouge," or the Red Death. Since then Philip had pointed his canoe straight UP the Dubawnt waterways, and was a hundred and twenty miles nearer to civilization. He had been through these waterways twice before, and he knew that there was not a white man within a hundred and fifty miles of him. And as for a white woman -

Weyman stopped his paddling where there was no current, and leaned back in his canoe for a breathing space, and to fill his pipe. A WHITE WOMAN! Would he stare at her like a fool when he saw her again for the first time? Eighteen months ago he had seen a white woman over at Fort Churchill - the English clerk's wife, thirty, with a sprinkle of gray in her blond hair, and pale blue eyes. Fresh from the Garden of Eden, he had wondered why the half-dozen white men over there regarded her as they did. Long ago, in the maddening gloom of the Arctic night, he had learned to understand. At Fond du Lac, when Weyman had first come up into the forest country, he had said to the factor: "It's glorious! It's God's Country!" And the factor had turned his tired, empty eyes upon him with the words: "It was - before SHE went. But no country is God's Country without a woman," and then he took Philip to the lonely grave under a huge lob-stick spruce, and told him in a few words how one woman had made life for him. Even then Philip could not fully understand. But he did now.

He resumed his paddling, his gray eyes alert. His aloneness and the bigness of the world in which, so far as he knew, he was the only human atom, did not weigh heavily upon him. He loved this bigness and emptiness and the glory of solitude. It was middle autumn, and close to noon of a day unmarred by cloud above, and warm with sunlight. He was following close to the west shore of the lake. The opposite shore was a mile away. He was so near to the rock-lined beach that he could hear the soft throat-cries of the moose-birds. And what he saw, so far as his eyes could see in all directions, was "God's Country" - a glory of colour that was like a great master painting. The birch had turned to red and gold. From out of the rocks rose trees that were great crimson splashes of mountain-ash berries framed against the dark lustre of balsam and cedar and spruce.

Without reason, Philip was listening again to the quiet lifeless words of Jasper, the factor over at Fond du Lac, as he described the day when he and his young wife first came up through the wonderland of the North. "No country is God's Country without a woman!" He found the words running in an unpleasant monotone through his brain. He had made up his mind that he would strike Fond du Lac on his way down, for Jasper's words and the hopeless picture he had made that day beside the little cross under the spruce had made them brothers in a strange sort of way. Besides, Jasper would furnish him with a couple of Indians, and a sledge and dogs if the snows came early.

In a break between the rocks Philip saw a white strip of sand, and turned his canoe in to shore. He had been paddling since five o'clock, and in the six hours had made eighteen miles. Yet he felt no fatigue as he stood up and stretched himself. He remembered how different it had been four years ago when Hill, the Hudson's Bay Company's man down at Prince Albert, had looked him over with skeptical and uneasy eyes, encouraging him with the words: "You're going to a funeral, young man, and it's your own. You won't make God's House, much less Hudson's Bay!"

Weyman laughed joyously.

"Fooled 'em - fooled 'em all!" he told himself. "We'll wager a dollar to a doughnut that we're the toughest looking specimen that ever drifted down from Coronation Gulf, or any other gulf. A DOUGHNUT! I'd trade a gold nugget as big as my fist for a doughnut or a piece of pie right this minute. Doughnuts an' pie - real old pumpkin pie - an' cranberry sauce, 'n' POTATOES! Good Lord, and they're only six hundred miles away, carloads of 'em!"

He began to whistle as he pulled his rubber dunnage sack out of the canoe. Suddenly he stopped, his eyes staring at the smooth white floor of sand. A bear had been there before him, and quite recently. Weyman had killed fresh meat the day before, but the instinct of the naturalist and the woodsman kept him from singing or whistling, two things which he was very much inclined to do on this particular day. He had no suspicion that a bear which he was destined never to see had become the greatest factor in his life. He was philosopher enough to appreciate the value and importance of little things, but the bear track did not keep him silent because he regarded it as significant, because he wanted to kill. He would have welcomed it to dinner, and would have talked to it were it as affable and good-mannered as the big pop-eyed moose-birds that were already flirting about near him.

He emptied a half of the contents of the rubber sack out on the sand and made a selection for dinner, and he chuckled in his big happiness as he saw how attenuated his list of supplies was becoming. There was still a quarter of a pound of tea, no sugar, no coffee, half a dozen pounds of flour, twenty-seven prunes jealously guarded in a piece of narwhal skin, a little salt and pepper mixed, and fresh caribou meat.

"It's a lovely day, and we'll have a treat for dinner," he informed himself. "No need of starving. We'll have a real feast. I'll cook SEVEN prunes instead of five!"

He built a small fire, hung two small pots over it, selected his prunes, and measured out a tablespoonful of black tea. In the respite he had while the water heated he dug a small mirror out of the sack and looked at himself. His long, untrimmed hair was blond, and the inch of stubble on his face was brick red. There were tiny creases at the corners of his eyes, caused by the blistering sleet and cold wind of the Arctic coast. He grimaced as he studied himself. Then his face lighted up with sudden inspiration.

"I've got it!" he exclaimed. "I need a shave! We'll use the prune water."

From the rubber bag he fished out his razor, a nubbin of soap, and a towel. For fifteen minutes after that he sat cross-legged on the sand, with the mirror on a rock, and worked. When he had finished he inspected himself closely.

"You're not half bad," he concluded, and he spoke seriously now. "Four years ago when you started up here you were thirty - and you looked forty. Now you're thirty-four, and if it wasn't for the snow lines in your eyes I'd say you were a day or two younger. That's pretty good."

He had washed his face and was drying it with the towel when a sound made him look over beyond the rocks. It was the crackling sound made by a dead stick stepped upon, or a sapling broken down. Either meant the bear.

Dropping the towel, he unbuttoned the flap to the holster of his revolver, took a peep to see how long he could leave the water before it would boil, and stepped cautiously in the direction of the sound. A dozen paces beyond the bulwark of rocks he came upon a fairly well-worn moose trail; surveying its direction from the top of a boulder, he made up his mind that the bear was dining on mountain-ash berries where he saw one of the huge crimson splashes of the fruit a hundred yards away.

He went on quietly. Under the big ash tree there was no sign of a feast, recent or old. He proceeded, the trail turning almost at right angles from the ash tree, as if about to bury itself in the deeper forest. His exploratory instinct led him on for another hundred yards, when the trail swung once more to the left. He heard the swift trickling run of water among rocks, and again a sound. But his mind did not associate the sound which he heard this time with the one made by the bear. It was not the breaking of a stick or the snapping of brush. It was more a part of the musical water-sound itself, a strange key struck once to interrupt the monotone of a rushing stream.

Over a gray hog-back of limestone Philip climbed to look down into a little valley of smooth-washed boulders and age-crumbled rock through which the stream picked its way. He descended to the white margin of sand and turned sharply to the right, where a little pool had formed at the base of a huge rock. And there he stopped, his heart in his throat, every fibre in his body charged with a sudden electrical thrill at what he beheld. For a moment he was powerless to move. He stood - and stared.

At the edge of the pool twenty steps from him was kneeling a woman. Her back was toward him, and in that moment she was as motionless as the rock that towered over her. Along with the rippling drone of the stream, without reason on his part - without time for thought-there leaped through his amazed brain the words of Jasper, the factor, and he knew that he was looking upon the miracle that makes "God's Country" - a white woman!

The sun shone down upon her bare head. Over her slightly bent shoulders swept a glory of unbound hair that rippled to the sand. Black tresses, even velvety as the crow's wing, might have meant Cree or half-breed. But this at which he stared - all that he saw of her - was the brown and gold of the autumnal tintings that had painted pictures for him that day.

Slowly she raised her head, as if something had given her warning of a presence behind, and as she hesitated in that birdlike, listening poise a breath of wind from the little valley stirred her hair in a shimmering veil that caught a hundred fires of the sun. And then, as he crushed back his first impulse to cry out, to speak to her, she rose erect beside the pool, her back still to him, and hidden to the hips in her glorious hair.

Her movement revealed a towel partly spread out on the sand, and a comb, a brush, and a small toilet bag. Philip did not see these. She was turning, slowly, scanning the rocks beyond the valley.

Like a thing carven out of stone he stood, still speechless, still staring, when she faced him.

CHAPTER TWO

A face like that into which Philip looked might have come to him from out of some dream of paradise. It was a girl's face. Eyes of the pure blue of the sky above met his own. Her lips were a little parted and a little laughing. Before he had uttered a word, before he could rise out of the stupidity of his wonder, the change came. A fear that he could not have forgotten if he had lived through a dozen centuries leaped into the lovely eyes. The half-laughing lips grew tense with terror. Quick as the flash of powder there had come into her face a look that was not that of one merely startled. It was fear - horror - a great, gripping thing that for an instant seemed to crush the life from her soul. In another moment it was gone, and she swayed back against the face of the rock, clutching a hand at her breast.

"My God, how I frightened you!" gasped Philip.

"Yes, you frightened me," she said.

Her white throat was bare, and he could see the throb of it as she made a strong effort to speak steadily. Her eyes did not leave him. As he advanced a step he saw that unconsciously she cringed closer to the rock.

"You are not afraid - now?" he asked. "I wouldn't have frightened you for the world. And sooner than hurt you I'd - I'd kill myself. I just stumbled here by accident. And I haven't seen a white woman - for two years. So I stared - stared - and stood there like a fool."

James Oliver Curwood

Relief shot into her eyes at his words.

"Two years? What do you mean?"

"I've been up along the rim of h - I mean the Arctic, on a government wild-goose chase," he explained. "And I'm just coming down."

"You're from the North?"

There was an eager emphasis in her question.

"Yes. Straight from Coronation Gulf. I ran ashore to cook a mess of prunes. While the water was boiling I came down here after a bear, and found YOU! My name is Philip Weyman; I haven't even an Indian with me, and there are three things in the world I'd trade that name for just now: One is pie, another is doughnuts, and the third -"

She brushed back her hair, and the fear went from her eyes as she looked at him.

"And the third?" she asked.

"Is the answer to a question," he finished. "How do YOU happen to be here, six hundred miles from anywhere?"

She stepped out from the rock. And now he saw that she was almost as tall as himself, and that she was as slim as a reed and as beautifully poised as the wild narcissus that sways like music to every call of the wind. She had tucked up her sleeves, baring her round white arms close to the shoulders, and as she looked steadily at him before answering his question she flung back the shining masses of her hair and began to braid it. Her fear for him was entirely gone. She was calm. And there was something in the manner of her quiet and soul-deep study of him that held back other words which he might have spoken.

In those few moments she had taken her place in his life. She stood before him like a goddess, tall and slender and unafraid, her head a gold-brown aureole, her face filled with a purity, a beauty, and a STRENGTH that made him look at her speechless, waiting for the sound of her voice. In her look there was neither boldness nor suspicion. Her eyes were clear, deep pools of velvety blue that defied him to lie to her, He felt that under those eyes he could have knelt down upon the sand and emptied his soul of its secrets for their inspection.

"It is not very strange that I should be here" she said at last. "I have always lived here. It is my home."

"Yes, I believe that," breathed Philip. "It is the last thing in the world that one would believe - but I do; I believe it. Something - I don't know what - told me that you belonged to this world as you stood there beside the rock. But I don't understand. A thousand miles from a city - and you! It's unreal. It's almost like the dreams I've been dreaming during the past eighteen months, and the visions I've seen during that long, maddening night up on the coast, when for five months we didn't see a glow of the sun. But - you understand - it's hard to comprehend."

From her he glanced swiftly over the rocks of the coulee, as if expecting to see some sign of the home she had spoken of, or at least of some other human presence. She understood his questioning look. "I am alone," she said.

The quality of her voice startled him more then her words. There was a deeper, darker glow in her eyes as she watched their effect upon him. She swept out a gleaming white arm, still moist with the water of the pool, taking in the wide, autumn-tinted spaces about them.

"I am alone," she repeated, still keeping her eyes on his face. "Entirely alone. That is why you startled me - why I was afraid. This is my hiding-place, and I thought -"

He saw that she had spoken words that she would have

recalled. She hesitated. Her lips trembled. In that moment of suspense a little gray ermine dislodged a stone from the rock ridge above them, and at the sound of it as it struck behind her the girl gave a start, and a quick flash of the old fear leaped for an instant into her face. And now Philip beheld something in her which he had been too bewildered and wonder-struck to observe before. Her first terror had been so acute that he had failed to see what remained after her fright had passed. But it was clear to him now, and the look that came into his own face told her that he had made the discovery.

The beauty of her face, her eyes, her hair - the wonder of her presence six hundred miles from civilization - had held him spellbound. He had seen only the deep lustre and the wonderful blue of her eyes. Now he saw that those eyes, exquisite in their loveliness, were haunted by something which she was struggling to fight back - a questing, hunted look that burned there steadily, and of which he was not the cause. A deep-seated grief, a terror far back, shone through the forced calmness with which she was speaking to him. He knew that she was fighting with herself, that the nervously twitching fingers at her breast told more than her lips had confessed. He stepped nearer to her and held out a hand, and when he spoke his voice was vibrant with the thing that made men respect him and women have faith in him.

"Tell me - what you started to say," he entreated quietly. "This is your hiding-place, and you thought - what? I think that I can guess. You thought that I was some one else, whom you have reason to fear."

She did not answer. It was as if she had not yet completely measured him. Her eyes told him that. They were not looking AT him, but INTO him. And they were softly beautiful as wood violets. He found himself looking steadily into them - close, so close that he could have reached out and touched her. Slowly there came over them a filmy softness. And then, marvellously, he saw the tears gathering, as dew might gather over the sweet petals of a flower. And still for a moment she did not speak. There came a little quiver at her throat, and she caught herself with a quick, soft breath.

"Yes, I thought you were some one else - whom I fear," she said then. "But why should I tell you? You are from down there, from what you please to call civilization. I should distrust you because of that. So why - why should I tell you?"

In an instant Philip was at her side. In his rough, storm-beaten hand he caught the white fingers that trembled at her breast. And there was something about him now that made her completely unafraid.

"Why?" he asked. "Listen, and I will tell you. Four years ago I came up into this country from down there - the world they call Civilization. I came up with every ideal and every dream I ever had broken and crushed. And up here I found God's Country. I found new ideals and new dreams. I am going back with them. But they can never be broken as the others were - because - now - I have found something that will make them live. And that something is YOU! Don't let my words startle you. I mean them to be as pure as the sun that shines over our heads. If I leave you now - if I never see you again - you will have filled this wonderful world for me. And if I could do something to prove this - to make you happier - why, I'd thank God for having sent me ashore to cook a mess of prunes."

He released her hand, and stepped back from her.

"That is why you should tell me," he finished.

A swift change had come into her eyes and face. She was breathing quickly. He saw the sudden throbbing of her throat. A flush of colour had mounted into her cheeks. Her lips were parted, her eyes shone like stars.

"You would do a great deal for me?" she questioned breathlessly. "A great deal - and like - A MAN?"

"Yes."

"A MAN - one of God's men?" she repeated.

He bowed his head.

Slowly, so slowly that she scarcely seemed to move, she drew nearer to him.

"And when you had done this you would be willing to go away, to promise never to see me again, to ask no reward? You would swear that?"

Her hand touched his arm. Her breath came tense and fast as she waited for him to answer. "If you wished it, yes," he said.

"I almost believe," he heard, as if she were speaking the words to herself. She turned to him again, and something of faith, of hope transfigured her face.

"Return to your fire and your prunes," she said quickly, and the sunlight of a smile passed over her lips. "Then, half an hour from now, come up the coulee to the turn in the rocks. You will find me there."

She bent quickly and picked up the little bag and the brush from the sand. Without looking at him again she sped swiftly beyond the big rock, and Philip's last vision of her was the radiant glory of her hair as it rippled cloudlike behind her in the sunlight.

CHAPTER THREE

That he had actually passed through the experience of the last few minutes, that it was a reality and not some beautiful phantasm of the red and gold world which again lay quiet and lifeless about him, Philip could scarcely convince himself as he made his way back to the canoe and the fire. The discovery of this girl, buried six hundred miles in a wilderness that was almost a terra incognita to the white man, was sufficient to bewilder him. And only now, as he kicked the burning embers from under the pails, and looked at his watch to time himself, did he begin to realize that he had not sensed a hundredth part of the miracle of it.

Now that he was alone, question after question leapt unanswered through his mind, and every vein in his body throbbed with strange excitement. Not for an instant did he doubt what she had said. This world - the forests about him, the lakes, the blue skies above, were her home. And yet, struggling vainly for a solution of the mystery, he told himself in the next breath that this could not be possible. Her voice had revealed nothing of the wilderness - except in its sweetness. Not a break had marred the purity of her speech. She had risen before him like the queen of some wonderful kingdom, and not like a forest girl. And in her face he had seen the soul of one who had looked upon the world as the world lived outside of its forest walls. Yet he believed her. This was her home. Her hair, her eyes, the flowerlike lithesomeness of her beautiful body - and something more, something that he could not see but which he could FEEL in her presence, told him that this was so. This wonder-world about him was her home. But why - how?

He seated himself on a rock, holding the open watch in his hand. Of one thing he was sure. She was oppressed by a strange fear. It was not the fear of being alone, of being lost, of some happen-chance peril that she might fancy was threatening her. It was a deeper, bigger thing than that. And she had confessed to him - not wholly, but enough to make him know - that this fear was of man. He felt at this thought a little thrill of joy, of undefinable exultation. He sprang from the rock and went down to the shore of the lake, scanning its surface with eager, challenging eyes. In these moments he forgot that civilization was waiting for him, that for eighteen months he had been struggling between life and death at the naked and barbarous end of the earth. All at once, in the space of a few minutes, his world had shrunken until it held but two things for him - the autumn-tinted forests, and the girl. Beyond these he thought of nothing except the minutes that were dragging like thirty weights of lead.

As the hand of his watch marked off the twenty-fifth of the prescribed thirty he turned his steps in the direction of the pool. He half expected that she would be there when he came over the ridge of rock. But she had not returned. He looked up the coulee, end then at the firm white sand close to the water. The imprints of her feet were there - small, narrow imprints of a heeled shoe. Unconsciously he smiled, for no other reason than that each surprise he encountered was a new delight to him. A forest girl as he had known them would have worn moccasins - six hundred miles from civilization.

As he was about to leap across the narrow neck of the pool he noticed a white object almost buried in the dry sand, and picked it up. It was a handkerchief; and this, too, was a surprise. He had not particularly noticed her dress, except that it was soft and clinging blue. The handkerchief he looked at more closely. It was of fine linen with a border of lace, and so soft that he could have hidden it in the palm of his hand.

From it rose a faint, sweet scent of the wild rock violet. He knew that it was rock violet, because more than once he had crushed the blossoms between his hands. He thrust the bit of fabric in the breast of his flannel shirt, and walked swiftly up the coulee.

A hundred yards above him the stream turned abruptly, and here a strip of forest meadow grew to the water's edge. He sprang up the low bank, and stood face to face with the girl.

She had heard his approach, and was waiting for him, a little smile of welcome on her lips. She had completed her toilet. She had braided her wonderful hair, and it was gathered in a heavy, shimmering coronet about her head. There was a flutter of lace at her throat, and little fluffs of it at her wrists. She was more beautiful, more than ever like the queen of a kingdom as she stood before him now. And she was alone. He saw that in his first swift glance.

"You didn't eat the prunes?" she asked, and for the first time he saw a bit of laughter in her eyes.

"No - I - I kicked the fire from under them," he said.

He caught the significance of her words, and her sudden sidewise gesture. A short distance from them was a small tent, and on the grass in front of the tent was spread a white cloth, on which was a meal such as he had not looked upon for two years.

"I am glad," she said, and again her eyes met his with their glow of friendly humour. "They might have spoiled your appetite, and I have made up my mind that I want you to have dinner with me. I can't offer you pie or doughnuts. But I have a home-made fruit cake, and a pot of jam that I made myself. Will you join me?"

They sat down, with the feast between them, and the girl leaned over to turn him a cup of tea from a pot that was already made and waiting. Her lovely head was near him, and he stared with hungry adoration at the thick, shining braids, and the soft white contour of her cheek and neck. She leaned back suddenly, and caught him. The words that were on her lips remained unspoken. The laughter went from her eyes. In a hot wave the blood flushed his own face.

"Forgive me if I do anything you don't understand," he begged. "For weeks past I have been wondering how I would act when I met white people again. Perhaps you can't understand. But eighteen months up there - eighteen months without the sound of a white woman's voice, without a glimpse of her face, with only dreams to live on - will make me queer for a time. Can't you understand - a little?"

"A great deal," she replied so quickly that she put him at ease again. "Back there I couldn't quite believe you. I am beginning to now. You are honest. But let us not talk of ourselves until after dinner. Do you like the cake?"

She had given him a piece as large as his fist, and he bit off the end of it.

"Delicious!" he cried instantly. "Think of it - nothing but bannock, bannock, bannock for two years, and only six ounces of that a day for the last six months! Do you care if I eat the whole of it - the cake, I mean?"

Seriously she began cutting the remainder of the cake into quarters.

"It would be one of the biggest compliments you could pay me," she said. "But won't you have some boiled tongue with it, a little canned lobster, a pickle -"

"Pickles!" he interrupted. "Just cake and pickles - please! I've dreamed of pickles up there. I've had 'em come to me at night as big as mountains, and one night I dreamed of chasing a pickle with legs for hours, and when at last I caught up with the thing it had turned into an iceberg. Please let me have just pickles and cake!"

Behind the lightness of his words she saw the truth - the craving of famine. Ashamed, he tried to hide it from her. He refused the third huge piece of cake, but she reached over and placed it in his hand. She insisted that he eat the last piece, and the last pickle in the bottle she had opened.

When he finished, she said:

"Now - I know."

"What?"

"That you have spoken the truth, that you have come from a long time in the North, and that I need not fear - what I did fear."

"And that fear? Tell me -"

She answered calmly, and in her eyes and the lines of her face came a look of despair which she had almost hidden from him until now.

"I was thinking during those thirty minutes you away," she said. "And I realized what folly it was in me to tell you as much as I have. Back there, for just one insane moment, I thought that you might help me in a situation which is as terrible as any you may have faced in your months of Arctic night. But it is impossible. All that I can ask of you now - all that I can demand of you to prove that you are the man you said you were - is that you leave me, and never whisper a word into another ear of our meeting. Will you promise that?"

"To promise that - would be lying," he said slowly, and his hand unclenched and lay listlessly on his knee. "If there is a reason - some good reason why I should leave you - then I will go."

"Then - you demand a reason?"

"To demand a reason would be -"

He hesitated, and she added:

"Unchivalrous."

"Yes - more than that," he replied softly. He bowed his head, and for a moment she saw the tinge of gray in his blond hair, the droop of his clean, strong shoulders, the SOMETHING of hopelessness in his gesture. A new light flashed into her own face. She raised a hand, as if to reach out to him, and dropped it as he looked up.

"Will you let me help you?" he asked.

She was not looking at him, but beyond him. In her face he saw again the strange light of hope that had illumined it at the pool.

"If I could believe," she whispered, still looking beyond him. "If I could trust you, as I have read that the maidens of old trusted their knights. But - it seems impossible. In those days, centuries and centuries ago, I guess, womanhood was next to - God. Men fought for it, and died for it, to keep it pure and holy. If you had come to me then you would have levelled your lance and fought for me without asking a question, without demanding a reward, without reasoning whether I was right or wrong - and all because I was a woman. Now it is different. You are a part of civilization, and if you should do all that I might ask of you it would be because you have a price in view. I know. I have looked into you. I understand. That price would be - ME!"

She looked at him now, her breast throbbing, almost a sob in her quivering voice, defying him to deny the truth of her words.

"You have struck home," he said, and his voice sounded strange to himself. "And I am not sorry. I am glad that you have seen - and understand. It seems almost indecent for me to tell you this, when I have known you for such a short time. But I have known you for years - in my hopes and dreams. For you I would go to the end of the world. And I can do what other men have done, centuries ago. They called them knights. You may call me a MAN!"

At his words she rose from where she had been sitting. She faced the radiant walls of the forests that rolled billow upon billow in the distance, and the sun lighted up her crown of hair in a glory. One hand still clung to her breast. She was breathing even more quickly, and the flush had deepened in her cheek until it was like the tender stain of the crushed bakneesh. Philip rose and stood beside her. His shoulders were back. He looked where she looked, and as he gazed upon the red and gold billows of forest that melted away against the distant sky he felt a new and glorious fire throbbing in his veins. From the forests their eyes turned - and met. He held out his hand. And slowly her own hand fluttered at her breast, and was given to him.

"I am quite sure that I understand you now," he said, and his voice was the low, steady, fighting voice of the man new-born. "I will be your knight, as you have read of the knights of old. I will urge no reward that is not freely given. Now - will you let me help you?"

For a moment she allowed him to hold her hand. Then she gently withdrew it and stepped back from him.

"You must first understand before you offer yourself," she said. "I cannot tell you what my trouble is. You will never know. And when it is over, when you have helped me across the abyss, then will come the greatest trial of all for you. I believe - when I tell you that last thing which you must do - that you will regard me as a monster, and draw back. But it is necessary. If you fight for me, it must be in the dark. You will not know why you are doing the things I ask you to do. You may guess, but you would not guess the truth if you lived a thousand years. Your one reward will be the knowledge that you have fought for a woman, and that you have saved her. Now, do you still want to help me?'

"I can't understand," he gasped. "But - yes - I would still accept the inevitable. I have promised you that I will do as you have dreamed that knights of old have done. To leave you now would be" - he turned his head with a gesture of hopelessness - "an empty world forever. I have told you now. But you could not understand and believe unless I did. I love you."

He spoke as quietly and with as little passion in his voice as if he were speaking the words from a book. But their very quietness made them convincing. She started, and the colour left her face. Then it returned, flooding her cheeks with a feverish glow.

"In that is the danger," she said quickly. "But you have spoken the words as I would have had you speak them. It is this danger that must be buried - deep - deep. And you will bury it. You will urge no questions that I do not wish to answer. You will fight for me, blindly, knowing only that what I ask you to do is not sinful nor wrong. And in the end -"

She hesitated. Her face had grown as tense as his own.

"And in the end," she whispered, "your greatest reward can be only the knowledge that in living this knighthood for me you have won what I can never give to any man. The world can hold only one such man for a woman. For your faith must be immeasurable, your love as pure as the withered violets out there among the rocks if you live up to the tests ahead of you. You will think me mad when I have finished. But I am sane. Off there, in the Snowbird Lake country, is my home. I am alone. No other white man or woman is with me. As my knight, the one hope of salvation that I cling to now, you will return with me to that place - as my husband. To all but ourselves we shall be man and wife. I will bear your name - or the one by which you must be known. And at the very end of all, in that hour of triumph when you know that you have borne me safely over that abyss at the brink of which I am hovering now, you will go off into the forest, and -"

She approached him, and laid a hand on his arm. "You will not come back," she finished, so gently that he scarcely heard her words. "You will die - for me - for all who have known you."

"Good God!" he breathed, and he stared over her head to where the red and gold billows of the forests seemed to melt away into the skies.

CHAPTER FOUR

Thus they stood for many seconds. Never for an instant did her eyes leave his face, and Philip looked straight over her head into that distant radiance of the forest mountains. It was she whose emotions revealed themselves now. The blood came and went in her cheeks. The soft lace at her throat rose and fell swiftly. In her eyes and face there was a thing which she had not dared to reveal to him before - a prayerful, pleading anxiety that was almost ready to break into tears.

At last she had come to see and believe in the strength and wonder of this man who had come to her from out of the North, and now he stared over her head with that strange white look, as if the things she had said had raised a mountain between them. She could feel the throb of his arm on which her hand rested. All at once her calm had deserted her. She had never known a man like this, had never expected to know one; and in her face there shone the gentle loveliness of a woman whose soul and not her voice was pleading a great cause. It was pleading for her self. And then he looked down.

"You want to go - now," she whispered. "I knew that you would."

"Yes, I want to go," he replied, and his two hands took hers, and held them close to his breast, so that she felt the excited throbbing of his heart. "I want to go - wherever you go. Perhaps in those years of centuries ago there lived women like you to fight and die for. I no longer wonder at men fighting for them as they have sung their stories in books. I have nothing down in that world which you have called civilization - nothing except the husks of murdered hopes, ambitions, and things that were once joys. Here I have you to love, to fight for. For you cannot tell me that I must not love you, even though I swear to live up to your laws of chivalry. Unless I loved you as I do there would not be those laws."

"Then you will do all this for me - even to the end - when you must sacrifice all of that for which you have struggled, and which you have saved?"

"Yes."

"If that is so, then I trust you with my life and my honour. It is all in your keeping - all."

Her voice broke in a sob. She snatched her hands from him, and with that sob still quivering on her lips she turned and ran swiftly to the little tent. She did not look back as she disappeared into it, and Philip turned like one in a dream and went to the summit of the bare rock ridge, from which he could look over the quiet surface of the lake and a hundred square miles of the unpeopled world which had now become so strangely his own. An hour - a little more than that - had changed the course of his life as completely as the master-strokes of a painter might have changed the tones of a canvas epic. It did not take reason or thought to impinge this fact upon him. It was a knowledge that engulfed him over-whelmingly. So short a time ago that even now he could not quite comprehend it all, he was alone out on the lake, thinking of the story of the First Woman that Jasper had told him down at Fond du Lac. Since then he had passed through a lifetime. What had happened might well have covered the space of months - or of years. He had met a woman, and like the warm sunshine she had become instantly a part of his soul, flooding him with those emotions which make life beautiful. That he had told her of this love as calmly as if she had known of it slumbering within his breast for years seemed to him to be neither unreal nor remarkable.

He turned his face back to the tent, but there was no movement there. He knew that there - alone - the girl was recovering from the tremendous strain under which she had been fighting. He sat down, facing the lake. For the first time his mental faculties began to adjust themselves and his blood to flow less heatedly through his veins. For the first time, too, the magnitude of his promise - of what he had undertaken - began to impress itself upon him. He had thought that in asking him to fight for her she had spoken with the physical definition of that word in mind. But at the outset she had plunged him into mystery. If she had asked him to draw the automatic at his side and leap into battle with a dozen of his kind he would not have been surprised. He had expected something like that. But this other - her first demand upon him! What could it mean? Shrouded in mystery, bound by his oath of honour to make no effort to uncover her secret, he was to accompany her back to her home AS HER HUSBAND! And after that - at the end - he was to go out into the forest, and die - for her, for all who had known him. He wondered if she had meant these words literally, too. He smiled, and slowly his eyes scanned the lake. He was already beginning to reason, to guess at the mystery which she had told him he could not unveil if he lived a thousand years. But he could at least work about the edges of it.

Suddenly he concentrated his gaze at a point on the lake three quarters of a mile away. It was close to shore, and he was certain that he had seen some movement there - a flash of sunlight on a shifting object. Probably he had caught a reflection of light from the palmate horn of a moose feeding among the water-lily roots. He leaned forward, and shaded his eyes. In another moment his heart gave a quicker throb. What he had seen was the flash of a paddle. He made out a canoe, and then two. They were moving close in-shore, one following the other, and apparently taking advantage of the shadows of the forest. Philip's hand shifted to the butt of his automatic. After all there might be fighting of the good old-fashioned kind. He looked back in the direction of the tent.

The girl had reappeared, and was looking at him. She waved a hand, and he ran down to meet her. She had been crying. The dampness of tears still clung to her lashes; but the smile on her lips was sweet and welcoming, and now, so frankly that his face burned with pleasure, she held out a hand to him.

"I was rude to run away from you in that way," she apologized. "But I couldn't cry before you. And I wanted to cry."

"Because you were glad, or sorry?" he asked.

"A little of both," she replied. "But mostly glad. A few hours ago it didn't seem possible that there was any hope for me. Now -"

"There is hope," he urged.

"Yes, there is hope."

For an instant he felt the warm thrill of her fingers as they clung tighter to his. Then she withdrew her hand, gently, smiling at him with sweet confidence. Her eyes were like pure, soft violets. He wanted to kneel at her feet, and cry out his thanks to God for sending him to her. Instead of betraying his emotion, he spoke of the canoes.

"There are two canoes coming along the shore of the lake," he said. "Are you expecting some one?"

The smile left her lips. He was startled by the suddenness with which the colour ebbed from her face and the old fear leapt back into her eyes.

"Two? You are sure there are two?" Her fingers clutched his arm almost fiercely. "And they are coming this way?"

"We can see them from the top of the rock ridge," he said. "I am sure there are two. Will you look for yourself?"

She did not speak as they hurried to the bald cap of the ridge. From the top Philip pointed down the lake. The two canoes were in plain view now. Whether they contained three or four people they could not quite make out. At sight of them the last vestige of colour had left the girl's cheeks. But now, as she stood there breathing quickly in her excitement, there came a change in her. She threw back her head. Her lips parted. Her blue eyes flashed a fire in which Philip in his amazement no longer saw fear, but defiance. Her hands were clenched. She seemed taller. Back into her cheeks there burned swiftly two points of flame. All at once she put out a hand and drew him back, so that the cap of the ridge concealed them from the lake.

"An hour ago those canoes would have made me run off into the forest - and hide," she said. "But now I am not afraid! Do you understand?"

"Then you trust me?"

"Absolutely."

"But - surely - there is something that you should tell me: Who they are, what your danger is, what I am to do."

"I am hoping that I am mistaken," she replied. "They may not be those whom I am dreading - and expecting. All I can tell you is this: You are Paul Darcambal. I am Josephine, your wife. Protect me as a wife. I will be constantly at your side. Were I alone I would know what to expect. But - with you - they may not offer me harm. If they do not, show no suspicion. But be watchful. Don't let them get behind you. And be ready always - always - to use that - if a thing so terrible must be done!" As she spoke she lay a hand on his pistol. "And remember: I am your wife!"

"To live that belief, even in a dream, will be a joy as

unforgettable as life itself," he whispered, so low that, in turning her head, she made as if she had not heard him.

"Come," she said. "Let us follow the coulee down to the lake. We can watch them from among the rocks."

She gave him her hand as they began to traverse the boulder-strewn bed of the creek. Suddenly he said:

"You will not suspect me of cowardice if I suggest that there is not one chance in a hundred of them discovering us?"

"No," she replied, with a glance so filled with her confidence and faith that involuntarily he held her hand closer in his own. "But I want them to find us - if they are whom I fear. We will show ourselves on the shore."

He looked at her in amazement before the significance of her words had dawned upon him. Then he laughed.

"That is the greatest proof of your faith you have given me," he said. "With me you are anxious to face your enemies. And I am as anxious to meet them."

"Don't misunderstand me," she corrected him quickly. "I am praying that they are not the ones I suspect. But if they are - why, yes, I want to face them - with you."

They had almost reached the lake when he said:

"And now, I may call you Josephine?"

"Yes, that is necessary."

"And you will call me -"

"Paul, of course - for you are Paul Darcambal."

"Is that quite necessary?" he asked. "Is it not possible that you might allow me to retain at least a part of my name, and call me Philip? Philip Darcambal?"

"There really is no objection to that," she hesitated. "If you wish I will call you Philip, But you must also be Paul - your middle name, perhaps."

"In the event of certain exigencies," he guessed.

"Yes."

He had still assisted her over the rocks by holding to her hand, and suddenly her fingers clutched his convulsively. She pointed to a stretch of the open lake. The canoes were plainly visible not more than a quarter of a mile away. Even as he felt her trembling slightly he laughed.

"Only three!" he exclaimed. "Surely it is not going to demand a great amount of courage to face that number, Josephine?"

"It is going to take all the courage in the world to face one of them," she replied in a low, strained voice. "Can you make them out? Are they white men or Indians?"

"The light is not right - I can't decide," he said, after a moment's scrutiny. "If they are Indians -"

"They are friends," she interrupted. "Jean - my Jean Croisset - left me hiding here five days ago. He is part French and part Indian. But he could not be returning so soon. If they are white -"

"We will expose ourselves on the beach," he finished significantly.

She nodded. He saw that in spite of her struggle to remain calm she was seized again by the terror of what might be in the approaching canoes. He was straining his eyes to make out their occupants when a low cry drew his gaze to her.

"It is Jean," she gasped, and he thought that he could hear her heart beating. "It is Jean - and the others are Indians! Oh, my God, how thankful I am -"

She turned to him.

"You will go back to the camp - please. Wait for us there, I must see Jean alone. It is best that you should do this."

To obey without questioning her or expostulating against his sudden dismissal, he knew was in the code of his promise to her. And he knew by what he saw in her face that Jean's return had set the world trembling under her feet, that for her it was charged with possibilities as tremendous as if the two canoes had contained those whom she had at first feared.

"Go," she whispered. "Please go."

Without a word he returned in the direction of the camp.

CHAPTER FIVE

Close to the tent Philip sat down, smoked his pipe, and waited. Not only had the developments of the last few minutes been disappointing to him, but they had added still more to his bewilderment. He had expected and hoped for immediate physical action, something that would at least partially clear away the cloud of mystery. And at this moment, when he was expecting things to happen, there had appeared this new factor, Jean, to change the current of excitement under which Josephine was fighting. Who could Jean be? he asked himself. And why should his appearance at this time stir Josephine to a pitch of emotion only a little less tense than that roused by her fears of a short time before? She had told him that Jean was part Indian, part French, and that he "belonged to her." And his coming, he felt sure, was of tremendous significance to her.

He waited impatiently. It seemed a long time before he heard voices and the sound of footsteps over the edge of the coulee. He rose to his feet, and a moment later Josephine and her companion appeared not more than a dozen paces from him. His first glance was at the man. In that same instant Jean Croisset stopped in his tracks and looked at Philip. Steadily, and apparently oblivious of Josephine's presence, they measured each other, the half-breed bent a little forward, the lithe alertness of a cat in his posture, his eyes burning darkly. He was a man whose age Philip could not guess. It might have been forty. Probably it was close to that. He was bareheaded, and his long coarse hair, black as an Indian's, was shot with gray. At first it would have been difficult to name the blood that ran strongest in his veins. His hair, the thinness of his face and body, his eyes, and the tense position in which he had paused, were all Indian. Then, above these things, Philip saw the French. Swiftly it became the dominant part of the man before him, and he was not surprised when Jean advanced with outstretched hand, and said:

"M'sieur Philip, I am Jean - Jean Jacques Croisset - and I am glad you have come."

The words were spoken for Philip alone, and where she stood Josephine did not catch the strange flash of fire in the half-breed's eyes, nor did she hear his still more swiftly spoken words: "I am glad it is YOU that chance has sent to us, M'sieur Weyman!"

The two men gripped hands. There was something about Jean that inspired Philip's confidence, and as he returned the half-breed's greeting his eyes looked for a moment over the other's shoulder and rested on Josephine. He was astonished at the change in her. Evidently Jean had not brought her bad news. She held the pages of an open letter in her hand, and as she caught Philip's look she smiled at him with a gladness which he had not seen in her face before. She came forward quickly, and placed a hand on his arm.

"Jean's coming was a surprise," she explained. "I did not expect him for a number of days, and I dreaded what he might have to tell me. But this letter has brought me fresh cause for thankfulness, though it may enslave you a little longer to your vows of knighthood. We start for home this afternoon. Are you ready?"

"I have a little packing to do," he said, looking after Jean, who was moving toward the tent. "Twenty-seven prunes and -"

"Me," laughed Josephine. "Is it not necessary that you make room in your canoe for me?"

Philip's face flushed with pleasure.

"Of course it is," he cried. "Everything has seemed so wonderfully unreal to me that for a moment I forgot that you were my - my wife. But how about Jean? He called me M'sieur Weyman."

"He is the one other person in the world who knows what you and I know," she explained. "That, too, was necessary. Will you go and arrange your canoe now? Jean will bring down my things and exchange them for some of your dunnage." She left him to run into the tent, reappearing quickly with a thick rabbit-skin blanket and two canoe pillows.

"These make my nest - when I'm not working," she said, thrusting them into Philip's arms. "I have a paddle, too. Jean says that I am as good as an Indian woman with it."

"Better, M'sieur," exclaimed Jean, who had come out of the tent. "It makes you work harder to see her. She is - what you call it - gwan-auch-ewin - so splendid! Out of the Cree you cannot speak it."

A tender glow filled Josephine's eyes as Jean began pulling up the pegs of the tent.

"A little later I will tell you about Jean," she whispered. "But now, go to your canoe. We will follow you in a few minutes."

He left her, knowing that she had other things to say to Jean which she did not wish him to hear. As he turned toward the coulee he noticed that she still held the opened letter in her hand.

There was not much for him to do when he reached his canoe. He threw out his sleeping bag and tent, and arranged Josephine's robe and pillows so that she would sit facing him. The knowledge that she was to be with him, that they were joined in a pact which would make her his constant companion, filled him with joyous visions and anticipations. He did not stop to ask himself how long this mysterious association might last, how soon it might come to the tragic end to which she had foredoomed it. With the spirit of the adventurer who had more than once faced death with a smile, he did not believe in burning bridges ahead of him. He loved Josephine. To him this love had come as it had come to Tristan and Isolde, to Paola and Francesca - sudden and irresistible, but, unlike theirs, as pure as the air of the world which he breathed. That he knew nothing of her, that she had not even revealed her full name to him, did not affect the depth or sincerity of his emotion. Nor had her frank avowal that he could expect no reward destroyed his hope. The one big thought that ran through his brain now, as he arranged the canoe, was that there was room for hope, and that she had been free to accept the words he had spoken to her without dishonour to herself. If she belonged to some other man she would not have asked him to play the part of a husband. Her freedom and his right to fight for her was the one consuming fact of significance to him just now. Beside that all others were trivial and unimportant, and every drop of blood in his veins was stirred by a strange exultation.

He found himself whistling again as he refolded his blankets and straightened out his tent. When he had finished this last task he turned to find Jean standing close behind him, his dark eyes watching him closely. As he greeted the half-breed, Philip looked for Josephine.

"I am alone, M'sieur," said Jean, coming close to Philip. "I tricked her into staying behind until I could see you for a moment as we are, alone, man to man. Why is it that our Josephine has come to trust you as she does?"

His voice was low - it was almost soft as a woman's, but deep in his eyes Philip saw the glow of a strange, slumbering fire.

"Why is it?" he persisted.

"God only knows," exclaimed Philip, the significance of the question bursting upon him for the first time. "I hadn't thought of it, Jean. Everything has happened so quickly, so strangely, that there are many things I haven't thought of. It must be because - she thinks I'm a MAN!"

"That is it, M'sieur," replied Jean, as quietly as before. "That, and because you have come from two years in the North. I have been there. I know that it breeds men. And our Josephine knows. I could swear that there is not one man in a million she would trust as she has put faith in you. Into your hands she has given herself, and what you do means for her life or death. And for you -"

The fires in his eyes were nearer the surface now.

"What?" asked Philip tensely.

"Death - unless you play your part as a man," answered Jean. There was neither threat nor excitement in his voice, but in his eyes was the thing that Philip understood. Silently he reached out and gripped the half-breed's hand, For an instant they stood, their faces close, looking into each other's eyes. And as men see men where the fires of the earth burn low, so they read each other's souls, and their fingers tightened in a clasp of understanding.

"What that part is to be I cannot guess," said Philip, then. "But I will play it, and it is not fear that will hold me to my promise to her. If I fail, why - kill me!"

"That is the North," breathed Jean, and in his voice was the thankfulness of prayer.

Without another word he stooped and picked up the tent and blankets. Philip was about to stop him, to speak further with him, when he saw Josephine climbing over the bulwark of rocks between them and the trail. He hurried to meet her. Her arms were full, and she allowed him to take a part of her load.

With what Jean had brought this was all that was to go in Philip's canoe, and the half-breed remained to help them off.

"You will go straight across the lake," he said to Philip. "If you paddle slowly, I will catch up with you."

Philip seated himself near the stern, facing Josephine, and Jean gave the canoe a shove that sent it skimming like a swallow on the smooth surface of the lake. For a moment Philip did not dip his paddle. He looked at the girl who sat so near to him, her head bent over in pretence of seeing that all was right, the sun melting away into rich colours in the thick coils of her hair. There filled him an overwhelming desire to reach over and touch the shining braids, to feel the thrill of their warmth and sweetness, and something of this desire was in his face when she looked up at him, a look of gentle thankfulness disturbed a little by anxiety in her eyes. He had not noticed fully how wonderfully blue her eyes were until now, and soft and tender they were when free of the excitement of fear and mental strain. They were more than ever like the wild wood violets, flecked with those same little brown spots which had made him think sometimes that the flowers were full of laughter. There was something of wistfulness, of thought for him in her eyes now, and in pure joy he laughed.

"Why do you laugh?" she asked.

"Because I am happy," he replied, and sent the canoe ahead with a first deep stroke. "I have never been happier in my life. I did not know that it was possible to feel as I do."

"And I am just beginning to feel my selfishness," she said. "You have thought only of me. You are making a wonderful sacrifice for me. You have nothing to gain, nothing to expect but the things that make me shudder. And I have thought of myself alone, selfishly, unreasonably. It is not fair, and yet this is the only way that it can be."

"I am satisfied," he said. "I have nothing much to sacrifice, except myself."

She leaned forward, with her chin in the cup of her hands, and looked at him steadily.

"You have people?"

"None who cares for me. My mother was the last. She died before I came North."

"And you have no sisters - or brothers?"

"None living."

For a moment she was silent. Then she said gently, looking into his eyes:

"I wish I had known - that I had guessed - before I let you come this far. I am sorry now - sorry that I didn't send you away. You are different from other men I have known - and you have had your suffering. And now - I must hurt you again. It wouldn't be so bad if you didn't care for me. I don't want to hurt you - because - I believe in you."

"And is that all - because you believe me?"

She did not answer. Her hands clasped at her breast. She looked beyond him to the shore they were leaving.

"You must leave me," she said then, and her voice was as lifeless as his had been. "I am beginning to see now. It all happened so suddenly that I could not think. But if you love me you must not go on. It is impossible. I would rather suffer my own fate than have you do that. When we reach the other shore you must leave me."

She was struggling to keep back her emotion, fighting to hold it within her own breast.

"You must go back," she repeated, staring into his set face. "If you don't, you will be hurt terribly, terribly!"

And then, suddenly, she slipped lower among the cushions he had placed for her, and buried her face in one of them with a moaning grief that cut to his soul. She was sobbing now, like a child. In this moment Philip forgot all restraint. He leaned forward and put a hand on her shining head, and bent his face close down to hers. His free hand touched one of her hands, and he held it tightly.

"Listen, my Josephine," he whispered. "I am not going to turn back, I am going on with you. That is our pact. At the end I know what to expect. You have told me; and I, too, believe. But whatever happens, in spite of all that may happen, I will still have received more than all else in the world could give me. For I will have known you, and you will be my salvation. I am going on."

For an instant he felt the fluttering pressure of her fingers on his. It was an answer a thousand times more precious to him than words, and he knew that he had won. Still lower he bent his head, until for an instant his lips touched the soft, living warmth of her hair. And then he leaned back, freeing her hand, and into his face had leaped soul and life and fighting strength; and under his breath he gave new thanks to God, and to the sun, and the blue sky above, while from behind them came skimming over the water the slim birchbark canoe of Jean Jacques Croisset.

CHAPTER SIX

At the touch of Weyman's lips to her hair Josephine lay very still, and Philip wondered if she had felt that swift, stolen caress. Almost he hoped that she had. The silken tress where for an instant his lips had rested seemed to him now like some precious communion cup in whose sacredness he had pledged himself. Yet had he believed that she was conscious of his act he would have begged her forgiveness. He waited, breathing softly, putting greater sweep into his paddle to keep Jean well behind them.

Slowly the tremulous unrest of Josephine's shoulders ceased. She raised her head and looked at him, her lovely face damp with tears, her eyes shimmering like velvety pools through their mist. She did not speak. She was woman now - all woman. Her strength, the bearing which had made him think of her as a queen, the fighting tension which she had been under, were gone. Until she looked at him through her tears her presence had been like that of some wonderful and unreal creature who held the control to his every act in the cup of her hands. He thought no longer of himself now. He knew that to him she had relinquished the mysterious fight under which she had been struggling. In her eyes he read her surrender. From this hour the fight was his. She told him, without speaking. And the glory of it all thrilled him with a sacred happiness so that he wanted to drop his paddle, draw her close into his arms, and tell her that there was no power in the world that could harm her now. But instead of this he laughed low and joyously full into her eyes, and her lips smiled gently back at him. And so they understood without words.

Behind them, Jean had been coming up swiftly, and now they heard him break for an instant into the chorus of one of the wild half-breed songs, and Philip listened to the words of the chant which is as old in the Northland as the ancient brass cannon and the crumbling fortress rocks at York Factory:

> "O, ze beeg black bear, he go to court,
> He go to court a mate;
> He court to ze Sout',
> He court to ze Nort',
> He court to ze shores of ze Indian Lake."

And then, in the moment's silence that followed, Philip threw back his head, and in a voice almost as wild and untrained as Jean Croisset's, he shouted back:

> "Oh! the fur fleets sing on Temiskaming,
> As the ashen paddles bend,
> And the crews carouse at Rupert's House,
> At the sullen winter's end.
> But my days are done where the lean wolves run,
> And I ripple no more the path
> Where the gray geese race 'cross the red moon's face
> From the white wind's Arctic wrath."

The suspense was broken. The two men's voices, rising in their crude strength, sending forth into the still wilderness both triumph and defiance, brought the quick flush of living back into Josephine's face. She guessed why Jean had started his chant - to give her courage. She KNEW why Philip had responded. And now Jean swept up beside them, a smile on his thin, dark face.

"The Good Virgin preserve us, M'sieur, but our voices are like those of two beasts," he cried.

"Great, true, fighting beasts," whispered Josephine under her breath. "How I would hate almost -"

She had suddenly flushed to the roots of her hair.

"What?" asked Philip.

"To hear men sing like women," she finished.

As swiftly as he had come up Jean and his canoe had sped on ahead of them.

"You should have heard us sing that up in our snow hut, when for five months the sun never sent a streak above the horizon," said Philip. "At the end - in the fourth month - it was more like the wailing of madmen. MacTavish died then: a young half Scot, of the Royal Mounted. After that Radisson and I were alone, and sometimes we used to see how loud we could shout it, and always, when we came to those two last lines -"

She interrupted him:

> "Where the gray geese race 'cross the red moon's face
> From the white wind's Arctic wrath."

"Your memory is splendid!" he cried admiringly.

"Yes, always when we came to the end of those lines, the white foxes would answer us from out on the barrens, and we would wait for the sneaking yelping of them before we went on. They haunted us like little demons, those foxes, and never once could we catch a glimpse of them during the long night. They helped to drive MacTavish mad. He died begging us to keep them away from him. One day I was wakened by Radisson crying like a baby, and when I sat up in my ice bunk he caught me by the shoulders and told me that he had seen something that looked like the glow of a fire thousands and thousands of miles away. It was the sun, and it came just in time."

"And this other man you speak of, Radisson?" she asked.

"He died two hundred miles back," replied Philip quietly. "But that is unpleasant to speak of. Look ahead. Isn't that ridge of the forest glorious in the sunlight?"

She did not take her eyes from his face.

"Do you know, I think there is something wonderful about you," she said, so gently and frankly that the blood rushed to his cheeks. "Some day I want to learn those words that helped to keep you alive up there. I want to know all of the story, because I think I can understand. There was more to it - something after the foxes yelped back at you?"

"This," he said, and ahead of them Jean Croisset rested on his paddle to listen to Philip's voice:

"My seams gape wide, and I'm tossed aside
To rot on a lonely shore,
While the leaves and mould like a shroud enfold,
For the last of my trails are o'er;
But I float in dreams on Northland streams
That never again I'll see,
As I lie on the marge of the old Portage,
With grief for company."

"A canoe!" breathed the girl, looking back over the sunlit lake.

"Yes, a canoe, cast aside, forgotten, as sometimes men and women are forgotten when down and out."

"Men and women who live in dreams," she added. "And with such dreams there must always be grief."

There was a moment of the old pain in her face, a little catch in her breath, and then she turned and looked at the forest ridge to which he had called her attention.

"We go deep into that forest," she said. "We enter a creek just beyond where Jean is waiting for us, and Adare House is a hundred miles to the south and east." She faced him with a quick smile. "My name is Adare," she explained, "Josephine Adare."

"Is - or was?" he asked.

"Is," she said; then, seeing the correcting challenge in his eyes she added quickly: "But only to you. To all others I am Madame Paul Darcambal."

"Paul?"

"Pardon me, I mean Philip."

They were close to shore, and fearing that Jean might become suspicious of his tardiness, Philip bent to his paddle and was soon in the half-breed's wake. Where he had thought there was only the thick forest he saw a narrow opening toward which Jean was speeding in his canoe. Five minutes later they passed under a thick mass of overhanging spruce boughs into a narrow stream so still and black in the deep shadows of the forest that it looked like oil. There was something a little awesome in the suddenness and completeness with which they were swallowed up. Over their heads the spruce and cedar tops met and shut out the sunlight. On both sides of them the forest was thick and black. The trail of the stream itself was like a tunnel, silent, dark, mysterious. The paddles dipped noiselessly, and the two canoes travelled side by side.

"There are few who know of this break into the forest," said Jean in a low voice. "Listen, M'sieur!"

From out of the gloom ahead of them there came a faint, oily splashing.

"Otter," whispered Jean. "The stream is like this for many miles, and it is full of life that you can never see because of the darkness."

Something in the stillness and the gloom held them silent. The canoes slipped along like shadows, and sometimes they bent their heads to escape the low-hanging boughs. Josephine's face shone whitely in the dusk. She was alert and listening. When she spoke it was in a voice strangely subdued.

"I love this stream," she whispered. "It is full of life. On all sides of us, in the forest, there is life. The Indians do not come here, because they have a superstitious dread of this eternal gloom and quiet. They call it the Spirit Stream. Even Jean is a little oppressed by it. See how closely he keeps to us. I love it, because I love everything that is wild. Listen! Did you hear that?"

"Mooswa," spoke Jean out of the gloom close to them.

"Yes, a moose," she said. "Here is where I saw my first moose, so many years ago that it is time for me to forget," she laughed softly. "I think I had just passed my fourth birthday."

"You were four on the day we started, ma Josephine," came Jean's voice as his canoe shot slowly ahead where the stream narrowed; and then his voice came back more faintly: "that was sixteen years ago to-day."

A shot breaking the dead stillness of the sunless world about him could not have sent the blood rushing through Philip's veins more swiftly than Jean's last words. For a moment he stopped his paddling and leaned forward so that he could look close into Josephine's face.

"This is your birthday?"

"Yes. You ate my birthday cake."

She heard the strange, happy catch in his breath as he straightened back and resumed his work. Mile after mile they wound their way through the mysterious, subterranean-like stream, speaking seldom, and listening intently for the breaks in the deathlike stillness that spoke of life. Now and then they caught the ghostly flutter of owls in the gloom, like floating spirits; back in the forest saplings snapped and brush crashed underfoot as caribou or moose caught the man-scent; they heard once the panting, sniffing inquiry of a bear close at hand, and Philip reached forward for his rifle. For an instant Josephine's hand fluttered to his own, and held it back, and the dark glow of her eyes said: "Don't kill." Here there were no big-eyed moose-birds, none of the mellow throat sounds of the brush sparrow, no harsh janglings of the gaudily coloured jays. In the timber fell the soft footpads of creatures with claw and fang, marauders and outlaws of darkness. Light, sunshine, everything that loved the openness of day were beyond. For more than an hour they had driven their canoes steadily on, when, as suddenly as they had entered it, they slipped out from the cavernous gloom into the sunlight again.

Josephine drew a deep breath as the sunlight flooded her face and hair.

"I have my own name for that place," she said. "I call it the Valley of Silent Things. It is a great swamp, and they say that the moss grows in it so deep that caribou and deer walk over it without breaking through."

The stream was swelling out into a narrow, finger-like lake that stretched for a mile or more ahead of them, and she turned to nod her head at the spruce and cedar shores with their colourings of red and gold, where birch, and poplar, and ash splashed vividly against the darker background.

"From now on it is all like that." she said. "Lake after lake, most of them as narrow as this, clear to the doors of Adare House. It is a wonderful lake country, and one may easily lose one's self - hundreds of lakes, I guess, running through the forests like Venetian canals."

"I would not be surprised if you told me you had been in Venice," he replied. "To-day is your birthday - your twentieth.

Have you lived all those years here?"

He repressed his desire to question her, because he knew that she understood that to be a part of his promise to her. In what he now asked her he could not believe that he was treading upon prohibited ground, and in the face of their apparent innocence he was dismayed at the effect his words had upon her. It seemed to him that her eyes flinched when he spoke, as if he had struck at her. There passed over her face the look which he had come to dread: a swift, tense betrayal of the grief which he knew was eating at her soul, and which she was fighting so courageously to hide from him. It had come and gone in a flash, but the pain of it was left with him. She smiled at him a bit tremulously.

"I understand why you ask that," she said, "and it is no more than fair that I should tell you. Of course you are wondering a great deal about me. You have just asked yourself how I could ever hear of such a place as Venice away up here among the Indians. Why, do you know" - she leaned forward, as if to whisper a secret, her blue eyes shilling with a sudden laughter - "I've even read the 'Lives' of Plutarch, and I'm waiting patiently for the English to bang a few of those terrible Lucretia Borgias who call themselves militant suffragettes!"

"I - I - beg your pardon," he stammered helplessly.

She no longer betrayed the hurt of his question, and so sweet was the laughter of her eyes and lips that he laughed back at her, in spite of his embarrassment. Then, all at once, she became serious.

"I am terribly unfair to you," she apologized gently; and then, looking across the water, she added: "Yes, I've lived almost all of those twenty years up here - among the forests. They sent me to the Mission school at Fort Churchill, over on Hudson's Bay, for three years; and after that, until I was seventeen, I had a little white-haired English governess at Adare House. If she had lived - " Her hands clenched the sides of the canoe, and she looked straight away from Philip. She seemed to force the words that came from her lips then: "When I was eighteen I went to Montreal - and lived there a year, That is all - that one year - away from - my forests -"

He almost failed to hear the last words, and he made no effort to reply. He kept his canoe nearer to Jean's, so that frequently they were running side by side. In the quick fall of the early northern night the sun was becoming more and more of a red haze in the sky as it sank farther toward the western forests. Josephine had changed her position, so that she now sat facing the bow of the canoe. She leaned a little forward, her elbows resting in her lap, her chin tilted in the cup of her hands, looking steadily ahead, and for a long time no sound but the steady dip, dip, dip of the two paddles broke the stillness of their progress. Scarcely once did Philip take his eyes from her. Every turn, every passing of shadow and light, each breath of wind that set stirring the shimmering tresses of her hair, made her more beautiful to him. From red gold to the rich and lustrous brown of the ripened wintel berries he marked the marvellous changing of her hair with the setting of the sun. A quick chill was growing in the air now and after a little he crept forward and slipped a light blanket about the slender shoulders. Even then Josephine did not speak, but looked up at him, and smiled her thanks. In his eyes, his touch, even his subdued breath, were the whispers of his adoration.

Movement roused Jean from his Indian-like silence. As Philip moved back, he called:

"It is four o'clock, M'sieur. We will have darkness in an hour. There is a place to camp and tepee poles ready cut on the point ahead of us."

Fifteen minutes later Philip ran his canoe ashore close to Jean Croisset's on a beach of white sand. He could not help seeing that, from the moment she had answered his question out on the lake, a change had come over Josephine. For a short time that afternoon she had risen from out of the thing that oppressed her, and once or twice there had been almost happiness in her smile and laughter. Now she seemed to have sunk again under its smothering grip. It was as if the chill and dismal gloom of approaching night had robbed her cheeks of colour, and had given a tired droop to her shoulders as she sat silently, and waited for them to make her tent comfortable. When it was up, and the blankets spread, she went in and left them alone, and the last glimpse that he had of her face left with Philip a cameo-like impression of hopelessness that made him want to call out her name, yet held him speechless. He looked closely at Jean as they put up their own tent, and for the first time he saw that the mask had fallen from the half-breed's face, and that it was filled with that same mysterious hopelessness and despair. Almost roughly he caught him by the shoulder.

"See here, Jean Croisset," he cried impatiently, "you're a man. What are you afraid of?"

"God," replied Jean so quietly that Philip dropped his hand from his shoulder in astonishment. "Nothing else in the world am I afraid of, M'sieur!"

"Then why - why in the name of that God do you look like this?" demanded Philip. "You saw her go into the tent. She is disheartened, hopeless because of something that I can't guess at, cold and shivering and white because of a FEAR of something. She is a woman. You are a man. Are YOU afraid?"

"No, not afraid, M'sieur. It is her grief that hurts me, not fear. If it would help her I would let you take this knife at my side and cut me into pieces so small that the birds could carry them away. I know what you mean. You think I am not a fighter. Our Lady in Heaven, if fighting could only save her!"

"And it cannot?"

"No, M'sieur. Nothing can save her. You can help, but you cannot save her. I believe that nothing like this terrible thing that has come to her has happened before since the world began. It is a mistake that it has come once. The Great God would not let it happen twice."

He spoke calmly. Philip could find no words with which to reply. His hand slipped from Jean's arm to his hand, and their fingers gripped. Thus for a space they stood. Philip broke the silence.

"I love her, Jean," he spoke softly.

"Every one loves her, M'sieur. All our forest people call her 'L'Ange.'"

"And still you say there is no hope?"

"None."

"Not even - if we fight -?"

Jean's fingers tightened about his like cords of steel.

"We may kill, M'sieur, but that will not save hearts crushed like - See! - like I crush these ash berries under my foot! I tell you again, nothing like this has ever happened before since the world began, and nothing like it will ever happen again!"

Steadily Philip looked into Jean's eyes.

"You have seen something of the world, Jean?"

"A good deal, M'sieur. For seven years I went to school at Montreal, and prepared myself for the holy calling of Missioner. That was many years ago. I am now simply Jean Jacques Croisset, of the forests."

"Then you know - you must know, that where there is life there is hope," argued Philip eagerly, "I have promised not to pry after her secret, to fight for her only as she tells me to fight.

But if I knew, Jean. If I knew what this trouble is - how and where to fight! Is this knowledge - impossible?"

"Impossible, M'sieur!"

Slowly Jean withdrew his hand.

"Don't take it that way, man," exclaimed Philip quickly. "I'm not ferreting for her secret now. Only I've got to know - is it impossible for her to tell me?"

"As impossible, M'sieur, as it would be for me. And Our Lady herself could not make me do that if I heard Her voice commanding me out of Heaven. All that I can do is to wait, and watch, and guard. And all that you can do, M'sieur, is to play the part she has asked of you. In doing that, and doing it well, you will keep the last bit of life in her heart from being trampled out. If you love her" - he picked up a tepee pole before he finished, and then, said - "you will do as you have promised!"

There was a finality in the shrug of Jean's shoulders which Philip did not question. He picked up an axe, and while Jean arranged the tepee poles began to chop down a dry birch. As the chips flew his mind flew faster. In his optimism he had half believed that the cloud of mystery in which Josephine had buried him would, in time, be voluntarily lifted by her. He had not been able to make himself believe that any situation could exist where hopelessness was as complete as she had described. Without arguing with himself he had taken it for granted that she had been labouring under a tremendous strain, and that no matter what her trouble was it had come to look immeasurably darker to her than it really was. But Jean's attitude, his low and unexcited voice, and the almost omniscient decisiveness of his words had convinced him that Josephine had not painted it as blackly as she might. She, at least, had seemed to see a ray of hope. Jean saw none, and Philip realized that the half-breed's calm and unheated judgment was more to be reckoned with than hers. At the same time, he did not feel dismayed. He was of the sort who have born in them the fighting instinct, And with this instinct, which is two thirds of life's battle won, goes the sort of optimism that has opened up raw worlds to the trails of men. Without the one the other cannot exist.

As the blows of his axe cut deep into the birch, Philip knew that so long as there is life and freedom and a sun above it is impossible for hope to become a thing of char and ash. He did not use logic. He simply LIVED! He was alive, and he loved Josephine.

The muscles of his arms were like sinews of rawhide. Every fibre in his body was strung with a splendid strength. His brain was as clear as the unpolluted air that drifted over the cedar and spruce. And now to these tremendous forces had come the added strength of the most wonderful thing in the world: love of a woman. In spite of all that Josephine and Jean had said, in spite of all the odds that might be against him, he was confident of winning whatever fight might be ahead of him.

He not only felt confident, but cheerful. He did not try to make Jean understand what it meant to be in camp with the company of a woman for the first time in two years. Long after the tents were up and the birch-fire was crackling cheerfully in the darkness Josephine still remained in her tent. But the mere fact that she was there lifted Philip's soul to the skies.

And Josephine, with a blanket drawn about her shoulders, lay in the thick gloom of her tent and listened to him. His far-reaching, exuberant whistling seemed to warm her. She heard him laughing and talking with Jean, whose voice never came to her; farther back, where he was cutting down another birch, she heard him shout out the words of a song between blows; and once, sotto voce, and close to her tent, she quite distinctly heard him say "Damn!" She knew that he had stumbled with an armful of wood, and for the first time in that darkness and her misery she smiled. That one word alone Philip had not intended that she should hear. But when it was out he picked himself up and laughed.

He did not meddle with Jean's cook-fire, but he built a second fire where the cheer of it would light up Josephine's tent, and piled dry logs on it until the flame of it lighted up the gloom about them for a hundred feet. And then, with a pan in one hand and a stick in the other, he came close and beat a din that could have been heard a quarter of a mile away.

Josephine came out full in the flood-light of the fire, and he saw that she had been crying. Even now there was a tremble of her lips as she smiled her gratitude. He dropped his pan and stick, and went to her. It seemed as if this last hour in the darkness of camp had brought her nearer to him, and he gently took her hands in his own and held them for a moment close to him. They were cold and trembling, and one of them that had rested under her cheek was damp with tears.

"You mustn't do this any more," he whispered.

"I'll try not to," she promised. "Please let me stand a little in the warmth of the fire. I'm cold."

He led her close to the flaming birch logs and the heat soon brought a warm flush into her cheeks. Then they went to where Jean had spread out their supper on the ground. When she had seated herself on the pile of blankets they had arranged for her, Josephine looked across at Philip, squatted Indian-fashion opposite her, and smiled apologetically.

"I'm afraid your opinion of me isn't getting better," she said. "I'm not much of a - a - sport - to let you men get supper by yourselves, am I? You see - I'm taking advantage of my birthday."

"Oui, ma belle princesse," laughed Jean softly, a tender look coming into his thin, dark face. "And do you remember that other birthday, years and years ago, when you took advantage of Jean Croisset while he was sleeping? Non, you do not remember?"

"Yes, I remember."

"She was six, M'sieur," explained Jean, "and while I slept, dreaming of one gr-r-rand paradise, she cut off my moustaches. They were splendid, those moustaches, but they would never grow right after that, and so I have gone shaven."

In spite of her efforts to appear cheerful, Philip could see that Josephine was glad when the meal was over, and that she was forcing herself to sip at a second cup of tea on their account. He accompanied her back to the tent after she had bade Jean good-night, and as they stood for a moment before the open flap there filled the girl's face a look that was partly of self-reproach and partly of wistful entreaty for his understanding and forgiveness.

"You have been good to me," she said. "No one can ever know how good you have been to me, what it has meant to me, and I thank you."

She bowed her head, and again he restrained the impulse to gather her close up in his arms. When she looked up he was holding something toward her in the palm of his hand. It was a little Bible, worn and frayed at the edges, pathetic in its raggedness.

"A long time ago, my mother gave me this Bible," he said. "She told me that as long as I carried it, and believed in it, no harm could come to me, and I guess she was right. It was her first Bible, and mine. It's grown old and ragged with me, and the water and snow have faded it. I've come to sort of believe that mother is always near this Book. I'd like you to have it, Josephine. It's the only thing I've got to offer you on your birthday."

While he was speaking he had taken one of her hands and thrust his precious gift into it. Slowly Josephine raised the little Bible to her breast. She did not speak, but for a moment Philip saw in her eyes the look for which he would have sacrificed the world; a look that told him more than all the volumes of the earth could have told of a woman's trust and faith.

He bent his head lower and whispered:

"To-night, my Josephine - just this night - may I wish you all the hope and happiness that God and my Mother can bring you, and kiss you - once -"

In that moment's silence he heard the throbbing of her heart. She seemed to have ceased breathing, and then, slowly, looking straight into his eyes, she lifted her lips to him, and as one who meets a soul of a thing too sanctified to touch with hands, he kissed her. Scarcely had the warm sweetness of her lips thrilled his own than she had turned from him, and was gone.

CHAPTER SEVEN

For a time after they had cleared up the supper things Philip sat with Jean close to the fire and smoked. The half-breed had lapsed again into his gloom and silence. Two or three times Philip caught Jean watching him furtively. He made no effort to force a conversation, and when he had finished his pipe he rose and went to the tent which they were to share together. At last he found himself not unwilling to be alone. He closed the flap to shut out the still brilliant illumination of the fire, drew a blanket about him, and stretched himself out on the top of his sleeping bag. He wanted to think.

He closed his eyes to bring back more vividly the picture of Josephine as she had given him her lips to kiss. This, of all the unusual happenings of that afternoon, seemed most like a dream to him, yet his brain was afire with the reality of it. His mind struggled again with the hundred questions which he had asked himself that day, and in the end Josephine remained as completely enshrouded in mystery as ever. Yet of one thing was he convinced. The oppression of the thing under which Jean and the girl were fighting had become more acute with the turning of their faces homeward. At Adare House lay the cause of their hopelessness, of Josephine's grief, and of the gloom under which the half-breed had fallen so completely that night. Until they reached Adare House he could guess at nothing. And there - what would he find?

In spite of himself he felt creeping slowly over him a shuddering fear that he had not acknowledged before. The darkness deepening as the fire died away, the stillness of the night, the low wailing of a wind growing out of the north roused in him the unrest and doubt that sunshine and day had dispelled. An uneasy slumber came at last with this disquiet. His mind was filled with fitful dreams. Again he was back with Radisson and MacTavish, listening to the foxes out on the barrens. He heard the Scotchman's moaning madness and listened to the blast of storm. And then he heard a cry - a cry like that which MacTavish fancied he had heard in the wind an hour before he died. It was this dream-cry that roused him.

He sat up, and his face and hands were damp. It was black in the tent. Outside even the bit of wind had died away. He reached out a hand, groping for Jean. The half-breed's blankets had not been disturbed. Then for a few moments he sat very still, listening, and wondering if the cry had been real. As he sat tense and still in the half daze of the sleep it came again. It was the shrill laughing carnival of a loon out on the lake. More than once he had laughed at comrades who had shivered at that sound and cowered until its echoes had died away in moaning wails. He understood now. He knew why the Indians called it moakwa - "the mad thing." He thought of MacTavish, and threw the blanket from his shoulders, and crawled out of the tent.

Only a few faintly glowing embers remained where he had piled the birch logs. The sky was full of stars. The moon, still full and red, hung low in the west. The lake lay in a silvery and unruffled shimmer. Through the silence there came to him from a great distance the coughing challenge of a bull moose inviting a rival to battle. Then Philip saw a dark object huddled close to Josephine's tent.

He moved toward it, his moccasined feet making no sound. Something impelled him to keep as quiet as the night itself. And when he came near - he was glad. For the object was Jean. He sat with his back to a block of birch twenty paces from the door of Josephine's tent. His head had fallen forward on his chest. He was asleep, but across his knees lay his rifle, gripped tightly in both hands. Quick as a flash the truth rushed upon Philip. Like a faithful dog Jean was guarding the girl. He had kept awake as long as he could, but even in slumber his hands did not give up their hold on the rifle.

Against whom was he guarding her? What danger could there be in this quiet, starlit night for Josephine? A sudden chill ran through Philip. Did Jean mistrust HIM? Was it possible that Josephine had secretly expressed a fear which made the Frenchman watch over her while she slept? As silently as he had approached he moved away until he stood in the sand at the shore of the lake. There he looked back. He could just see Jean, a dark blot; and all at once the unfairness of his suspicion came upon him. To him Josephine had given proofs of her faith which nothing could destroy. And he understood now the reason for that tired, drawn look in Jean's face. This was not the first night he had watched. Every night he had guarded her until, in the small hours of dawn, his eyes had closed heavily as they were closed now.

The beginning of the gray northern dawn was not far away. Philip knew that without looking at the hour. He sensed it. It was in the air, the stillness of the forest, in the appearance of the stars and moon. To prove himself he looked at his watch with the match with which he lighted his pipe. It was half-past three. At this season of the year dawn came at five.

He walked slowly along the strip of sand between the dark wall of the forest and the lake. Not until he was a mile away from the camp did he stop. Then something happened to betray the uneasy tension to which his nerves were drawn. A sudden crash in the brush close at hand drew him about with a start, and even while he laughed at himself he stood with his automatic in his hand.

He heard the whimpering, babyish-like complaint of the porcupine that had made the sound, and still chuckling over his nervousness he seated himself on a white drift-log that had lain bleaching for half a century in the sand.

The moon had fallen behind the western forests; the stars were becoming fainter in the sky, and about him the darkness was drawing in like a curtain. He loved this hour that bridged the northern night with the northern day, and he sat motionless and still, covering the glow of fire in his pipe bowl with the palm of his hand.

Out of the brush ambled the porcupine, chattering and talking to itself in its queer and good-humoured way, fat as a poplar bud ready to burst, and so intent on reaching the edge of the lake that it passed in its stupid innocence so close that Philip might have struck it with a stick. And then there swooped down from out of the cover of the black spruce a gray cloudlike thing that came with the silence and lightness of a huge snowflake, hovered for an instant over the porcupine, and disappeared into the darkness beyond. And the porcupine, still oblivious of danger and what the huge owl would have done to him had he been a snowshoe rabbit instead of a monster of quills, drank his fill leisurely and ambled back as he had come, chattering his little song of good-humour and satisfaction.

One after another there came now the sounds that merged dying night into the birth of day, and for the hundredth time Philip listened to the wonders that never grew old for him. The laugh of the loon was no longer a raucous, mocking cry of exultation and triumph, but a timid, question note - half drowsy, half filled with fear; and from the treetops came the still lower notes of the owls, their night's hunt done, and seeking now the densest covers for the day. And then, from deep back in the forests, came a cry that was filled with both hunger and defiance - the wailing howl of a wolf. With these night sounds came the first cheep, cheep, cheep of the little brush sparrow, still drowsy and uncertain, but faintly heralding the day. Wings fluttered in the spruce and cedar thickets. From far overhead came the honking of Canada geese flying southward. And one by one the stars went out, and in the south-eastern skies a gray hand reached up slowly over the forests and wiped darkness from the earth. Not until then did Philip rise from his seat and turn his face toward camp.

He tried to throw off the feeling of oppression that still clung to him. By the time he reached camp he had partly succeeded. The fire was burning brightly again, and Jean was busy preparing breakfast. To his surprise he saw Josephine standing outside of her tent. She had finished brushing her hair, and was plaiting it in a long braid. He had wondered how they would meet that morning. His face flushed warm as he approached her. The thrill of their kiss was still on his lips, and his heart sent the memory of it burning in his eyes as he came up, Josephine turned to greet him. She was pale and calm. There were dark lines under her eyes, and her voice was steady and without emotion as she said "Good morning." It was as if he had dreamed the thing that had passed the night before. There was neither glow of tenderness, of regret, nor of memory in her eyes. Her smile was wan and forced. He knew that she was calling upon his chivalry to forget that one moment before the door of her tent. He bowed, and said simply:

"I'm afraid you didn't sleep well, Josephine. Did I disturb you when I stole out of camp?"

"I heard nothing," she replied. "Nothing but the cries of that terrible bird out on the lake. I'm afraid I didn't sleep much."

The atmosphere of the camp that morning weighted Philip's heart with a heaviness which he could not throw off. He performed his share of the work with Jean, and tried to talk to him, but Croisset would only reply to his most pointed remarks. He whistled. He shouted out a song back in the timber as he cut an armful of dry birch, and he returned to Jean and the girl laughing, the wood piled to his chin and the axe under his arm. Neither showed that they had heard him. The meal was eaten in a chilly silence that filled him with deepest foreboding. Josephine seemed at ease. She talked with him when he spoke to her, but there seemed now to be a mysterious restraint in every word that she uttered. She excused herself before Jean and he were through, and went to her tent. A moment later Philip rose and went down to his canoe.

In the rubber sack was the last of his tobacco. He was fumbling for it when his heart gave a great jump. A voice had spoken softly behind him:

"Philip."

Slowly, unbelieving, he turned. It was Josephine. For the first time she had called him by his name. And yet the speaking of it seemed to put a distance between them, for her voice was calm and without emotion, as she might have spoken to Jean.

"I lay awake nearly all of the night, thinking," she said. "It was a terrible thing that we did, and I am sorry - sorry -"

In the quickening of her breath he saw how heroically she was fighting to speak steadily to him.

"You can't understand," she resumed, facing him with the steadiness of despair. "You cannot understand - until you reach Adare House. And that is what I dread, the hour when you will know what I am, and how terrible it was for me to do what I did last night. If you were like most other men, I wouldn't care so much. But you have been different."

He replied in words which he would not dare to have uttered a few hours before.

"And yet, back there when you first asked me to go with you as your husband, you knew what I would find at Adare House?" he asked, his voice low and tense. "You knew?"

"Yes."

"Then what has produced the change that makes you fear to have me go on? Is it because" - he leaned toward her, and his face was bloodless - "Is it because you care a little for me?"

"Because I respect you, yes," she said in a voice that disappointed him. "I don't want to hurt you. I don't want you to go back into the world thinking of me as you will. You have been honest with me. I do not blame you for what happened last night. The fault was mine. And I have come to you now, so that you will understand that, no matter how I may appear and act, I have faith and trust in you. I would give anything that last night might be wiped out of our memories. That is impossible, but you must not think of it and you must not talk to me any more as you have, until we reach Adare House. And then -"

Her white face was pathetic as she turned away from him.

"You will not want to," she finished. "After that you will fight for me simply because you are a knight among men, and because you have promised. There will not even be the promise to bind you, for I release you from that."

Philip stood silent as she left him. He knew that to follow her and to force further conversation upon her after what she had said would be little less than brutal. She had given him to understand that from now on he was to hold himself toward her with greater restraint, and the blood flushed hot and uncomfortable into his face as he realized for the first time how he had overstepped the bounds.

All his life womanhood had been the most beautiful thing in the world to him. And now there was forced upon him the dread conviction that he had insulted it. He did not stop to argue that the overwhelming completeness of his love had excused him. What he thought of now was that he had found Josephine alone, had declared that love for her before he knew her name, and had followed it up by act and word which he now felt to be dishonourable. And yet, after all, would he have recalled what had happened if he could? He asked himself that question as he returned to help Jean. And he found no answer to it until they were in their canoes again and headed up the lake, Josephine sitting with her back to him, her thick silken braid falling in a sinuous and sunlit rope of red gold over her shoulders. Then he knew that he would not.

Jean gave little rest that day, and by noon they had covered twenty miles of the lake-way. An hour for dinner, and they went on. At times Josephine used her paddle, and not once during the day did she sit with her face to Philip. Late in the afternoon they camped on a portage fifty miles from Adare House.

There were no stars or moon in the sky this night. The wind had changed, and came from the north. In it was the biting chill of the Arctic, and overhead was a gray-dun mass of racing cloud. A dozen times Jean turned his face anxiously from the fire into the north, and held wet fingers high over his head to see if in the air was that peculiar sting by which the forest man forecasts the approach of snow.

At last he said to Philip: "The wind will grow, M'sieur," and picked up his axe.

Philip followed with his own, and they piled about Josephine's tent a thick protection of spruce and cedar boughs. Then together they brought three or four big logs to the fire. After that Philip went into their own tent, stripped off his outer garments, and buried himself in his sleeping bag. For a long time he lay awake and listened to the increasing wail of the wind in the tall spruce tops. It was not new to him. For months he had fallen asleep with the thunderous crash of ice and the screaming fury of storm in his ears. But to-night there was something in the sound which sunk him still deeper into the gloom which he had found it impossible to throw off. At last he fell asleep.

When he awoke he struck a match and looked at his watch. It was four o'clock, and he dressed and went outside. The wind had died down. Jean was already busy over the cook-fire, and in Josephine's tent he saw the light of a candle. She appeared a little later, wrapped close in a thick red Hudson's Bay coat, and with a marten-skin cap on her head. Something in her first appearance, the picturesqueness of her dress, the jauntiness of the little cap, and the first flush of the fire in her face filled him with the hope that sleep had given her better spirit. A closer glance dashed this hope. Without questioning her he knew that she had spent another night of mental torture. And Jean's face looked thinner, and the hollows under his eyes were deeper.

All that day the sky hung heavy and dark with cloud, and the water was rough. Early in the afternoon the wind rose again, and Croisset ran alongside them to suggest that they go ashore. He spoke to Philip, but Josephine interrupted quickly:

"We must go on, Jean," she demanded. "If it is not impossible we must reach Adare House to-night."

"It will be late - midnight," replied Jean. "And if it grows rougher -"

A dash of spray swept over the bow into the girl's face.

"I don't care for that," she cried. "Wet and cold won't hurt us." She turned to Philip, as if needing his argument against Jean's. "Is it not possible to get me home to-night?" she asked.

"It is two o'clock," said Philip. "How far have we to go, Jean?"

"It is not the distance, M'sieur - it is that," replied Jean, as a wave sent another dash of water over Josephine. "We are twenty miles from Adare House."

Philip looked at Josephine.

"It is best for you to go ashore and wait until to-morrow, Josephine. Look at that stretch of water ahead - a mass of whitecaps."

"Please, please take me home," she pleaded, and now she spoke to Philip alone. "I'm not afraid. And I cannot live through another night like last night. Why, if anything should happen to us" - she flung back her head and smiled bravely at him through the mist of her wet hair and the drenching spray - "if anything should happen I know you'd meet it gloriously. So I'm not afraid. And I want to go home."

Philip turned to the half-breed, who had drifted a canoe length away.

"We'll go on, Jean," he called. "We can make it by keeping close inshore. Can you swim?"

"Oui, M'sieur; but Josephine -"

"I can swim with her," replied Philip, and Josephine saw the old life and strength in his face again as she turned to the white-capped seas ahead of them.

Hour after hour they fought their way on after that, the wind rising stronger in their faces, the seas burying them deeper; and each time that Josephine looked back she marvelled at the man behind her, bare-headed, his hair drenched, his arms naked to the elbows, and his clear gray eyes always smiling confidence at her through the gloom of mist. Not until darkness was falling about them did Jean drop near enough to speak again. Then he shouted:

"Another hour and we reach Snowbird River, M'sieur. That is four miles from Adare House. But ahead of us the wind rushes across a wide sweep of the lake. Shall we hazard it?"

"Yes, yes," cried the girl, answering for Philip. "We must go on!"

Without another word Croisset led the way. The wind grew stronger with each minute's progress. Shouting for Jean to hold his canoe for a space, Philip steadied his own canoe while he spoke to the girl.

"Come back to me as quietly as you can, Josephine," he said. "Pass the dunnage ahead of you to take the place of your weight. If anything happens, I want you near me."

Cautiously Josephine did as he bade her, and as she added slowly to the ballast in the bow she drew little by little nearer to Philip, Her hand touched an object in the bottom of the canoe as she came close to him. It was one of his moccasins. She saw now his naked throat and chest. He had stripped off his heavy woollen shirt as well as his footwear. He reached out, and his hand touched her lightly as she huddled down in front of him.

"Splendid!" he laughed. "You're a little brick, Josephine, and the best comrade in a canoe that I ever saw. Now if we go over all I've got to do is to swim ashore with you. Is it good walking to Adare House?"

He did not hear her reply; but a fresh burst of the wind sent a loose strand of her hair back into his face, and he was happy. Happy in spite of a peril which neither he nor Jean would have thought of facing alone. In the darkness he could no longer see Croisset or his canoe. But Jean's shout came back to him every minute on the wind, and over Josephine's head he answered. He was glad that it was so dark the girl could not see what was ahead of them now. Once or twice his own breath stopped short, when it seemed that the canoe had taken the fatal plunge which he was dreading. Every minute he figured the distance from the shore, and his chances of swimming it if they were overturned. And then, after a long time, there came a sudden lull in the wind, and the seas grew less rough. Jean's voice came from near them, filled with a thrill of relief.

"We are behind the point," he shouted. "Another mile and we will enter the Snowbird, M'sieur!"

Philip leaned forward in the gloom. Josephine's cap had fallen off, and for a moment his hand rested on her wet and wind-blown hair.

"Did you hear that?" he cried. "We're almost home."

"Yes," she shivered. "And I'm glad - glad -"

Was it an illusion of his own, or did she seem to shiver and draw away from him AT THE TOUCH OF HIS HAND? Even in the blackness he could FEEL that she was huddled forward, her face in her hands. She did not speak to him again. When they entered the smooth water of the Snowbird, Jean's canoe drew close in beside them, but not a word fell from Croisset. Like shadows they moved up the stream between two black walls of forest. A steadily increasing excitement, a feeling that he was upon the eve of strange events, grew stronger in Philip. His arms and back ached, his legs were cramped, the last of his splendid strength had been called upon in the fight with wind and seas, but he forgot this exhaustion in anticipation of the hour that was drawing near. He knew that Adare House would reveal to him things which Josephine had not told him. She had said that it would, and that he would hate her then. That they were burying themselves deeper into the forest he guessed by the lessening of the wind.

Half an hour passed, and in that time his companion did not move or speak. He heard faintly a distant wailing cry. He recognized the sound. It was not a wolf-cry, but the howl of a husky. He fancied then that the girl moved, that she was gripping the sides of the canoe with her hands. For fifteen minutes more there was not a sound but the dip of the paddles and the monotone of the wind sweeping through the forest tops. Then the dog howled again, much nearer; and this time he was joined by a second, a third, and a fourth, until the night was filled with a din that made Philip stare wonderingly off into the blackness. There were fifty dogs if there was one in that yelping, howling horde, he told himself, and they were coming with the swiftness of the wind in their direction.

From his canoe Croisset broke the silence.

"The wind has given the pack our scent, ma Josephine, and they are coming to meet you," he said.

The girl made no reply, but Philip could see now that she was sitting tense and erect. As suddenly as it had begun the cry of the pack ceased. The dogs had reached the water, and were waiting. Not until Jean swung his canoe toward shore and the bow of it scraped on a gravelly bar did they give voice again, and then so close and fiercely that involuntarily Philip held his canoe back. In another moment Josephine had stepped lightly over the side in a foot of water. He could not see what happened then, except that the bar was filled with a shadowy horde of leaping, crowding, yelping beasts, and that Josephine was the centre of them. He heard her voice clear and commanding, crying out their names - Tyr, Captain, Bruno, Thor, Wamba - until their number seemed without end; he heard the metallic snap of fangs, quick, panting breaths, the shuffling of padded feet; and then the girl's voice grew more clear, and the sounds less, until he heard nothing but the bated breath of the pack and a low, smothered whine.

In that moment the wind-blown clouds above them broke in a narrow rift across the skies, and for an instant the moon shone through What he saw then drew Philip's breath from him in a wondering gasp.

On the white bar stood Josephine. The wind on the lake had torn the strands of her long braid loose and her hair swept in a damp and clinging mass to her hips. She was looking toward him, as if about to speak. But it was the pack that made him stare. A sea of great shaggy heads and crouching bodies surrounded her, a fierce yellow and green-eyed horde flattened like a single beast upon their bellies their heads turned toward her, their throats swelling and their eyes gleaming in the joyous excitement of her return. An instant of that strange and thrilling picture, and the night was black again. The girl's voice spoke softly. Bodies shuffled out of her path. And then she said, quite near to him;

"Are you coming, Philip?"

CHAPTER EIGHT

Not without a slight twinge of trepidation did Philip step from his canoe to her. He had not heard Croisset go ashore, and for a moment he felt as if he were deliberately placing himself at the mercy of a wolf-pack. Josephine may have guessed the effect of the savage spectacle he had beheld from the canoe, for she was close to the water's edge to meet him. She spoke, and in the pitch darkness he reached out. Her hand was groping for him, and her fingers closed firmly about his own.

"They are my bodyguard, and I have trained them all from puppies," she explained. "They don't like strangers, but will fight for anything that I touch. So I will lead you." She turned with him toward the pack, and cried in her clear, commanding voice: "Marche, boys! - Tyr, Captain, Thor, Marche! Hoosh, hoosh, Marche!"

It seemed as if a hundred eyes gleamed out of the blackness; then there was a movement, a whining, snarling, snapping movement, and as they walked up the bar and into a narrow trail Philip could hear the pack falling out to the side and behind them. Also he knew that Jean was ahead of them now. He did not speak, nor did Josephine offer to break the silence again. Still letting her hand rest in his she followed close behind the half-breed. Her hand was so cold that Philip involuntarily held it tighter in his own, as if to give it warmth. He could feel her shivering, and yet something told him that what he sensed in the darkness was not caused by chill alone. Several times her fingers closed shudderingly about his.

They had not walked more than a couple of hundred yards when a turn brought them out of the forest trail, and the blackness ahead was broken by a solitary light, a dimly lighted window in a pit of gloom.

"Marja is not expecting us to-night," apologized the girl nervously. "That is Adare House."

The loneliness of the spot, its apparent emptiness of life, the silence save for the snuffling and whining of the unseen beasts about them, stirred Philip with a curious sensation of awe. He had at least expected light and life at Adare House. Here were only the mystery of darkness and a deathlike quiet. Even the one light seemed turned low. As they advanced toward it a great shadow grew out of the gloom; and then, all at once, it seemed as if a curtain of the forest had been drawn aside, and away beyond the looming shadow Philip saw the glow of a camp-fire. From that distant fire there came the challenging howl of a dog, and instantly it was taken up by a score of fierce tongues about them. As Josephine's voice rose to quell the disturbance the light in the window grew suddenly brighter, and then a door opened and in it stood the figures of a man and woman. The man was standing behind the woman, looking over her shoulder, and for one moment Philip caught the flash of the lamp-glow on the barrel of a rifle.

Josephine paused.

"You will forgive me if I ask you to let me go on alone, and you follow with Jean?" she whispered. "I will try and see you again to-night, when I have dressed myself, and I am in better condition to show you hospitality."

Jean was so close that he overheard her. "We will follow," he said softly. "Go ahead, ma cheri."

His voice was filled with an infinite gentleness, almost of pity; and as Josephine drew her hand from Philip's and went on ahead of them he dropped back close to the other's side.

"Something will happen soon which may turn your heart to stone and ice, M'sieur," he said, and his voice was scarce above a whisper. "I wanted her to tell you back there, two days ago, but she shrank from the ordeal then. It is coming to-night. And, however it may effect you, M'sieur, I ask you not to show the horror of it, but to have pity. You have perhaps known many women, but you have never known one like our Josephine. In her soul is the purity of the blue skies, the sweetness of the wild flowers, the goodness of our Blessed Lady, the Mother of Christ. You may disbelieve, and what is to come may eat at the core of your heart as it has devoured life and happiness from mine. But you will love L'Ange - our Josephine - just the same."

Even as he felt himself trembling strangely at Jean Croisset's words, Philip replied:

"Always, Jean, I swear that."

In the open door Josephine had paused for a moment, and was looking back. Then she disappeared.

"Come," said Jean. "And may God have pity on you if you fail to keep your word in all you have promised, M'sieur Philip Darcambal. For from this hour on you are Philip Darcambal, of Montreal, the husband of Josephine Adare, our beloved lady of the forests. Come, M'sieur!"

CHAPTER NINE

Without another word Jean led the way to the door, which had partly closed after Josephine. For a moment he paused with his hand upon it, and then entered. Philip was close behind him. His first glance swept the room in search of the girl. She had disappeared with her two companions. For a moment he heard voices beyond a second door in front of him. Then there was silence.

In wonder he stared about him, and Jean did not interrupt his gaze. He stood in a great room whose walls were of logs and axe-hewn timbers. It was a room forty feet long by twenty in width, massive in its build, with walls and ceiling stained a deep brown. In one end was a fireplace large enough to hold a pile of logs six feet in length, and in this a small fire was smouldering. In the centre of the room was a long, massive table, its timber carved by the axe, and on this a lamp was burning. The floor was strewn with fur rugs, and on the walls hung the mounted heads of beasts. These things impressed themselves upon Philip first. It was as if he had stepped suddenly out of the world in which he was living into the ancient hall of a wild and half-savage thane whose bones had turned to dust centuries ago.

Not until Jean spoke to him, and led the way through the room, was this first impression swept back by his swift and closer observation of detail. About him extreme age was curiously blended with the modern. His breath stopped short when he saw in the shadow of the farther wall a piano, with a bronze lamp suspended from the ceiling above it. His eyes caught the shadowy outline of cases filled with books; he saw close to the fireplace wide, low-built divans covered with cushions; and over the door through which they passed hung a framed copy of da Vinci's masterpiece, "La Joconde," the Smiling Woman.

Into a dimly lighted hall he followed Jean, who paused a moment later before another door, which he opened. Philip waited while he struck a match and lighted a lamp. He knew at a glance that this was to be his sleeping apartment, and as he took in its ample comfort, the broad low bed behind its old-fashioned curtains, the easy chairs, the small table covered with books and magazines, and the richly furred rugs on the floor, he experienced a new and strange feeling of restfulness and pleasure which for the moment overshadowed his more excited sensations. Jean was already on his knees before a fireplace touching a match to a pile of birch, and as the inflammable bark spurted into flame and the small logs began to crackle he rose to his feet and faced Philip. Both were soaked to the skin. Jean's hair hung lank and wet about his face, and his hollow cheeks were cadaverous. In spite of the hour and the place, Philip could not restrain a laugh.

"I'm glad Josephine was thoughtful enough to come in ahead of us, Jean," he chuckled. "We look like a couple of drowned water-rats!"

"I will bring up your sack, M'sieur," responded Jean. "If you haven't dry clothes of your own you will find garments behind the curtains. I think some of them will fit you. After we are warmed and dried we will have supper."

A few moments after Jean left him an Indian woman brought him a pail of hot water. He was half stripped and enjoying a steaming sponge bath when Croisset returned with his dunnage sack. The Arctic had not left him much to choose from, but behind the curtains which Jean had pointed out to him he found a good-sized wardrobe. He glowed with warmth and comfort when he had finished dressing. The chill was gone from his blood. He no longer felt the ache in his arms and back. He lighted his pipe, and for a few moments stood with his back to the crackling fire, listening and waiting. Through the thick walls no sound came to him. Once he thought that he heard the closing of a distant door. Even the night was strangely silent, and he walked to the one large window in his room and stared out into the darkness. On this side the edge of the forest was not far away, for he could hear the soughing of the wind in the treetops.

For an hour he waited with growing impatience for Jean's return or some word from Josephine. At last there came another knock at the door. He opened it eagerly. To his disappointment neither Jean nor the girl stood there, but the Indian woman who had brought him the hot water, carrying in her hands a metal server covered with steaming dishes. She moved silently past him, placed the server on the table, and was turning to go when he spoke to her.

"Tan'se a itumuche hooyun?" he asked in Cree.

She went out as if she had not heard him, and the door closed behind her. With growing perplexity, Philip directed his attention to the food. This manner of serving his supper partly convinced him that he would not see Josephine again that night. He was hungry, and began to do justice to the contents of the dishes. In one dish he found a piece of fruit cake and half a dozen pickles, and he knew that at least Josephine had helped to prepare his supper. Half an hour later the Indian woman returned as silently as before and carried away the dishes. He followed her to the door and stood for a few moments looking down the hall. He looked at his watch. It was after ten o'clock. Where was Jean? he wondered. Why had Josephine not sent some word to him - at least an explanation telling him why she could not see him as she had promised? Why had Croisset spoken in that strange way just before they entered the door of Adare House? Nothing had happened, and he was becoming more and more convinced that nothing would happen - that night.

He turned suddenly from the door, facing the window in his room. The next instant he stood tense and staring. A face was glued against the pane: dark, sinister, with eyes that shone with the menacing glare of a beast. In a flash it was gone. But in that brief space Philip had seen enough to hold him like one turned to stone, still staring where the face had been, his heart beating like a hammer. As the face disappeared he had seen a hand pass swiftly through the light, and in the hand was a pistol. It was not this fact, nor the suddenness of the apparition, that drew the gasping breath from his lips. It was the face, filled with a hatred that was almost madness - the face of Jean Jacques Croisset!

Scarcely was it gone when Philip sprang to the table, snatched up his automatic, and ran out into the hall. The end of the hall he believed opened outdoors, and he ran swiftly in that direction, his moccasined feet making no sound. He found a door locked with an iron bar. It took him but a moment to throw this up, open the door, and leap out into the night. The wind had died away, and it was snowing. In the silence he stood and listened, his eyes trying to find some moving shadow in the gloom. His fighting blood was up. His one impulse now was to come face to face with Jean Croisset and demand an explanation. He knew that if he had stood another moment with his back to the window Jean would have killed him. Murder was in the half-breed's eyes. His pistol was ready. Only Philip's quick turning from the door had saved him. It was evident that Jean had fled from the window as quickly as Philip had run out into the hall. Or, if he had not fled, he was hiding in the gloom of the building. At the thought that Jean might be crouching in the shadows Philip turned suddenly and moved swiftly and silently along the log wall of Adare House. He half expected a shot out of the darkness, and with his thumb he pressed down the safety lever of his automatic. He had almost reached his own window when a sound just beyond the pale filter of light that came out of it drew him more cautiously into the pitch darkness of the deep shadow next the wall. In another moment he was sure. Some other person was moving through the gloom beyond the streak of light.

With his pistol in readiness, Philip darted through the illuminated path. A startled cry broke out of the night, and with that cry his hand gripped fiercely in the deep fur of a coat. In the same breath an exclamation of astonishment came from his own lips as he looked into the white, staring face of Josephine. His pistol arm had dropped to his side. He believed that she had not seen the weapon, and he thrust it in his trousers pocket.

"You, Josephine!" he gasped. "What are you doing here?"

"And you?" she counter demanded. "You have no coat, no hat ..." Her hands gripped his arm. "I saw you run through the light. You had a pistol."

An impulse which he could not explain prompted him to tell her a falsehood.

"I came out - to see what the night looked like," he said. "When I heard you in the darkness it startled me for a moment, and I drew my pistol."

It seemed to him that her fingers clutched deeper and more convulsively into his arm.

"You have seen no one else?" she asked.

Again he was prompted to keep his secret.

"Is it possible that any one else is awake and roaming about at this hour?" he laughed. "I was just returning to my room to go to bed, Josephine. I thought that you had forgotten me. And Jean - where is he?"

"We hadn't forgotten you," shivered Josephine. "But unexpected things have happened since we came to Adare

House to-night. I was on my way to you. And Jean is back in the forest. Listen!"

From perhaps half a mile away there came the howl of a dog, and scarcely had that sound died away when there followed it the full-throated voice of the pack whose silence Philip had wondered at. A strange cry broke from Josephine.

"They are coming!" she almost sobbed. "Quick, Philip! My last hope of saving you is gone, and now you must be good to me - if you care at all!" She seized him by the hand and half ran with him to the door through which they had entered a short time before. In the great room she threw off her hood and the long fur cape that covered her, and then Philip saw that she had not dressed for the night and the storm. She had on a thin, shimmering dress of white, and her hair was coiled in loose golden masses about her head. On her breast, just below her white, bare throat, she wore a single red rose. It did not seem remarkable that she should be wearing a rose. To him the wonderful thing was that the rose, the clinging beauty of her dress, the glowing softness of her hair had been for him, and that something unexpected had taken her out into the night. Before he could speak she led him swiftly through the hall beyond, and did not pause until they had entered through another door and stood in the room which he knew was her room. In a glance he took in its exquisite femininity. Here, too, the bed was set behind curtains, and the curtains were closely drawn.

She had faced him now, standing a few steps away. She was deathly white, but her eyes had never met his more unflinchingly or more beautiful. Something in her attitude restrained him from approaching nearer. He looked at her, and waited. When she spoke her voice was low and calm. He knew that at last she had come to the hour of her greatest fight, and in that moment he was more unnerved than she.

"In a few minutes my mother and father will be here, Philip," she said. "The letter Jean brought me back there, where we first saw each other, came up by way of Wollaston House, and told me I need not expect them for a number of weeks. That was what made me happy for a little while. They were in Montreal, and I didn't want them to return. You will understand why - very soon. But my father changed his mind, and almost with the mailing of the letter he and my mother started home by way of Fond du Lac. Only an hour ago an Indian ran to us with the news that they were coming down the river. They are out there now - less than half a mile away - with Jean and the dogs!"

She turned a little from him, facing the bed.

"You remember - I told you that I had spent a year in Montreal," she went on. "I was there - alone - when it happened. See -"

She moved to the bed and gently drew the curtains aside. Scarcely breathing, Philip followed her.

"It's my baby," she whispered, "My little boy."

He could not see her face. She bowed her head and continued softly, as if fearing to awaken the baby asleep on the bed:

"No one knows - but Jean. My mother came first, and then my father. I lied to them. I told them that I was married, and that my husband had gone into the North. I came home with the baby - to meet this man I called Paul Darcambal, and whom they thought was my husband. I didn't want it to happen down there, but I planned on telling them the truth when we all got back in our forests. But after I returned I found that - I couldn't. Perhaps you may understand. Up here - among the forest people - the mother of a baby - like that - is looked upon as the most terrible thing in the world. She is called La bete noir - the black beast. Day by day I came to realize that I couldn't tell the truth, that I must live a great lie to save other hearts from being crushed as life has been crushed out of mine. I thought of telling them that my husband had died up here - in the North. And I was fearing suspicion ... the chance that my father might learn the untruth of it, when you came. That is all, Philip. You understand now. You know why - some day - you must go away and never come back. It is to save the boy, my father, my mother, and me!"

Not once in her terrible recital had the girl's voice broke. And now, as if bowing herself in silent prayer, she kneeled beside he bed and laid her head close to the baby's. Philip stood motionless, his unseeing eyes staring straight through the log walls and the black night to a city a thousand miles away. He understood now. Josephine's story was not the strangest thing in the world after all. It was perhaps the oldest of all stories. He had heard it a hundred times before, but never had it left him quite so cold and pulseless as he was now. And yet, even as the palace of the wonderful ideal he had builded crumbled about him in ruin, there rose up out of the dust of it a thing new-born and tangible for him. Slowly his eyes turned to the beautiful head bowed in its attitude of prayer. The blood began to surge back into his heart. His hands unclenched. She had told him that he would hate her, that he would want to leave her when he heard the story of her despair. And instead of that he wanted to kneel beside her now and take her close in his arms, and whisper to her that the sun had not set for them, but that it had only begun to rise.

And then, as he took a step toward her, there flashed through his brain like a disturbing warning the words with which she had told him that he would never know the real cause of her grief. "YOU MAY GUESS, BUT YOU WOULD NOT GUESS THE TRUTH IF YOU LIVED A THOUSAND YEARS." And could this that he had heard, and this that he looked upon be anything but the truth? Another step and he was at her side. For a moment all barriers were swept from between them. She did not resist him as he clasped her close to his breast. He kissed her upturned face again and again, and his voice kept whispering: "I love you, my Josephine - I love you - I love you -"

Suddenly there came to them sounds from out of the night. A door opened, and through the hall there came the great, rumbling voice of a man, half laughter, half shout; and then there were other voices, the slamming of the door, and THE voice again, this time in a roar that reached to the farthest walls of Adare House.

"Ho, Mignonne - Ma Josephine!"

And Philip held Josephine still closer and whispered:

"I love you!"

CHAPTER TEN

Not until the sound of approaching steps grew near did Josephine make an effort to free herself from Philip's arms. Unresisting she had given him her lips to kiss; for one rapturous moment he had felt the pressure of her arms about his shoulders; in the blue depths of her eyes he had caught the flash of wonderment and disbelief, and then the deeper, tenderer glow of her surrender to him. In this moment he forgot everything except that she had bared her secret to him, and in baring it had given herself to him. Even as her hands pressed now against his breast he kissed her lips again, and his arms tightened about her.

"They are coming to the door, Philip," she panted, straining against him. "We must not be found like this!"

The voice was booming in the hall again, calling her name, and in a moment Philip was on his feet raising Josephine to him. Her face still was white. Her eyes were still on the verge of fear, and as the steps came nearer he brushed back the warm masses of her hair and whispered for the twentieth time, as if the words must convince her: "I love you!" He slipped an arm about her waist, and Josephine's fingers nervously caught his hand.

Then the door was flung open. Philip knew that it was the master of Adare House who stood on the threshold - a great, fur-capped giant of a man who seemed to stoop to enter, and in whose eyes as they met Philip's there was a wild and half-savage inquiry. Such a man Philip had not expected to see; awesome in his bulk, a Thorlike god of the forests, gray-bearded, deep-chested, with shaggy hair falling out from under his cap, and in whose eyes there was the glare which Philip understood and which he met unflinchingly.

For a moment he felt Josephine's fingers grip tighter about his own; then with a low cry she broke from him, and John Adare opened his arms to her and crushed his bearded face down to hers as her arms encircled his neck. In the gloom of the hall beyond them there appeared for an instant the thin, dark face of Jean Jacques Croisset. In a flash it had come and gone. In that flash the half-breed's eyes had met Philip's, and in them was a look that made the latter take a quick step forward. His impulse was to pass John Adare and confront Jean in the hall. He held himself back, and looked at Josephine and her father. She had pushed the cap from the giant's head and had taken his bearded face between her two hands, and John Adare was smiling down into her white, pleading face with the gentleness and worship of a woman. In a moment he broke forth into a great rumbling laugh, and looked over her head at Philip.

"God bless my soul, if I don't almost believe my little girl thought I was coming home to murder her!" he cried. "I guess she thought I'd hate you for stealing her away from me the way you did. I have contemplated disliking you, quite seriously, too. But you're not the sort of looking chap I thought you'd be with that oily French name. You've shown good judgment. There isn't a man in the world good enough for my Jo. And if you'll excuse my frankness, I like your looks!"

As he spoke he held out a hand, and Josephine eagerly faced Philip. A flush grew in her cheeks as the two men shook hands. Her eyes were on Philip, and her heart beat a little quicker. She had not hoped that he would rise to the situation so completely. She had feared that there would be some betrayal in voice or action. But he was completely master of himself, and the colour in her face deepened beautifully. Before this moment she had not wholly perceived how splendidly clear and fearless were his eyes. His long blond hair, touched with its premature gray, was still windblown from his rush out into the night, giving to his head a touch of leonine strength as he faced her father.

Quietly she slipped aside and looked at them, and neither saw the strange, proud glow that came like a flash of fire into her eyes. They were wonderful, these two strong men who were hers. And in this moment they WERE her own. Neither spoke for a space, as they stood, hand clasping hand, and in that space, brief as it was, she saw that they measured each other as completely as man ever measured man; and that it was not satisfaction alone, but something deeper and more wonderful to her, that began to show in their faces. It was as if they had forgotten her presence in this meeting, and for a moment she, too, forgot that everything was not real. Moved by an impulse that made her breath quicken, she darted to them and caught their two clasped hands in both her own. Her face was glorious as she looked up at them,

"I'm glad, glad that you like each other," she cried softly. "I knew that it would be so, because -"

The master of Adare House had drawn her to him again. She put out a hand, and it rested on Philip's shoulder. Her eyes turned directly to him, and he alone saw the swift ebbing of the joyous light from them. John Adare's voice rumbled happily, and with his grizzled face bowed in Josephine's hair he said:

"I guess I'm not sorry - but glad, Mignonne." He looked at Philip again. "Paul, my son, you are welcome to Adare House!"

"Philip, Mon Pere," corrected Josephine. "I like that better than Paul."

"And you?" said Philip, smiling straight into Adare's eyes. "I am almost afraid to keep my promise to Josephine. It was that I should call you mon pere, too."

"There was one other promise, Philip," replied Adare quickly. "There must have been one other promise, that you would never take my girl away from me. If you did not swear to that, I am your enemy!"

"That promise was unnecessary," said Philip. "Outside of my Josephine's world there is nothing for me. If there is room for me in Adare House -"

"Room!" interrupted Adare, beginning to throw off his great fur coat. "Why, I've dreamed of the day when there'd be half a dozen babies under my feet. I -" His huge frame suddenly stiffened. He looked at Josephine, and his voice dropped to a hoarse whisper: "Where's the kid?" he asked.

Philip saw Josephine turn at the question. Silently she pointed to the curtained bed. As her father moved toward it she went to the door, but not before Philip had taken a step to intercept her. He felt her shuddering.

"I must go to my mother," she whispered for him alone. "I will return soon. If he asks - tell him that we named the baby after him." With a swift glance in her father's direction she whispered still lower: "He knows nothing about you, so you may tell him the truth about yourself - except that you met me in Montreal eighteen months ago, and married me there."

With this warning she was gone. From the curtains Philip heard a deep breath. When he came to the other's side John Adare stood staring down upon the sleeping baby.

"I came in like a monster and didn't wake 'im," he was whispering to himself. "The little beggar!"

He reached out a great hand behind him, gropingly, and it touched a chair. He drew it to him, still keeping his eyes on the baby, and sat down, his huge, bent shoulders doubled over the edge of the bed, his hands hovering hesitatingly over the counterpane. In wonderment Philip watched him, and he heard him whisper again:

"You blessed little beggar!"

Then he looked up suddenly. In his face was the transformation that might have come into a woman's. There was something awesome in its animal strength and its tenderness. He seized one of Philip's hands and held it for a moment in a grip that made the other's fingers ache.

"You're sure it's a boy?" he asked anxiously.

"Quite sure," replied Philip. "We've named him John."

The master of the Adare House leaned over the bed again. Philip heard him mumbling softly in his thick beard, and very cautiously he touched the end of a big forefinger to one of the baby's tiny fists. The little fingers opened, and then they closed tightly about John Adare's thumb. The older man looked again at Philip, and from him his eyes sought Josephine. His voice trembled with ecstasy.

"Where is Josephine?"

"Gone to her mother," replied Philip.

"Bring her - quick!" commanded Adare. "Tell her to bring her mother and wake the kid or I'll yell. I've got to hear the little beggar talk." As Philip turned toward the door he flung after him in a sibilant whisper: "Wait! Maybe you know how to do it -"

"We'd better have Josephine," advised Philip quickly, and before Adare could argue his suggestion he hurried into the hall.

Where he would find her he had no idea, and as he went down the hall he listened at each of the several doors he passed. The door into the big living-room was partly ajar, and he looked in. The room was empty. For a few moments he stood silent. From the size and shape of the building whose outside walls he had followed in his hunt for Jean he knew there must be many other rooms, and probably other shorter corridors leading to some of them.

Just now his greatest desire was to come face to face with Croisset - and alone. He had already determined upon a course of action if such a meeting occurred. Next to that he wanted to see Josephine's mother. It had struck him as singular that she had not accompanied her husband to Josephine's room, and his curiosity was still further aroused by the girl's apparent indifference to this fact. Jean Croisset and the mistress of Adare House had hung behind when the older man came into the room where they were standing. For an instant Jean had revealed himself, and he was sure that Adare's wife was not far behind him, concealed in the deeper gloom.

Suddenly the sound of a falling object came to his ears, as if a book had dropped from a table, or a chair had overturned. It was from the end of the hall - almost opposite his room. At his own door he stopped again and listened. This time he could hear voices, a low and unintelligible murmur. It was quite easy for him to locate the sound. He moved across to the other door, and hesitated. He had already disobeyed Josephine's injunction to remain with her father. Should he take a further advantage by obeying John Adare's command to bring his wife and daughter? A strange and subdued excitement was stirring him. Since the appearance of the threatening face at his window - the knowledge that in another moment he would have invited death from out of the night - he felt that he was no longer utterly in the hands of the woman he loved. And something stronger than he could resist impelled him to announce his presence at the door.

At his knock there fell a sudden silence beyond the thick

panels. For several moments he waited, holding his breath. Then he heard quick steps, the door swung slowly open, and he faced Josephine.

"Pardon me for interrupting you," he apologized in a low voice. "Your father sent me for you and your mother. He says that you must come and wake the baby."

Slowly Josephine held out a hand to him. He was startled by its coldness.

"Come in, Philip," she said. "I want you to meet my mother."

He entered into the warm glow of the room. Slightly bending over a table stood the slender form of a woman, her back toward him. Without seeing her face he was astonished at her striking resemblance to Josephine - the same slim, beautiful figure, the same thick, glowing coils of hair crowning her head - but darker. She turned toward him, and he was still more amazed by this resemblance. And yet it was a resemblance which he could not at first define. Her eyes were very dark instead of blue. Her heavy hair, drawn smoothly back from her forehead, was of the deep brown that is almost black in the shadow. Slimness had given her the appearance of Josephine's height. She was still beautiful. Hair, eyes, and figure gave her at first glance an appearance of almost girlish loveliness.

And then, all at once, the difference swept upon him. She was like Josephine as he had seen her in that hour of calm despair when she had come to him at the canoe. Home-coming had not brought her happiness. Her face was colourless, her cheeks slightly hollowed, in her eyes he saw now the lustreless glow which frequently comes with a fatal sickness. He was smiling and holding out his hand to her even as he saw these things, and at his side he heard Josephine say:

"Mother, this is Philip."

The hand she gave him was small and cold. Her voice, too, was wonderfully like Josephine's.

"I was not expecting to see you to-night, Philip," she said. "I am almost ill. But I am glad now that you joined us. Did I hear you say that my husband sent you?"

"The baby is holding his thumb," laughed Philip. "He says that you must come and wake him. I doubt if you can get him out of the baby's room to-night."

The voice of Adare himself answered from the door: "Was holding it," he corrected. "He's squirming like an eel now and making grimaces that frightened me. Better hurry to him, Josephine!" He went directly to his wife, and his voice was filled with an infinite tenderness as he slipped an arm about her and caressed her smooth hair with one of his big hands. "You're tired, aren't you?" he asked gently. "The jaunt was almost too much for my little girl, wasn't it? It will do you good to see the baby before you go to bed. Won't you come, Miriam?"

Josephine alone saw the look in Philip's face. And for one moment Philip forgot himself as he stared at John Adare and his wife. Beside this flowerlike slip of a woman Adare was more than ever a giant, and his eyes glowed with the tenderness that was in his voice. Miriam's lips trembled in a smile as she gazed up at her husband. In her eyes shone a responsive gentleness; and then Philip turned to find Josephine looking at him from the door, her lips drawn in a straight, tense line, her face as white as the bit of lace at her throat. He hurried to her. Behind him rumbled the deep, joyous voice of the master of Adare House, and passing through the door he glanced behind and saw them following, Adare's arm about his wife's waist. Josephine caught Philip's arm, and whispered in a low voice:

"They are always like that, always lovers. They are like two wonderful children, and sometimes I think it is too beautiful to be true. And now that you have met them I am going to ask you to go to your room. You have been my true knight - more than I dared to hope, and to-morrow -"

She interrupted herself as Adare and his wife appeared at the door.

"To-morrow?" he persisted.

"I will try and thank you," she replied. Then she said, and Philip saw she spoke directly to her father: "You will excuse Philip, won't you, Mon Pere? I will go with you, for I have taken the care of baby from Moanne to-night. Her husband is sick."

Adare shook hands with Philip.

"I'm up mornings before the owls have gone to sleep," he said. "Will you breakfast with me? I'm afraid that if you wait for Miriam and Mignonne you will go hungry. They will sleep until noon to make up for to-night."

"Nothing would suit me better," declared Philip. "Will you knock at my door if I fail to show up?"

Adare was about to answer, but caught himself suddenly as he looked from Philip to Josephine.

"What! this soon, Mignonne?" he demanded, chuckling in his beard. "Your rooms at the two ends of the house already! That was never the way with Miriam and me. Can you remember such a thing, Ma Cheri?"

"It - it is the baby," gasped Josephine, backing from the light to hide the wild rush of blood to her face. "Philip cannot sleep," she finished desperately.

"Then I disapprove of his nerves," rejoined her father. "Good-night, Philip, my boy!"

"Good-night!" said Philip.

He was looking at Adare's wife as they moved away. In the dim light of the hall a strange look had come into her face at her husband's jesting words. Was it the effect of the shadows, or had he seen her start - almost as if for an instant she had been threatened by a blow? Was it imagination, or had he in that same instant caught a sudden look of alarm, of terror, in her eyes? Josephine had told him that her mother knew nothing of the tragedy of the child's birth. If this were so, why had she betrayed the emotions which Philip was sure he had seen?

A chaotic tangle of questions and of doubts rushed through his mind. John Adare alone had acted a natural and unrestrained part in the brief space that had intervened since his home-coming. Philip had looked upon the big man's love and happiness, his worship of the woman who was his wife, his ecstasy over the baby, his affection for Josephine, and it seemed to him that he KNEW this man now. The few moments he had stood in the room with mother and daughter had puzzled him most. In their faces he had seen no sign of gladness at their reunion, and he asked himself if Josephine had told him all the truth - if her mother were not, after all, a partner to her secret.

And then there swept upon him in all its overwhelming cloud of mystery that other question which until now he had not dared to ask himself: HAD JOSEPHINE HERSELF TOLD HIM ALL THE TRUTH? He did not dare to tell himself that it was possible that she was NOT the mother of the child which she had told him was her own. And yet he could not kill the whispering doubt deep back in his brain. It had come to him in the room, quick as a flashlight, when she had made her confession; it was insistent now as he stood looking at the closed door through which they had disappeared.

For him to believe wholly and unquestioned Josephine's confession was like asking him to believe that da Vinci's masterpiece hanging in the big room had been painted by a blind man. In her he had embodied all that he had ever dreamed of as pure and beautiful in a woman, and the thought came now. Had Josephine, for some tremendous reason known only to herself and Jean, tried to destroy his great love for her by revealing herself in a light that was untrue?

Instantly he told himself that this could not be so. If he believed in Josephine at all, he must believe that she had told him the truth. And he did believe, in spite of the whispering doubt. He felt that he could not sleep until he had seen Josephine alone. In her room John Adare had interrupted them a minute too soon. In spite of the mysterious and unsettling events of the night his heart still beat with the wild and joyous hope that had come with Josephine's surrender to his arms and lips.

Instead of accepting the confession of her misfortune as the final barrier between them, he had taken it as the key that had unlocked the chains of her bondage. If she had told him the truth - if this were what separated them - she belonged to him; and he wanted to tell her this again before he slept, and hear from her lips the words that would give her to him forever.

Despairing of this, he opened the door to his room.

CHAPTER ELEVEN

Scarcely had he crossed the threshold when an exclamation of surprise rose to Philip's lips. A few minutes before he had left his room even uncomfortably warm. A cold draught of air struck his face now, and the light was out. He remembered that he had left the lamp burning. He groped his way through the darkness to the table before he lighted a match.

As he touched the flame to the wick he glanced toward the window. It was open. A film of snow had driven through and settled upon the rug under it. Replacing the chimney, he took a step or two toward the window. Then he stopped, and stared at the floor. Some one had entered his room through the open window and had gone to the door opening into the hall. At each step had fallen a bit of snow, and close to the door was a space of the bare floor soppy and stained. At that point the intruder had stood for some moments without moving.

For several seconds Philip stared at the evidences of a prowling visitor without making a move himself. It was not without a certain thrill of uneasiness that he went to the window and closed it. It did not take him long to assure himself that nothing in the room had been touched. He could find no other marks of feet except those which led directly from the window to the door, and this fact was sufficient proof that whoever had visited his room had come as a listener and a spy and not as a thief.

It occurred to Philip now that he had found his door

unlatched and slightly ajar when he entered. That the eavesdropper had seen them in the hall and had possibly overheard a part of their conversation he was quite certain from the fact that the window had been left open in a hurried flight.

For some time the impulse was strong in him to acquaint both Josephine and her father with what had happened, and with Jean Croisset's apparent treachery. He did not need to ask himself if it was the half-breed who had stolen into his room. He was as certain of that as he was of the identity of the face he had seen at the window some time before. And yet something held him from communicating these events of the night to the master of Adare House and the girl. He was becoming more and more convinced that there existed an unaccountable and mysterious undercurrent of tragic possibilities at Adare House of which Josephine was almost ignorant, and her father entirely so. Josephine's motherhood and the secret she was guarding were not the only things that were clouding his mental horizon now. There was something else. And he believed that Jean was the key to the situation.

He felt a clammy chill creep over him as he asked himself how closely Jean Jacques Croisset himself was associated with the girl he loved. It was a thought that almost made him curse himself for giving it birth. And yet it clung to him like a grim and haunting spectre that he would have crushed if he could. Josephine's confession of motherhood had not made him love her less. In those terrible moments when she had bared her soul to him, his own soul had suffered none of the revulsion with which he might have sympathized in others. It was as if she had fallen at his feet, fluttering in the agony of a terrible wound, a thing as pure as the heavens, hurt for him to cherish in his greater strength - such was his love. And the thought that Jean loved her, and that a jealousy darker than night was burning all that was human out of his breast, was a possibility which he found unpleasant to admit to himself.

So deeply was he absorbed in these thoughts that he forgot any

James Oliver Curwood

immediate danger that might be threatening himself. He passed and repassed the window, smoking his pipe, and fighting with himself to hit upon some other tangible reason for Jean's unexpected change of heart. He could not forget his first impression of the dark-faced half-breed, nor the grip in which they had pledged their fealty. He had accepted Jean as one of ten thousand - a man he would have trusted to the ends of the earth, and yet he recalled moments now when he had seen strange fires smouldering far back in the forest man's eyes. The change in Jean alone he felt that he might have diagnosed, but almost simultaneously with his discovery of this change he had met Adare's wife - and she had puzzled him even more than the half-breed.

Restlessly he moved to his door again, opened it, and looked down the hall. The door of Josephine's room was closed, and he reentered his room. For a moment he stood facing the window. In the same instant there came the report of a rifle and the crashing of glass. A shower of shot-like particles struck his face. He heard a dull smash behind him, and then a stinging, red-hot pain shot across his arm, as if a whiplash had seared his naked flesh. He heard the shot, the crashing glass, the strike of the bullet behind him before he felt the pain - before he reeled back toward the wall. His heel caught in a rug and he fell. He knew that he was not badly hurt, but he crouched low, and with his right hand drew his automatic and levelled it at the window.

Never in his life had his blood leaped more quickly through his body than it did now. It was not merely excitement - the knowledge that he had been close to death, and had escaped. From out of the darkness Jean Croisset had shot at him like a coward. He did not feel the burn of the scratch on his arm as he jumped to his feet. Once more he ran swiftly through the hall. At the end door he looked back. Apparently the shot had not alarmed the occupants of Josephine's room, to whom the report of a rifle - even at night - held no special significance.

Another moment and Philip was outside. It had stopped

snowing, and the clouds were drifting away from under the moon. Crouched low, his pistol level at his side, he ran swiftly in the direction from which the shot must have come. The moon revealed the dark edge of the forest a hundred yards away, and he was sure that his attempted murderer had stood somewhere between Adare House and the timber when he fired. He was not afraid of a second shot. Even caution was lost in his mad desire to catch Jean red-handed and choke a confession of several things from his lips. If Jean had suddenly risen out of the snow he would not have used his pistol unless forced to do so. He wanted to be hand to hand with the treacherous half-breed, and his breath came in panting eagerness as he ran.

Suddenly he stopped short. He had struck the trail. Here Croisset had stood, fifty yards from his window, when he fired. The snow was beaten down, and from the spot his retreating footsteps led toward the forest. Like a dog Philip followed the trail. The first timber was thinned by the axe, and the moon lighted up the white spaces ahead of him. He was half across the darker wall of the spruce when his heart gave a sudden jump. He had heard the snarl of a dog, the lash of a whip, a man's low voice cursing the beast he was striking. The sounds came from the dense cover of the spruce, and told him that Jean was not looking for immediate pursuit. He slipped in among the shadows quietly, and a few steps brought him to a smaller open space where few trees had been cut. In this little clearing a slim dark figure of a man was straightening out the tangled traces of a sledge-team.

Philip could not see his face, but he knew that it was Jean. It was Jean's figure, Jean's movement, his low, sharp voice as he spoke to the dogs. Man and huskies were not twenty steps from him. With a tense breath Philip replaced his pistol in its holster. He did not want to kill, and he possessed a proper respect for the hair-trigger mechanism of his automatic. In the fight he anticipated with Jean the weapon would be safer in its holster than in his hand. Jean was at present unarmed, except for his hunting-knife. His rifle leaned against a tree, and in another moment Philip was between the gun and the half-breed.

One of the sledge dogs betrayed him. At its low and snarling warning the half-breed whirled about with the alertness of a lynx, and he was half ready when Philip launched himself at his throat. They went down free of the dogs, the forest man under. One of Philip's hands had reached his enemy's throat, but with a swift movement of his arm the half-breed wrenched it off and slipped out from under his assailant with the agility of an eel. Both were on their feet in an instant, facing each other in the tiny moonlit arena a dozen feet from the silent and watchful dogs.

Even now Philip could not see the half-breed's features because of a hood drawn closely about his face. The "breed" had made no effort to draw a weapon, and Philip flung himself upon him again. Thus in open battle his greater physical strength and advantage of fifty pounds in weight would have won for Philip. But the forest man's fighting is filled with the elusive ermine's trickery and the lithe quickness of the big, fur-padded cat of the trap-lines.

The half-breed made no effort to evade Philip's assault. He met the shock of attack fairly, and went down with him. But this time his back was to the watchful semicircle of dogs, and with a sharp, piercing command he pitched back among them, dragging Philip with him. Too late Philip realized what the cry meant. He tried to fling himself out of reach of the threatening fangs, and freed one hand to reach for his pistol. This saved him from the dogs, but gave the half-breed his opportunity. Again he was on his feet, the butt of his dog whip in his hand. As the moonlight glinted on the barrel of the automatic, he brought the whip down with a crash on Philip's head - and then again and again, and Philip pitched backward into the snow.

He was not wholly unconscious. He knew that as soon as he had fallen the half-breed had turned again to the dogs. He could hear him as he straightened out the traces. In a subconscious sort of way, Philip wondered why he did not take advantage of his opportunity and finish what he had failed to do with the bullet through the window. Philip heard him run back for his gun, and tried to struggle to his knees. Instead of the shot he half expected there came the low "Hoosh - hoosh - marche!" of the forest man's voice. Dogs and sledge moved. He fought himself up and swayed on his knees, staring after the retreating shadows. He saw his automatic in the snow and crawled to it. It was another minute before he could stand on his feet, and then he was dizzy. He staggered to a tree and for a space leaned against it.

It was some minutes before he was steady enough to walk, and by that time he knew that it would be futile to pursue the half-breed and his swift-footed dogs, weakened and half dressed as he was. Slowly he returned to Adare House, cursing himself for not having used his pistol to compel Jean's surrender. He acknowledged that he had been a fool, and that he had deserved what he got. The hall was still empty when he reentered it. His adventure had roused no one, and with a feeling of relief he went to his room.

If the walls had fallen about his ears he could not have received a greater shock than when he entered through the door.

Seated in a chair close to the table, looking at him calmly as he entered, was Jean Jacques Croisset!

CHAPTER TWELVE

Unable to believe that what he saw was not an illusion, Philip stood and stared at the half-breed. No word fell from his lips. He did not move. And Jean met his eyes calmly, without betraying a tremor of excitement or of fear. In another moment Philip's hand went to his pistol. As he half drew it his confused brain saw other things which made him gasp with new wonder.

Croisset showed no signs of the fight in the forest which had occurred not more than ten minutes before. He was wearing a pair of laced Hudson's Bay boots. In the struggle in the snow Philip's hand had once gripped his enemy's foot, and he knew that he had worn moccasins. And Jean was not winded. He was breathing easily. And now Philip saw that behind the calmness in his eyes there was a tense and anxious inquiry. Slowly the truth broke upon him. It could not have been Jean with whom he had fought in the edge of the forest! He advanced a step or two toward the half-breed, his hand still resting uncertainly on his pistol. Not until then did Jean speak, and there was no pretence in his voice:

"The Virgin be praised, you are not badly hurt, M'sieur?" he exclaimed, rising. "There is a little blood on your face. Did the glass cut you?"

"No," said Philip. "I overtook him in the edge of the forest."

Not for an instant had his eyes left Croisset. Now he saw him start. His dark face took on a strange pallor. He leaned forward, and his breath came in a quick gasp.

"The result?" he demanded. "Did you kill him?"

"He escaped."

The tense lines on Croisset's face relaxed. Philip turned and bolted the door.

"Sit down, Croisset," he commanded. "You and I are going to square things up in this room to-night. It is quite natural that you should be glad he escaped. Perhaps if you had fired the shot in place of putting the affair into the hands of a hired murderer the work would have been better done. Sit down!"

Something like a smile flickered across Jean's face as he reseated himself. There was in it no suggestion of bravado or of defiance. It was rather the facial expression of one who was looking beyond Philip's set jaws, and seeing other things - the betrayal which comes at times when one has suffered quietly for another. It was a look which made Philip uneasy as he seated himself opposite the half-breed, and made him ashamed of the fact that he had exposed his right hand on the table, with the muzzle of his automatic turned toward Jean's breast. Yet he was determined to have it out with Jean now.

"You are glad that the man who tried to kill me escaped?" he repeated.

The promptness and quiet decisiveness of Jean's answer amazed him.

"Yes, M'sieur, I am. But the shot was not for you. It was intended for the master of Adare House. When I heard the shot to-night I did not know what it meant. A little later I came to your room and found the broken window and the bullet mark in the wall. This is M'sieur Adare's old room, and the bullet was intended for him. And now, M'sieur Philip, why do you say that I am responsible for the attempt to kill you, or the master?"

"You have convicted yourself," declared Philip, his eyes ablaze. "A moment ago you said you were glad the assassin escaped!"

"I am, M'sieur," replied Jean in the same quiet voice. "Why I am glad I will leave to your imagination. Unless I still had faith in you and was sure of your great love for our Josephine, I would have lied to you. You were told that you would meet with strange things at Adare House. You gave your oath that you would make no effort to discover the secret which is guarded here. And this early, the first night, you threaten me at the end of a pistol!"

Like fire Jean's eyes were burning now. He gripped the edges of the table with his thin fingers, and his voice came with a sudden hissing fury.

"By the great God in Heaven, M'sieur, are you accusing me of turning traitor to the Master and to her, to our Josephine, whom I have watched and guarded and prayed for since the day she first opened her eyes to the world? Do you accuse me of that - I, Jean Jacques Croisset, who would die a thousand deaths by torture that she might be freed from her own suffering?"

He leaned over the table as if about to spring. And then, slowly, his fingers relaxed, the fire died out of his eyes, and he sank back in his chair. In the face of the half-breed's outburst Philip had remained speechless. Now he spoke:

"Call it threatening, if you like. I do not intend to break my word to Josephine. I demand no answer to questions which may concern her, for that is my promise. But between you and me there are certain things which must be explained. I concede that I was mistaken in believing that it was you with whom I fought in the forest. But it was you who looked through my window earlier in the night, with a pistol in your hand. You would have killed me if I had not turned."

Genuine surprise shot into Jean's face.

"I have not been near your window, M'sieur. Until I returned with M'sieur Adare I was waiting up the river, several miles from here. Since then I have not left the house. Josephine and her father can tell you this, if you need proof."

"Your words are impossible!" exclaimed Philip. "I could not have been mistaken. It was you."

"Will you believe Josephine, M'sieur? She will tell you that I could not have been at the window."

"If it was not you - who was it?"

"It must have been the man who shot at you," replied Jean.

"And you know who that man is, and yet refuse to tell me in order that he may have another opportunity of finishing what he failed to do to-night. The most I can do is to inform John Adare."

"You will not do that," said Jean confidently. Again he showed excitement. "Do you know what it would mean?" he demanded.

"Trouble for you," volunteered Philip,

"And ruin for Josephine and every soul in the House of Adare!" added Croisset swiftly. "As soon as Adare could lace his moccasins he would take up that trail out there. He would come to the end of it, and then - mon Dieu! - in that hour the world would smash about his ears!"

"Either you are mad or I am," gasped Philip, staring into the half-breed's tense face. "I don't think you are lying, Jean. But you must be mad. And I am mad for listening to you. You insist on giving this murderer another chance. You as much as say that by giving him a second opportunity to kill John Adare you are proving your loyalty to Josephine and her father. Can that be anything but madness?"

An almost gentle smile nickered over Jean's lips. He looked at Philip as if marvelling that the other could not understand.

"Within an hour it will be Jean Jacques Croisset who will take up the trail," he replied softly, and without boastfulness. "It is I, and not the master of Adare House, who will come to the end of that trail. And there will be no other shot after that, and no one will ever know - but you and me."

"You mean that you will follow and kill him - and that John Adare must never know that an attempt has been made on his life?"

"He must never know, M'sieur. And what happens in the forest at the end of the trail the trees will never tell."

"And the reason for this secrecy you will not confide in me?"

"I dare not, M'sieur."

Philip leaned across the table.

"Perhaps you will, Jean, when you know there is no longer anything between Josephine and me," he said. "To-night she told me everything. I have seen the baby. Her secret she has given to me freely - and it has made no difference. I love her. Tomorrow I shall ask her to end all this make-believe, and my heart tells me that she will. We can be married secretly. No one will ever know."

His face was filled with the flush of hope. One of his hands caught Jean's in the old grip of friendship - of confidence. Jean did not reply. But his face betrayed what he did not speak. Once or twice before Philip had seen the same look of anguish in his eyes, the tightening of the lines about the corners of his mouth. Slowly the half-breed rose from the table and turned a little from Philip. In a moment Philip was at his side.

"Jean!" he cried softly, "you love Josephine!"

No sign of passion was in Jean's face as he met the other's eyes.

"How do you mean, M'sieur?" he asked quietly. "As a father and a brother, or as a man?"

"A man," said Philip.

Jean smiled. It was a smile of deep understanding, as if suddenly there had burst upon him a light which he had not seen before.

"I love her as the flowers love the sunshine, as the wood violets love the rains," he said, touching Philip's arm. "And that, M'sieur, is not what you understand as the love of a man. There is one other whom I love in another way, whose voice is the sweetest music in the world, whose heart beats with mine, whose soul leads me day and night through the forests, and who whispers to me of our sweet love in my dreams - Iowaka, my wife! Come, M'sieur; I will take you to her."

"It is late - too late," voiced Philip wonderingly.

But as he spoke he followed Jean. The half-breed seemed to have risen out of his world now. There was a wonderful light in his face, a something that seemed to reach back through centuries that were gone - and in this moment Philip thought of Marechal, of Prince Rupert, of le Chevalier Grosselier - of the adventurous and royal blood that had first come over to the New World to form the Great Company, and he knew that of such men as these was Jean Jacques Croisset, the forest man. He understood now the meaning of the soft and faultless speech of this man who had lived always under the stars and the open skies. He was not of to-day, but a harkening back to that long-forgotten yesterday; in his veins ran the blood red and strong of the First Men of the North. Out into the night Philip followed him, bare-headed, with the moonlight streaming down from above; and he stopped only when Jean stopped, close to a little plot where a dozen wooden crosses rose above a dozen snow-covered mounds.

Jean stopped, and his hand fell on Philip's arm.

"These are Josephine's," he said softly, with a sweep of his other hand. "She calls it her Garden of Little Flowers. They are children, M'sieur. Some are babies. When a little one dies - if it is not too far away - she brings it to Le Jardin - her garden, so that it may not sleep alone under the lonely spruce, with the wolves howling over it on winter nights. They must be lonely in the woodsy graves, she says. I have known her to bring an Indian baby a hundred miles, and some of these I have seen die in her arms, while she crooned to them a song of Heaven. And five times as many little ones she has saved, M'sieur. That is why even the winds in the treetops whisper her name, L'Ange! Does it not seem to you that even the moon shines brighter here upon these little mounds and the crosses?"

"Yes," breathed Philip reverently.

Jean pointed to a larger mound, the one guardian mound of them all, rising a little above the others, its cross lifted watchfully above the other crosses; and he said, as if the spirits themselves were listening to him:

"M'sieur, there is my wife, my Iowaka. She died three years ago, but she is with me always, and even now her beloved voice is singing in my heart, telling me that it is not black and cold where she and the little ones are waiting, but that all is light and beautiful. M'sieur" - his voice dropped to a whisper - "Could I sell my hereafter with her for the price of another woman's love on earth?"

Philip tried to speak; and strange after a moment he succeeded in saying:

"Jean, an hour ago, I thought I was a man. I see how far short of that I have fallen. Forgive me, and let me be your brother. Such a love as yours is my love for Josephine. And to-morrow -"

"Despair will open up and swallow you to the depths of your soul," interrupted Jean gently. "Return to your room, M'sieur. Sleep. Fight for the love that will be yours in Heaven, as I live for my Iowaka's. For that love will be yours, up there. Josephine has loved but one man, and that is you. I have watched and I have seen. But in this world she can never be more to you than she is now, for what she told you to-night is the least of the terrible thing that is eating away her soul on earth. Good-night, M'sieur!"

Straight out into the moonlight Jean walked, head erect, in the face of the forest. And Philip stood looking after him over the little garden of crosses until he had disappeared.

CHAPTER THIRTEEN

Alone and with the deadening depression that had come with Jean's last words, Philip returned to his room. He had made no effort to follow the half-breed who had shamed him to the quick beside the grave of his wife. He felt no pleasure, no sense of exultation, that his suspicions of Croisset's feelings toward Josephine had been dispelled. Since the hour MacTavish had died up in the madness of Arctic night, deep and hopeless gloom had not laid its hand more heavily upon him,

He bolted his door, drew the curtain to the window, and added a bit of wood to the few embers that still remained alive in the grate. Then he sat down, with his face to the fire. The dry birch burst into flame, and for half an hour he sat staring into it with almost unseeing eyes. He knew that Jean would keep his word - that even now he was possibly on the fresh trail that led through the forest. For him there was something about the half-breed now that was almost omniscient. In him Philip had seen incarnated the things which made him feel like a dwarf in manhood. In those few moments close to the graves, Jean had risen above the world. And Philip believed in him. Yet with his belief, his optimism did not quite die.

In the same breath Jean had told him that he could never possess Josephine, and that Josephine loved him. This in itself, Jean's assurance of her love, was sufficient to arouse a spirit like his with new hope. At last he went to bed, and in spite of his mental and physical excitement of the night, he fell asleep.

John Adare did not fail in his promise to rouse Philip early in the day. When Philip jumped out of bed in response to Adare's heavy knock at the door, he judged that it was not later than seven o'clock, and the room was still dark. Adare's voice came booming through the thick panels in reply to Philip's assurance that he was getting up.

"This is the third time," he cried. "I've cracked the door trying to rouse you. And we've got a caribou porterhouse two inches thick waiting for us."

The giant was walking back and forth in the big living-room when Philip joined him a few minutes later. He wore an Indian-made jacket and was smoking a big pipe. That he had been up for some time was evident from the logs fully ablaze in the fireplace. He rubbed his hands briskly as Philip entered. Every atom of him disseminated good cheer.

"You don't know how good it seems to get back home," he exclaimed, as they shook hands. "I feel like a boy - actually like a boy, Philip! Didn't sleep two winks after I went to bed, and Miriam scolded me for keeping her awake. Bless my soul, I wouldn't live in Montreal if they'd make me a present of the whole Hudson's Bay Company."

"Nor I," said Philip. "I love the North."

"How long?"

"Four years - without a break."

"One can live a long time in the North in four years," mused the master of Adare. "But Josephine said she met you in Montreal?"

"True," laughed Philip, catching himself. "That was a break - and I thank God for it. Outside of that I spent all of the four years north of the Hight of Land. For eighteen months I lived along the edges of the Arctic trying to take an impossible census of the Eskimo for the government."

"I knew something of the sort when I first looked at you," said Adare. "I can tell an Arctic man, just as I can pick a Herschel dog or an Athabasca country malemute from a pack of fifty. We have much to talk about, my boy. We will be great friends. Just now we are going to that caribou steak."

Out into the hall, through another door, and down a short corridor, he led Philip. Here a third door was open, and Adare stood aside while Philip entered.

"This is my private sanctuary," he said proudly. "What do you think of it?"

Philip looked about him. He was in a room almost as large as the one from which they had come. In a huge fireplace a pile of logs were blazing. One end of the room was given up almost entirely to shelves and weighted down with books. Philip was amazed at their number. The other end was still partially hidden in glooms but he could make out that it was fitted up as a laboratory, and on shelves he caught the white gleam of scores of wild beast skulls. Comfortably near to the fire was a large table scattered with books, papers, and piles of manuscript, and behind this was a small iron safe. Here, Philip thought, was the adytum of no ordinary man; it was the study of a scholar and a scientist. He marked the absence of mounted heads from the walls, but in spite of that the very atmosphere of the room breathed of the forests and the beast. Here and there he saw the articulated skeletons of wild animals. From among the books themselves the jaws and ivory fangs of skulls gleamed out at him. Before he had finished his wondering survey of the strange room, John Adare stepped to the table and picked up a skull.

"This is my latest specimen," he said, his voice eager with enthusiasim. "It is perfect. Jean secured it for me while I was away. It is the skull of a beaver, and shows in three distinct and remarkable gradations how nature replaces the soft enamel as it is worn from the beaver's teeth. You see, I am a hobbyist. For twenty years I have been studying wild animals. And there -"

He replaced the skull on the table to point to an isolated shelf filled with books and magazines.

"- there is my most remarkable collection," he added, a gleam of humour in his eyes. "They are the books and magazine stories of nature fakirs, the 'works' of naturalists who have never heard the howl of a wolf or the cry of a loon; the wild dreams of fictionists, the rot of writers who spend two weeks or a month each year on some blazed trail and return to the cities to call themselves students of nature. When I feel in bad humour I read some of that stuff and laugh."

He leaned over to press a button under the table,

"One of my little electrical arrangements," he explained. "That will bring our breakfast. To use a popular expression of the uninformed, I'm as hungry as a bear. As a matter of fact, you know, a bear is the lightest eater of all brute creation for his size, strength, and fat supply. That row of naturalists over there have made him out a pig. The beast's a genius, for it takes a genius to grow fat on poplar buds!"

Then he laughed good humouredly.

"I suppose you are tired of this already. Josephine has probably been filling you with a lot of my foolishness. She says I must be silly or I would have my stuff published in books. But I am waiting, waiting until I have come down to the last facts. I am experimenting now with the black and the silver fox. And there are many other experiments to come, many of them. But you are tired of this."

"Tired!"

Philip had listened to him without speaking. In this room John Adare had changed. In him he saw now the living, breathing soul of the wild. His own face was flushed with a new enthusiasm as he replied:

"Such things could never tire me. I only ask that I may be your companion in your researches, and learn something of the wonders which you must already have discovered. You have studied wild animals - for twenty years?"

"Twenty and four, day and night; it has been my hobby."

"And you have written about them?"

"A score of volumes, if they were in print."

Philip drew a deep breath.

"The world would give a great deal for what you know," he said. "It would give a great deal for those books, more than I dare to estimate, undoubtedly it would be a vast sum in dollars."

Adare laughed softly in his beard.

"And what would I do with dollars?" he asked. "I have sufficient with which to live this life here. What more could money bring me? I am the happiest man in the world!"

For a moment a cloud overshadowed his face.

"And yet of late I have had a worry," he added thoughtfully. "It is because of Miriam, my wife. She is not well. I had hoped that the doctors in Montreal would help her. But they have failed. They say she possesses no malady, no sickness that they can discover. And yet she is not the old Miriam. God knows I hope the tonic of the snows will bring her back to health this winter!"

"It will," declared Philip. "The signs point to a glorious winter, crisp and dry - the sledge and dog kind, when you can hear the crack of a whiplash half a mile away."

"You will hear that frequently enough if you follow Josephine," chuckled Adare. "Not a trail in these forests for a hundred miles she does not know. She trains all of the dogs, and they are wonderful."

It was on the point of Philip's tongue to ask a reason for the silence of the fierce pack he had seen the night before, when he caught himself. At the same moment the Indian woman appeared through the door with a laden tray. Adare helped her arrange their breakfast on a small table near the fire.

"I thought we would be more congenial here than alone in the dining-room, Philip," he explained. "Unless I am mistaken the ladies won't be up until dinner time. Did you ever see a steak done to a finer turn than this? Marie, you are a treasure." He motioned Philip to a seat, and began serving. "Nothing in the world is better than a caribou porterhouse cut well back," he went on. "Don't fry or roast it, but broil it. An inch and a half is the proper thickness, just enough to hold the heart of it ripe with juice. See it ooze from that cut! Can you beat it?"

"Not with anything I have had along the Arctic," confessed Philip. "A steak from the cheek of a cow walrus is about the best thing you find up in the 'Big Icebox' - that is, at first. Later, when the aurora borealis has got into your marrow, you gorge on seal blubber and narwhal fat and call it good. As for me, I'd prefer pickles to anything else in the world, so with your permission I'll help myself. Just now I'd eat pickles with ice cream."

It was a pleasant meal. Philip could not remember when he had known a more agreeable host. Not until they had finished, and Adare had produced cigars of a curious length and slimness, did the older man ask the question for which Philip had been carefully preparing himself.

"Now I want to hear about you," he said. "Josephine told me

very little - said that she wanted me to get my impressions first hand. We'll smoke and talk. These cigars are clear Havanas. I have the tobacco imported by the bale and we make the cigars ourselves. Reduces the cost to a minimum, and we always have a supply. Go on, Philip, I'm listening."

Philip remembered Josephine's words telling him to narrate the events of his own life to her father - except that he was to leave open, as it were, the interval in which he was supposed to have known her in Montreal. It was not difficult for him to slip over this. He described his first coming into the North, and Adare's eyes glowed sympathetically when Philip quoted Hill's words down at Prince Albert and Jasper's up at Fond du Lac. He listened with tense interest to his experiences along the Arctic, his descriptions of the death of MacTavish and the passing of Pierre Radisson. But what struck deepest with him was Philip's physical and mental fight for new life, and the splendid way in which the wilderness had responded.

"And you couldn't go back now," he said, a tone of triumph in his voice. "When the forests once claim you - they hold."

"Not alone the forests, Mon Pere."

"Ah, Mignonne. No, there is neither man nor beast in the world that would leave her. Even the dogs are chained out in the deep spruce that they may not tear down her doors in the night to come near her. The whole world loves my Josephine. The Indians make the Big Medicine for her in a hundred tepees when they learn she is ill. They have trimmed five hundred lob-stick trees in her memory. Mon Dieu, in the Company's books there are written down more than thirty babes and children grown who bear her name of Josephine! She is different than her mother. Miriam has been always like a flower - a timid wood violet, loving this big world, yet playing no part in it away from my side. Sometimes Josephine frightens me. She will travel a hundred miles by sledge to nurse a sick child, and only last winter she buried herself in a shack filled with smallpox and brought six souls out of it alive! For two weeks she was buried in that hell. That is Mignonne, whom Indian, breed, and white man call L'Ange. Miriam they call La Fleurette. We are two fortunate men, my son!"

A dozen questions burned on Philip's lips, but he held them back, fearing that some accidental slip of the tongue might betray him. He was convinced that Josephine's father knew absolutely nothing of the trouble that was wrecking the happiness of Adare House, and he was equally positive that all, even Miriam herself, were fighting to keep the secret from him.

That Josephine's motherhood was not the sole cause of the mysterious and tragic undercurrent that he had been made to feel he was more than suspicious. A few hours would tell him if he was right, for he would ask Josephine to become his wife. And he already knew what John Adare did not know.

Miriam was not sick with a physical illness. The doctors whom Adare had not believed were right. And he wondered, as he sat facing her husband, if it was fear for his life that was breaking her down. Were they shielding him from some great and ever-menacing peril - a danger with which, for some inconceivable reason, they dared not acquaint him?

In the short time he had known him, a strange feeling for John Adare had found a place in Philip's heart. It was more than friendship, more than the feeling which his supposed relationship might have roused. This big-hearted, tender, rumbling voiced giant of a man he had grown to love. And he found himself struggling blindly now to keep from him what the others were trying to conceal, for he knew that John Adare's heart would crumble down like a pile of dust if he knew the truth. He was thinking of the baby, and it seemed as if his thoughts flashed like fire to the other.

Adare was laughing softly in his beard.

"You should have seen the kid last night, Philip. When they

woke 'im he stared at me for a time as though I was an ogre, then he grinned, kicked me, and grabbed my whiskers, I've just one fault to find. I wish he was a dozen instead of me. The little rascal! I wonder if he is awake?"

He half rose, as if about to investigate, then reseated himself.

"Guess I'd better not take a chance of waking him," he reflected. "If Jean should catch me rousing Josephine or the baby he'd throttle me."

"Jean is - a sort of guardian," ventured Philip.

"More than that. Sometimes I think he is a spirit," said Adare impressively. "I have known him for twenty years. Since the day Josephine was born he has been her watch-dog. He came in the heart of a great storm, years and years ago, nearly dead from cold and hunger. He never went away, and he has talked but little about himself. See -"

Adare went to a shelf and returned with a bundle of manuscript.

"Jean gave me the idea for this," he went on.

There are two hundred and eighty pages here. I call it 'The Aristocracy of the North.' It is true - and it is wonderful!

"You have seen a spring or New Year's gathering of the forest people at a Company's post - the crowd of Indians, half-breeds, and whites who follow the trap-lines? And would you guess that in that average foregathering of the wilderness people there is better blood than you could find in a crowded ballroom of New York's millionaires? It is true. I have given fish to hungry half-breeds in whose veins flows the blood of royalty. I have eaten with Indian women whose lineage reaches back to names that were mighty before the first Astors and the first Vanderbilts were born. The descendant of a king has hunted me caribou meat at two cents a pound. In a smoke-blackened tepee, over beyond the Gray Loon waterway, there lives a girl with hair and eyes as black as a raven's wing who could go to Paris to-morrow and say: 'I am the descendant of a queen,' and prove it. And so it is all over the Northland.

"I have hunted down many curious facts, and I have them here in my manuscript. The world cannot sneer at me, for records have been kept almost since the day away back in the seventeenth century when Prince Rupert landed with his first shipload of gentlemen adventurers. They intermarried with our splendid Crees - those first wanderers from the best families of Europe. They formed the English-Cree half-breed. Prince Rupert himself had five children that can be traced to him. Le Chevalier Grosselier had nine. And so it went on for a hundred years, the best blood in England giving birth to a new race among the Crees, and the best of France sowing new generations among the Chippewyans on their way up from Quebec.

"And for another hundred years and more the English-Cree half-breed and the French-Chippewyan half-breed have been meeting and intermarrying, forming the 'blood,' until in all this Northland scarce a man or a woman cannot call back to names that have long become dust in history.

"From the blood of some mighty king of France - of some splendid queen - has come Jean Croisset. I have always felt that, and yet I can trace him no farther than a hundred years back, to the quarter-strain wife of the white factor at Monsoon. Jean has lost interest in himself now - since his wife died three years ago. Has Josephine told you of her?"

"Very little," said Philip.

The flush of enthusiasm faded from Adare's eyes. It was replaced by a look that was grief deep and sincere.

"Iowaka's death was the first great blow that came to Adare

House," he said gently. "For nine years they were man and wife lovers. God's pity they had no children. She was French - with a velvety touch of the Cree, lovable as the wild flowers from which she took her name. Since she went Jean has lived in a dream. He says that she is constantly with him, and that often he hears her voice. I am glad of that. It is wonderful to possess that kind of a love, Philip! - the love that lives like a fresh flower after death and darkness. And we have it - you and I."

Philip murmured softly that it was so. He felt that it was dangerous to tread upon the ground which Adare was following. In these moments, when this great bent-shouldered giant's heart lay like an open book before him, he was not sure of himself. The other's unbounded faith, his happiness, the idyllic fulness of his world as he found it, were things which added to the heaviness and fear at Philip's heart instead of filling him with similar emotions. Of these things he was not a part. A voice kept whispering to him with maddening insistence that he was a fraud. One by one John Adare was unlocking for him hallowed pictures in which Jean had told him he could never share possession. His desire to see Josephine again was almost feverish, and filled him with a restlessness which he knew he must hide from Adare. So when Adare's eyes rested upon him in a moment's silence, he said:

"Last night Jean and I were standing beside her grave. It seemed then as though he would have been happier if he had lain near her - under the cross."

"You are wrong," said Adare quickly. "Death is beautiful when there is a perfect love. If my Miriam should die it would mean that she had simply gone from my SIGHT. In return for that loss her hand would reach down to me from Heaven, as Iowaka reaches down to Jean. I love life. My heart would break if she should go. But it would be replaced by something almost like another soul. For it must be wonderful to be over-watched by an angel."

He rose and went to the window, and with a queer thickening in his throat Philip stared at his broad back. He thought he saw a moment's quiver of his shoulders. Then Adare's voice changed.

"Winter brings close to our doors the one unpleasant feature of this country," he said, turning to light a second cigar. "Thirty-five miles to the north and west of us there is what the Indians call 'Muchemunito Nek' - the Devil's Nest. It's a Free Trader's house. A man down in Montreal by the name of Lang owns a string of them, and his agent over at the Devil's Nest is a scoundrel of the first water. His name is Thoreau. There are a score of half-breeds and whites in his crowd, and not a one of them with an honest hair in his head. It's the one criminal rendezvous I know of in all this North country. Bad Indians who have lost credit at the Hudson's Bay Company's posts go to Thoreau's. Whites and half-breeds who have broken the laws are harboured there. A dozen trappers are murdered each winter for their furs, and the assassins are among Thoreau's men. One of these days there is going to be a big clean-up. Meanwhile, they are unpleasant company. There is a deep swamp between our house and Thoreau's, so that during the open water seasons it means we are a hundred miles away from them by canoe. When winter comes we are only thirty-five miles, as the sledge-dogs run. I don't like it. You can snow-shoe the distance in a few hours."

"I know of such a place far to the west," replied Philip. "Both the Hudson's Bay Company and Reveillon Freres have threatened to put it out of business, but it still remains. Perhaps that is owned by Lang, too."

He had joined Adare at the window. The next moment both men were staring at the same object in a mutual surprise. Into the white snow space between the house and the forest there had walked swiftly the slim, red-clad figure of Josephine, her face turned to the forest, her hair falling in a long braid down her back.

The master of Adare chuckled exultantly.

"There goes our little Red Riding Hood!" he rumbled. "She beat us after all, Philip. She is going after the dogs!"

Philip's heart was beating wildly. A better opportunity for seeing Josephine alone could not have come to him. He feared that his voice might betray him as he laid a hand on Adare's arm.

"If you will excuse me I will join her," he said. "I know it doesn't seem just right to tear off in this way, but - you see -"

Adare interrupted him with one of his booming laughs.

"Go, my lad. I understand. If it was Miriam instead of Mignonne running away like that, John Adare wouldn't be waiting this long."

Philip turned and left the room, every pulse in his body throbbing with an excitement roused by the knowledge that the hour had come when Josephine would give herself to him forever, or doom him to that hopelessness for which Jean Croisset had told him to prepare himself.

CHAPTER FOURTEEN

In his eagerness to join Josephine Philip had reached the outer door before it occurred to him that he was without hat or coat and had on only a pair of indoor moccasin slippers. He would still have gone on, regardless of this utter incongruity of dress, had he not known that John Adare would see him through the window. He partly opened the hall door and looked out. Josephine was halfway to the forest. He turned swiftly back to his room, threw on a coat, put his moccasins on over the soft caribou skin slippers, caught up his cap, and hurried back to the door. Josephine had disappeared into the edge of the forest. He held himself to a walk until he reached the cover of the spruce, but no sooner was he beyond Adare's vision than he began to run. Three or four hundred yards in the forest he overtook Josephine.

He had come up silently in the soft snow, and she turned, a little startled, when be called her name.

"You, Philip!" she exclaimed, the colour deepening quickly in her cheeks. "I thought you were with father in the big room."

She had never looked lovelier to him. From the top of her hooded head to the hem of her short skirt she was dressed in a soft and richly glowing red. Her eyes shone gloriously this morning, and about her mouth there was a tenderness and a sweetness which had not been there the night before. The lines that told of her strain and grief were gone. She seemed like a different Josephine now, confessing in this first thrilling moment of their meeting that she, too, had been living in the memory of what had passed between them a few hours before. And yet in the gentle welcome of her smile there was a mingling of sadness and of pathos that tempered Philip's joy as he came to her and took her hands.

"My Josephine," he cried softly.

She did not move as he bent down. Again he felt the warm, sweet thrill of her lips. He would have kissed her again, have clasped her close in his arms, but she drew away from him gently.

"I am glad you saw me - and followed, Philip," she said, her clear, beautiful eyes meeting his. "It is a wonderful thing that has happened to us. And we must talk about it. We must understand. I was on my way to the pack. Will you come?"

She offered him her hand, so childishly confident, so free of her old restraint now, that he took it without a word and fell in at her side. He had rushed to her tumultuously. On his lips had been a hundred things that he had wanted to say. He had meant to claim her in the full ardour of his love - and now, quietly, without effort, she had worked a wonderful change in him. It was as if their experience had not happened yesterday, but yesteryear; and the calm, sweet yielding of her lips to him again, the warm pressure of her hand, the illimitable faith in him that shone in her eyes, filled him with emotions which for a space made him speechless. It was as if some wonderful spirit had come to them while they slept, so that now there was no necessity for explanation or speech. In all the fulness of her splendid womanhood Josephine had accepted his love, and had given him her own in return. Every fibre in his being told him that this was so. And yet she had uttered no word of love, and he had spoken none of the things that had been burning in his soul.

They had gone but a few steps when Josephine paused close to the fallen trunk of a huge cedar. With her mittened hands she brushed off the snow, seated herself, and motioned Philip to sit beside her.

"Let us talk here," she said. And then she asked, a little anxiously, "You left my father believing in you - in us?"

"Fully," replied Philip. He took her face between his two hands and turned it up to him. Her fingers clasped his arms. But they made no effort to pull down the hands that held her eyes looking straight into his own.

"He believes in us," he repeated. "And you, Josephine, you love me?"

He saw the tremulous forming of a word on her lips, but she did not speak. A deeper glow came into her eyes. Gently her fingers crept to his wrists, and she took down his hands from her face, and drew him to the seat at her side.

"Yes, Philip," she said then, in a voice so low and calm that it roused a new sense of fear in him. "There can be no sin in telling you that - after last night. For we understand each other now. It has filled me with a strange happiness. Do you remember what you said to me in the canoe? It was this: 'In spite of all that may happen, I will receive more than all else in the world could give me. For I will have known you, and you will be my salvation.' Those words have been ringing in my heart night and day. They are there now. And I understand them; I understand you. Hasn't some one said that it is better to have loved and lost than never to have loved at all? Yes, it is a thousand times better. The love that is lost is often the love that is sweetest and purest, and leads you nearest Heaven. Such is Jean's love for his lost wife. Such must be your love for me. And when you are gone my life will still be filled with the happiness which no grief can destroy. I did not know these things - until last night. I did not know what it meant to love as Jean must love. I do now. And it will be my salvation up in these big forests, just as you have said that it will be yours down in that other world to which you will go."

He had listened to her like one stricken by a sudden grief. He understood her, even before she had finished, and his voice came in a sudden broken cry of protest and of pain.

"Then you mean - that after this - you will still send me away? After last night? It is impossible! You have told me, and it makes no difference, except to make me love you more. Become my wife. We can be married secretly, and no one will ever know. My God, you cannot drive me away now, Josephine! It is not justice. If you love me - it is a crime!"

In the fierceness of his appeal he did not notice how his words were driving the colour from her face. Still she answered him calmly, in her voice a strange tenderness. Strong in her faith in him, she put her hands to his shoulders, and looked into his eyes.

"Have you forgotten?" she asked gently. "Have you forgotten all that you promised, and all that I told you? There has been no change since then - no change that frees me. There can be no change. I love you, Philip. Is that not more than you expected? If one can give one's soul away, I give mine to you. It is yours for all eternity. Is it not enough? Will you throw that away - because - my body - is not free?"

Her voice broke in a dry sob; but she still looked into his eyes, waiting for him to answer - for the soul of him to ring true. And he knew what must be. His hands lay clenched between them. Jean seemed to rise up before him again at the grave-sides, and from his lips he forced the words:

"Then there is something more - than the baby?"

"Yes," she replied, and dropped her hands from his shoulders. "There is that of which I warned you - something which you could not know if you lived a thousand years."

He caught her to him now, so close that his breath swept her face.

"Josephine, if it was the baby alone, you would give yourself to me? You would be my wife?"

"Yes."

Strength leaped back into him, the strength that made her love him. He freed her and stood back from the log, his face ablaze with the old fighting spirit. He laughed, and held out his arms without taking her.

"Then you have not killed my hope!" he cried.

His enthusiasm, the strength and sureness of him as he stood before her, sent the flush back into her own face. She rose, and reached to one of his outstretched hands with her own.

"You must hope for nothing more than I have given you," she said. "A month from to-day you will leave Adare House, and will never return."

"A month!" He breathed the words as if in a dream.

"Yes, a month from to-day. You will go off on a snowshoe journey. You will never return, and they will think that you have died in the deep snows. You have promised me this. And you will not fail me?"

"What I have promised I will do," he replied, and his voice was now as calm as her own. "And for this one month - you are mine!"

"To love as I have given you love, yes."

For a moment he folded her in his arms; and then he drew back her hood so that he might lay a hand on her shining hair, and his eyes were filled with a wonderful illumination as he looked into her upturned face.

"A month is a long time, my Josephine," he whispered. "And

after that month there are other months - years and years of them, and through years, if it must be, my hope will live. You cannot destroy it, and some day, somewhere, you will send word to me. Will you promise to do that?"

"If such a thing becomes possible, yes."

"Then I am satisfied," he said. "I am going to fight for you, Josephine. No man ever fought for a woman as I am going to fight for you. I don't know what this strange thing is that separates us. But I can think of nothing terrible enough to frighten me. I am going to fight, mentally and physically, day and night - until you are my own. I cannot lose you now. That will be what God never meant to be. I shall keep all my promises to you. You have given me a month, and much can happen in that time. If at the end of the month I have failed - I will go. But you will not send me away. For I shall win!"

So sure was he, so filled with the conviction of his final triumph, so like a god to her in this moment of his greatest strength, that Josephine drew slowly away from him, her breath coming quickly, her eyes filled with the star-like pride and glory of the Woman who has found a Master. For a moment they stood facing each other in the white stillness of the forest, and in that moment there came to them the low and mourning wail of a dog beyond them. And then the full voice of the pack burst through the wilderness, a music that was wild and savage, and yet through which there ran a strange and plaintive note for Josephine.

"They have caught us in the wind," she said, holding out her hand to him. "Come, Philip. I want you to love my beasts."

CHAPTER FIFTEEN

After a little the trail through the thick spruce grew narrow and dark, and Josephine went ahead of Philip. He followed so close that he could reach out a hand and touch her. She had not replaced her hood. Her face was flushed and her lips parted and red when she turned to him now and then. His heart beat with a tumultuous joy as he followed. A few moments before he had not spoken to her boastfully, or to keep up a falling spirit. He had given voice to what was in his heart, what was there now, telling him that she belonged to him, that she loved him, that there could be nothing in the world that would long stand between them.

The voice of the pack came to them stronger each moment, yet for a space it was unheard by him. His mind - all the senses he possessed - travelled no farther than the lithesome red and gold figure ahead of him. The thick strands of her braid had become partly undone, covering her waist and hips in a shimmering veil of gold. He wanted to touch that rare treasure with his hands. He was filled with the desire to stop her, and hold her close in his arms. And yet he knew that this was a thing which he must not do. For him she had risen above a thing merely physical. The touching of her hair, her lips, her face, were no longer the first passions of love with him. And because Josephine knew these things rose the joyous flush in her face and the wonder-light in her eyes. The still, deep forests had long ago brought her dreams of this man. And these same forests seemed to whisper to Philip that her beauty was a part of her soul, and that it was not to be desecrated in such moments of desire as he was fighting back in himself now.

Suddenly she ran a little ahead of him, and then stopped. A moment later he stood at her side. They were peering into what looked like a great, dimly lighted and carpeted hall. For the space of a hundred feet in diameter the spruce had been thinned out. The trees that remained were lopped of their lower branches, leaving their upper parts crowding in a dense shelter that shut out cold and storm. No snow had filtered through their tops, and on the ground lay cedar and balsam needles two inches deep, a brown and velvety carpet that shone with the deep lustre of a Persian rug.

The place was filled with moving shapes and with gleaming eyes that were half fire in the gloom. Here were leashed the forty fierce and wolfish beasts of the pack. The dogs had ceased their loud clamour, and at sight of Josephine and sound of her voice, as she cried out greeting to them, there ran through the whole space a whining and a clinking of chains, and with that a snapping of jaws that sent a momentary shiver up Philip's back.

Josephine took him by the hand now. With him she ran in among them, calling out their names, laughing with them, caressing the shaggy heads that were thrust against her - until it seemed to Philip that every beast in the pit was straining at the end of his chain to get at them and rend them into pieces. And yet, above this thought, the nervousness that he could not fight it out of himself, rose the wonder of it all.

Philip had seen a husky snap off a man's hand at a single lunge; he knew it was a creature of the whip and the club, with the hatred of men inborn in it from the wolf. What he looked on now filled him with a sort of awe - and a fear for Josephine. He gave a warning cry and half drew his pistol when she dropped on her knees and flung her arms about the shaggy head of a huge beast that could have torn the life from her in an instant. She looked up at him, laughing, the inch-long fangs of Captain, the lead-dog, gleaming in brute happiness close to her soft, flushed face.

"Don't be afraid, Philip!" she cried. "They are my pets - all of them. This is Captain, who leads my sledge team. Isn't he magnificent?"

"Good God!" breathed Philip, looking about him. "I know something of sledge-dogs, Josephine. These are not from mongrel breeds. There are no hounds, no malemutes, none of the soft-footed breeds here. They are WOLF!"

She rose and stood beside him, panting, triumphant, glorious.

"Yes - they've all got the strain of wolf," she said. "That is why I love them, Philip. They are of the forests. AND I HAVE MADE THEM LOVE ME!"

A yellow beast, with small, dangerous eyes, was leaping fiercely at the end of his chain close to them. Philip pointed to him.

"And you would trust yourself THERE?" he exclaimed, catching her by the arm.

"That is Hero," she said. "Once his name was Soldier. Three years ago a man from Thoreau's Place offered me an insult in the woods, and Soldier almost killed him. He would have killed him if I had not dragged him off. From that day I called him Hero. He is a quarter-strain wolf."

She went to the husky, and the yellow giant leaped up against her, so that her arms were about him, with his wolfish muzzle reaching for her face. Under the cedars Philip's face was as white as the snow out in the open. Josephine saw this, and came and put her arm through his fondly.

"You are afraid for me, Philip?" she asked, with a little laugh of pleasure at his anxiety. "You mustn't be, for you must love them - for my sake. I have brought them all up from puppyhood. And they would fight for me - just as you would fight for me, Philip. Once I was lost in a storm. Father turned the dogs loose. And they found me - miles and miles away. When you hear the wonderful stories I have to tell about them you will love them. They will not harm you. They will harm nothing that I have touched. I have taught them that. I am going to unleash them now. Metoosin is coming along the trail with their frozen fish."

Before she had moved, Philip went straight up to the yellow creature that she had told him was a quarter wolf.

"Hero," he spoke softly. "Hero -"

He held out his hands. The giant husky's eyes burned a deeper glow; for an instant his upper lip drew back, baring his stiletto-like fangs, and the hair along his neck and back stood up like a brush. Then, inch by inch, his muzzle drew nearer to Philip's steady hands, and a low whine rose in his throat. His crest drooped, his ears shot forward a little, and Philip's hand rested on the wolfish head.

"That is proof," he laughed, turning to Josephine. "If he had snapped off my hand I would say that you were wrong."

She passed quickly from one dog to another now, with Philip close at her side, and from the collar of each dog she snapped the chain. After she had freed a dozen, Philip began to help her. A few of the huskies snarled at him. Others accepted him already as a part of her. Yet in their eyes he saw the smouldering menace, the fire that wanted only a word from her to turn them into a horde of tearing demons.

At first he was startled by Josephine's confidence in them. Then he was only amazed. She was not only unafraid herself; she was unafraid for him. She knew that they would not touch him. When they were all free the pack gathered in close about them, and then Josephine came and stood at Philip's side, and put her hands to his shoulders. Thus she stood for a few moments, half facing the dogs, calling their names again; and they crowded up still closer about them, until Philip fancied he could feel their warm breath.

"They have all seen me with you now," she cried after that. "They have seen me touch you. Not one of them will snap at you after this."

The dogs swept on ahead of them in a great wave as they left the spruce shelter. Out in the clear light Philip drew a deep breath. He had never seen anything like this pack. They crowded shoulder to shoulder, body to body, in the open trail. Most of them were the tawny dun and gray and yellow of the wolf. There were a few blacks, and a few pure whites, but none that wore the mongrel spots of the soft-footed and softer-throated dogs from the south.

He shivered as he measured the pent-up power, the destructive possibilites of the whining, snapping, living sea of sinew and fang ahead of them. And they were Josephine's! They were her slaves! What need had she of his protection? What account would be the insignificant automatic at his side in the face of this wild horde that awaited only a word from her? What could there be in these forests that she feared, with them at her command? Ten men with rifles could not have stood in the face of their first mad rush - and yet she had told him that everything depended upon his protection. He had thought that meant physical protection. But it could not be. He spoke his thoughts aloud, pointing to the dogs:

"What danger can there be in this world that you need fear - with them?" he asked. "I don't understand. I can't guess."

She knew what he meant. The hand on his arm pressed a little closer to him.

"Please don't try to understand," she answered in a low voice. "They would fight for me. I have seen them tear a wolf-pack into shreds. And I have called them back from the throat of a wind-run deer, so that not a hair of her was harmed. But, Philip, I guess that sometimes mistakes were made in the creation of things. They have a brain. But it isn't REASON!"

"You mean -" he cried.

"That you, a man, unarmed, alone, are still their master," she interrupted him. "In the face of reason they are powerless. See, there comes Metoosin with the frozen fish! What if he were a stranger and the fish were poisoned?"

"I understand," he replied. "But others drive them besides you?"

"Only those very near to the family. Twenty of them are used in the traces. The others are my companions - my bodyguard, I call them."

Metoosin approached them now, weighted down under a heavy load in a gunny-sack, and Philip believed that he recognized in the silent Indian the man whom he had first seen at the door of Adare House with a rifle in his hands. At a few commands from Josephine the dogs gathered about them, and Metoosin opened the bag.

"I want you to throw them the fish, Philip," said Josephine. "Their brains comprehend the hand that feeds them. It is a sort of pledge of friendship between you and them."

With Metoosin she drew a dozen steps back, and Philip found that he had become the centre of interest for the pack. One by one he pulled out the fish. Snapping jaws met the frozen feast in midair. There was no fighting - no vengeful jealousy of fang. Once when a gray and yellow husky snapped at a fish already in the jaws of another, Josephine reprimanded him sharply, and at the sound of his name he slunk back. One by one Philip threw out the fish until they were all gone. Then he stood and looked down upon the flat-bellied pack, listening to the crunching of bones and frozen flesh, and Josephine came and stood beside him again.

Suddenly he felt her start. He looked up, and saw that her face was turned down the trail. He had caught the quick change in her eyes, the swift tenseness that flashed for an instant in her mouth. The vivid colour in her face had paled. She looked again as he had seen her for that short space at the door in Miriam's room. He followed the direction of her eyes.

A hundred yards away two figures were advancing toward them. One was her father, the master of Adare. And on his arm was Miriam his wife.

CHAPTER SIXTEEN

The strange effect upon Josephine of the unexpected appearance of Adare and his wife passed as quickly as it had come. When Philip looked at her again she was waving a hand and smiling. Adare's voice came booming up the trail. He saw Miriam laughing. Yet in spite of himself - even as he returned Adare's greeting - he could not keep himself from looking at the two women with curious emotions.

"This is rank mutiny!" cried Adare, as they came up. "I told them they must sleep until noon. I have already punished Miriam. And you, Mignonne? Does Philip let you off too easily?"

Adare's wife had given Philip her hand. A few hours' rest had brightened her eyes and brought colour into her face. She looked still younger, still more beautiful. And Adare was riotous with joy because of it.

"Look at your mother, Josephine," he commanded in a hoarse whisper, meant for all to hear. "I said the forests would do more than a thousand doctors in Montreal!"

"You do look splendid, Mikawe," said Josephine, slipping an arm about her mother's waist.

Adare had turned into a sudden volley of greetings to the feasting dogs, and for another moment Philip's eyes were on mother and daughter. Josephine was the taller of the two by half a head. She was more like her father. He noted that the colour had not returned fully into her cheeks, while the flush in Miriam's face had deepened. There was something forced in Josephine's laugh, a note that was unreal and make-believe, as she turned to Philip.

"Isn't my mother wonderful, Philip? I call her Mikawe because that means a little more than Mother in Cree - something that is almost undying and spirit-like. You will never grow old, my little mother!"

"Ponce de Leon made a great mistake when he didn't search in these forests for his fountain of eternal youth," said Adare, laying a hand on Philip's shoulder. "Would you guess that it was twenty-two years ago a month from to-day that she came to be mistress of Adare House? And you, Ma Cheri," added Adare tenderly, taking his wife by the hand, "Do you remember that it was over this same trail that we took our first walk - from home? We went to the Chasm."

"Yes, I remember."

"And here - where we stand - the wood violets were so thick they left perfume on our boots."

"And you made me a wreath of them - with the red bakneesh," said Miriam softly.

"And braided it in your hair."

"Yes."

She was breathing a little more quickly. For a moment it seemed as if these two had forgotten Philip and Josephine. Their eyes had turned to each other.

"Twenty-two years ago - A MONTH FROM TO-DAY!" repeated Josephine.

It seemed as if she had spoken the words that Philip might catch their hidden meaning.

Adare straightened with a sudden idea:

"On that day we shall have a great anniversary feast," he declared. "We will ask every soul - red and white - for a hundred miles about, with the exception of the rogues over at Thoreau's Place! What do you say, Philip?"

"Splendid!" cried Philip, catching triumphantly at this straw in the face of Josephine's plans for him. He looked straight into her eyes as he spoke. "A month from to-day these forests shall ring with our joy. And there will be a reason for it - MORE THAN ONE!"

She could not misunderstand that! And Philip's heart beat joyously as Josephine turned quickly to her mother, the colour flooding to the tips of her ears.

The dogs had eaten their fish and were crowding about them. For the first time Adare seemed to notice Metoosin, who had stood motionless twenty paces behind them.

"Where is Jean?" he asked.

Josephine shook her head.

"I haven't seen him since last night."

"I had almost forgotten what I believe he intended me to tell you," said Philip. "He has gone somewhere in the forest. He may be away all day."

Philip saw the anxious look that crept into Josephine's eyes. She looked at him closely, questioningly, yet he guessed that beyond what he had said she wanted him to remain silent. A little later, when Adare and his wife were walking ahead of them, she asked:

"Where is Jean? What did he tell you last night?"

Philip remembered Jean's warning.

"I cannot tell you," he replied evasively. "Perhaps he has gone out to reconnoitre for - game."

"You are true," she breathed softly. "I guess I understand. Jean doesn't want me to know. But after I went to bed I lay awake a long time and thought of you - out in the night with that gun in your hand. I can't believe that you were there simply because of a noise, as you said. A man like you doesn't hunt for a noise with a pistol, Philip. What is the matter with your arm?"

The directness of her question startled him.

"Why do you ask that?" he managed to stammer.

"You have flinched twice when I touched it - this arm."

"A trifle," he assured her. "It should have healed by this time."

She smiled straight up into his eyes.

"You are too true to tell me fairy stories in a way that I must believe them, Philip. Day before yesterday your sleeves were up when you were paddling, and there was nothing wrong with this arm - this forearm - then. But I'm not going to question you. You don't want me to know." In the same breath she recalled his attention to her father and mother. "I told you they were lovers. Look!"

As if she had been a little child John Adare had taken his wife up in his arms and sat her high on the trunk of a fallen tree that was still held four or five feet above the ground by a crippled spruce. Philip heard him laugh. He saw the wife lean over, still clinging for safety to her husband's shoulders.

"It is beautiful," he said.

Josephine spoke as if she had not heard him.

"I do not believe there is another man in the world quite like my father. I cannot understand how a woman could cease to love such a man as he even for a day - an hour. She couldn't forget, could she?"

There was something almost plaintive in her question. As if she feared an answer, she went on quickly:

"He has made her happy. She is almost forty - thirty-nine her last birthday. She does not look that old. She has been happy. Only happiness keeps one young. And he is fifty. If it wasn't for his beard, I believe he would appear ten years younger. I have never known him without a beard; I like him that way. It makes him look 'beasty' - and I love beasts."

She ran ahead of him, and John Adare lifted his wife down from the tree when they joined them. This time Josephine took her mother's arm. At the door to Adare House she turned to the two men, and said:

"Mother and I have a great deal to talk over, and we are scheming not to see you again until dinner time. Little Daddy, you can go to your foxes. And please keep Philip out of mischief."

The dogs had followed her close to the door. As the men entered after Josephine and her mother, Philip paused for a moment to look at the pack. A dozen of them had already settled themselves upon their bellies in the snow.

"The Grand Guard," chuckled Adare, waiting for him. "Come, Philip. I'm going to follow Mignonne's suggestion and do some work on my foxes. Jean had a splendid surprise for me when I returned - a magnificent black. This is the dull season, when I can amuse myself only by writing and experimenting.

A little later, when the furs begin to come in, there will be plenty of life at Adare House."

"Do you buy many furs?" asked Philip.

"Yes. But not because I am in the business for money. Josephine got me into it because of her love for the forest people." He led the way into his big study; and added, as he threw off his cap and coat:

"You know in all the world no people have a harder struggle than these men, women, and little children of the trap-lines. From Labrador westward to the Mackenzie it is the land of the caribou, the rabbit, and the fur-bearing animals, but the land is not suitable for farming. It has been, it will always be, the country of the hunter.

"To the south the Ojibway may grow a little corn and wheat. To the north the Eskimo might seem to dwell in a more barren land, but not so, for he has an ever abundant supply of game from the sea, seal in winter, fish in summer, but here are only the rabbit, the caribou, and small game. The Indians would starve if they could not trade their furs for a little flour, traps, guns, and cloth to fight the cold and aid the hunter. Even then it is hard. The Indians cannot live in villages, except at a post, like Adare House. Such a large number of people living in one spot could not feed themselves, and in the winter each family goes to its own allotted hunting grounds. From father to son for generations the same district has been handed down, each territory rich enough in fur to support one family. One - not two, for two would starve, and if a strange trapper poaches the fight is to the death, even in the normal year when game is plentiful and fur prime.

"But every seventh year there may be famine. Here in the North it is the varying hare, the rabbit, that feeds the children of the trap-lines and the marten and fox they trap, and every seventh year there comes a mysterious disease. One year there are rabbits in millions, the next there are none. The lynx and the wolf and the fox starve, there are no fur bearers in the traps, the trapper faces the blizzard and the cold to find empty deadfalls day after day, and however skillfully he may hunt there is no game for his gun. What would he do, but starve, if it were not for the fur trader and the post, where there is flour, a little food to help John the Trapper through the winter? The people about us are not thin in the waist. Josephine has made a little oasis of plenty where John the Trapper is safe in good years and bad. That's why I buy fur."

The giant's eyes were flushed with enthusiasm again. He pushed the cigars across the table to Philip, and one of his fists was knotted.

"She wants me to publish a lot of these things," he went on. "She says they are facts which would interest the whole world. Perhaps that is so. Fur is gotten with hardship and danger and suffering. It may be there are not many people who know that up here at the top end of the world there is a country of forest and stream twenty times as large as the State of Ohio, and in which the population per square mile is less than that of the Great African Desert. And it's all because everyone must live off the game. Everything goes back to that. Let something happen, some little thing - a migration of game, a case of measles. The Indians will die if there are not white men near to help them. That's why Josephine makes me buy fur."

He pointed to the wall behind Philip. Over the door through which they had just come hung a huge, old-fashioned flint-lock six feet in length. There was something like the snarl of an animal in John Adare's voice when he spoke again.

"That's the tool of the Northland," he said. "That is the only tool John the Trapper knows, all he can know in a land where even trees are stunted and there are no plows. His clothes and the blankets he weaves of twisted strips of rabbit fur are adapted to the cold, he is a master of the canoe and the most skilful trapper in the world, but in all else he must be looked after like a child. He is still largely one of God's men, this John the Trapper. He hasn't any measurements of value. He doesn't know what the dollar means. He measures his wealth in 'skins,' and when he trades the basis for whatever mental calculations he may make is in the form of lead bullets taken from one tin-pan and transferred to another. He doesn't keep track of figures. He trusts alone to the white man's word, and only those who understand him, who have dealt with him for years, can be trusted not to take advantage of his faith. That's why I buy fur - to give John his chance to live."

Adare laughed, and ran a hand through his shaggy hair as if rousing himself from thought of a relentless struggle. "But this isn't working on my foxes, is it? On second thought I think I shall postpone that until to-morrow, Philip. I have promised Miriam that I will have Metoosin trim my hair and beard before dinner. Shall I send him to you?"

"A hair cut would be a treat," said Philip, rising. He was surprised at the sudden change in the other's mood. But he was not sorry Adare had given him the opportunity to go. He had planned to say other things to Josephine that morning if they had not been interrupted, and he did not believe that she would be long with her mother.

In this, however, he was doomed to disappointment. When he returned to his room he found that Josephine had not forgotten the condition of his wardrobe, and he guessed immediately why she had surprised them all by rising so early. On his bed were spread several changes of shirts and underwear, a pair of new corduroy trousers, a pair of caribou skin leggings, and moccasins. In a box were a dozen linen handkerchiefs and a number of ties for the blue-gray soft shirts Josephine had chosen for him. He was not much ahead of Metoosin, who came in a few minutes later and clipped his hair. When this was done and he had clad himself in his new raiment he looked at himself in the mirror. Josephine had shown splendid judgment. Everything fitted him.

For an hour he listened for footsteps in the hall, and

occasionally looked out of the window. He wondered if Josephine had seen the small round hole with its myriad of out-shooting cracks where the bullet had pierced the glass. He had made up his mind that she had not, for no one could mistake it, and she would surely have spoken to him of it. He found that the hole was so high up on the pane that he could draw the curtain over it without shutting out much light. He did this.

Later he went outside, and found that the dogs regarded him with certain signs of friendship. In him was a growing presentiment that something had happened to Jean. He was sure that Croisset had taken up the trail of the man who had shot at him soon after they had separated at the gravesides. He was equally certain that the chase would be short. Jean was quick. Dogs and sledge would be an impediment for the other in the darkness of the night. Before this, hours ago, they must have met. If Jean had come out of that meeting unharmed, it was time for him to be showing up at Adare House. Still greater perturbation filled Philip's mind when he recalled the unpleasant skill of the mysterious forest man's fighting. He had been more than his equal in swiftness and trickery; he was certainly Jean's.

Should he make some excuse and follow Jean's trail? He asked himself this question a dozen times without arriving at an answer. Then it occurred to him that Jean might have some definite reason for not returning to Adare House immediately. The longer he reasoned with himself the more confident he became that Croisset had been the victor. He knew Jean. Every advantage was on his side. He was as watchful as a lynx. It was impossible to conceive of him walking into a trap. So he determined to wait, at least until that night.

It was almost noon when Adare sent word by Metoosin asking Philip to rejoin him in the big room. A little later Josephine and her mother came in. Again Philip noticed that in the face of Adare's wife was that strange look which he had first observed in her room. The colour of the morning had faded from her cheeks. The glow in her eyes was gone. Adare noted the change, and spoke to her tenderly.

Miriam and Josephine went ahead of them to the dining-room, and with his hand on Philip's arm John Adare whispered:

"Sometimes I am afraid, Philip. She changes so suddenly. This morning her cheeks and lips were red, her eyes were bright, she laughed - she was the old Miriam. And now! Can you tell me what it means? Is it some terrible malady which the doctors could not find?"

"No, it is not that," Philip felt his heart beat a little faster. Josephine had fallen a step behind her mother. She had heard Adare's words, and at Philip she flung back a swift, frightened look. "It is not that," he repeated. "See how much better she looks to-day than yesterday! You understand, Mon Pere, that oftentimes there comes a period of nervousness - of a sickness that is not sickness - in a woman's life. The winter will build her up."

The dinner passed too swiftly for Philip. They sat at a long table, and Josephine was opposite him. For a time he forgot the strain he was under, that he was playing a part in which he must not strike a single false key. Yet in another way he was glad when it came to an end, for it gave him an opportunity of speaking a few words with Josephine. Adare and Miriam went out ahead of them. At the door Philip held Josephine back.

"You are not going to leave me alone this afternoon?" he asked. "It is not quite fair, or safe, Josephine. I am travelling on thin ice. I -"

"You are doing splendidly, Philip," she protested. "To-morrow I will be different. Metoosin says there is a little half-breed girl very sick ten miles back in the forest, and you may go with me to visit her. There are reasons why I must be with my mother all of to-day. She has had a long journey and is worn out and nervous. Perhaps she will not want to appear at supper. If that is so, I will remain with her. But we will be together to-morrow. All day. Is that not recompense?"

She smiled up into his face as they followed Adare and his wife.

"You may help Metoosin with the dogs," she suggested. "I want you to be good friends - you and my beasts."

The hours that followed proved to be more than empty ones for Philip. Twice he went to the big room and found that Adare himself had yielded to the exhaustion of the long trip up from civilization, and was asleep. He accompanied Metoosin to the pit and assisted in chaining the dogs, but Metoosin was taciturn and uncommunicative. Josephine and her mother send down their excuses at supper time, and he sat down alone with Adare, who was delighted when he received word that they had been sleeping most of the afternoon, and would join them a little later. His face clouded, however, when he spoke of Jean.

"It is unusual," he said. "Jean is very careful to leave word of his movements. Metoosin says it is possible he went after fresh caribou meat. But that is not so. His rifle is in his room. He left during the night, or he would have spoken to us. I saw him as late as midnight, and he made no mention of it then. It has been snowing for two or three hours or I would send Metoosin on his trail."

"What possible cause for worry can you have?" asked Philip.

"Thoreau's cutthroats," replied Adare, a sudden fire in his eyes. "This winter may see - things happen. The force behind Thoreau's success in trade is whisky. That damnable stuff is his lure, or all the fur in this country would come to Adare House. If he could drive me out he would have nothing to fight against - his hands would be at the throat of every living soul in these regions, and all through whisky. Among those who were killed or turned up missing last winter were four of my best hunters. Twice Jean was shot at on the trail. I fear for him because he is my right arm."

When Philip left Adare he went to his room, put on heavier moccasins, and went quietly from the house. Three inches of fresh snow had fallen, and the air was thick with the white deluge. He hurried into the edge of the forest. A few minutes futile searching convinced him of the impossibility of following the trail made by Jean and the man he had pursued. Through the thickening darkness he returned to Adare House.

Again he changed his moccasins, and waited for the expected word from Josephine or Adare. Half an hour passed, and during this time his mind became still more uneasy. He had hoped that Croisset was hanging in the edge of the forest, waiting for darkness. Each minute now added to his fear that all had not gone well with the half-breed. He paced up and down his room, smoking, and looking at his watch frequently. After a time he went to the window and tried to peer out into the white swirl of the night. The opening of his door turned him about. He expected to see Adare. Words that were on his lips froze in a moment of speechless horror.

He knew that it was Jean Croisset who stood before him. But it did not look like Jean. The half-breed's cap was gone. He was swaying, clutching at the partly opened door to support himself. His face was disfigured with blood, the front of his coat was spattered with frozen clots of it. His long hair had fallen in ropelike strands over his eyes and frozen there. His lips were terrible.

"Good God!" gasped Philip.

He sprang forward and caught Jean as the half-breed staggered toward him. Jean's body hung a weight in his arms. His legs gave way under him, but for a moment the clutch of his fingers on Philip's shoulder were viselike.

"A little help, M'sieur," he gasped. "I am faint, sick. Whatever happens, as you love Our Lady, let no one know of this to-night!"

With a rattling breath his head dropped upon Philip's arm.

CHAPTER SEVENTEEN

Scarcely had Jean uttered the few words that preceded his lapse into unconsciousness than Philip heard the laughing voice of Adare at the farther end of the hall. Heavy footsteps followed the voice. Impulse rather than reason urged him into action. He lowered Jean to the floor, sprang to the partly open door, closed it and softly locked it. He was not a moment too soon. A few steps more and Adare was beating on the panel with his fist.

"What, ho!" he cried in his booming voice. "Josephine wants to know if you have forgotten her?" Adare's hand was on the latch.

"I am - undressed," explained Philip desperately. "Offer a thousand apologies for me, Mon Pere. I will finish my bath in a hurry!"

He dropped on his knees beside Jean as the master of Adare moved away from the door. A brief examination showed him where Croisset was hurt. The half-breed had received a scalp wound from which the blood had flowed down over his face and breast. He breathed easier when he discovered nothing beyond this. In a few minutes he had him partially stripped and on his bed. Jean opened his eyes as he bathed the blood from his face. He made an effort to rise, but Philip held him back.

"Not yet, Jean," he said.

Jean's glance shifted in a look of alarm toward the door.

"I must, M'sieur," he insisted. "It was the last few hundred yards that made me dizzy. I am better now. And there is no time to lose. I must get into my room - into other clothes!"

"We will not be interrupted," Philip assured him. "Is this your only hurt, Jean?"

"That alone, M'sieur. It was not bad until an hour ago. Then it broke out afresh, and made me so dizzy that with my last breath I stumbled into your room. The saints be praised that I managed to reach you!"

Philip left him, to return in a moment with a flask. Jean had pulled himself to a sitting posture on the side of the bed.

"Here's a drop of whisky, Jean. It will stir up your blood."

"Mon Dieu, it has been stirred up enough this night, tanike," smiled Jean feebly. "But it may give me voice, M'sieur. Will you get me fresh clothes? They are in my room - which is next to this on the right. I must be prepared for Josephine or Le M'sieur before I talk."

Philip went to the door and opened it cautiously. He could hear voices coming from the room through which he had first entered Adare House. The hall was clear. He slipped out and moved swiftly to Jean's room. Five minutes later he reentered his own room with an armful of Jean's clothes. Already Croisset was something like himself. He quickly put on the garments Philip gave him, brushed the tangles from his hair, and called upon Philip to examine him to make sure he had left no spot of blood on his face or neck.

"You have the time?" he asked then.

Philip looked at his watch.

"It is eight o'clock."

"And I must see Josephine - alone - before ten," said Jean quickly. "You must arrange it, M'sieur. No one must know that I have returned until I see her. It is important. It means -"

"What?"

"The great God alone can answer that," replied Jean in a strange voice. "Perhaps it will mean that to-morrow, or the next day, or the day after that M'sieur Weyman will know the secret we are keeping from him now, and will fight shoulder to shoulder with Jean Jacques Croisset in a fight that the wilderness will remember so long as there are tongues to tell of it!"

There was nothing of boastfulness or of excitement in his words. They were in the voice of a man who saw himself facing the final arbiter of things - a voice dead to visible hope, yet behind which there trembled a thing that made Philip face him with a new fire in his eyes.

"Why to-morrow or the next day?" he demanded. "Why shroud me in this damnable mystery any longer, Jean? If there is fighting to be done, let me fight!"

Jean's hollowed cheeks took on a flush.

"I would give my life if we two could go out and fight - as I want to fight," he said in a low, tense voice, "It would be worth your life and mine - that fight. It would be glorious. But I am a Catholic, M'sieur. I am a Catholic of the wilderness. And I have taken the most binding oath in the world. I have sworn by the sweet soul of my dead Iowaka to do only as Josephine tells me to do in this. Over her grave I swore that, with Josephine kneeling at my side. I have prayed that my Iowaka might come to me and tell me if I am right. But in this her voice has been silent. I have prayed Josephine to free me from my oath, and she has refused. I am afraid. I dare reveal nothing. I cannot act as I want to act. But to-night -"

His voice sank to a whisper. His fingers gripped deep into the flesh of Philip's hand.

"To-night may mean - something," he went on, his voice filled with an excitement strange to him. "The fight is coming, M'sieur. We cannot much longer evade what we have been trying to evade! It is coming. And then, shoulder to shoulder, we will fight!"

"And until then, I must wait?"

"Yes, you must wait, M'sieur."

Jean freed his hand and sat down in one of the chairs near the table. His eyes turned toward the window.

"You need not fear another shot, M'sieur," he said quietly. "The man who fired that will not fire again."

"You killed him?"

Jean bowed his head without replying. The movement was neither of affirmation nor denial:

"He will not fire again."

"It was more than one against one," persisted Philip. "Does your oath compel you to keep silent about that, too?"

There was a note of irritation in his voice which was almost a challenge to Jean. It did not prick the half-breed. He looked at Philip a moment before he replied:

"You are an unusual man, M'sieur," he said at last, as though he had been carefully measuring his words. "We have known each other only a few days, and yet it seems a long time. I had my suspicions of you back there. I thought it was Josephine's beauty you were after, and I have stood ready to kill you if I saw in you what I feared. But you have won, M'sieur. Josephine loves you. I have faith in you. And do you know why? It is because you have fought the fight of a strong man. It does not take great soul in a man to match knife against knife, or bullet against bullet. Not to keep one's word, to play a hopeless part in the dark, to leap when the numma wapew is over the eyes and you are blind - that takes a man. And now, when Jean Jacques Croisset says for the first time that there is a ray of hope for you, where a few hours ago no hope existed, will you give me again your promise to play the part you have been asked to play?"

"Hope!" Philip was at Jean's side in an instant. "Jean, what do you mean? Is it that you, even YOU - now give me hope of possessing Josephine?"

Slowly Jean rose from his chair.

"I am part Cree, M'sieur," he said. "And in our Cree there is a saying that the God of all things, Kisamunito, the Great Spirit, often sits on high and laughs at the tricks which he plays on men. Perhaps this is one of those times. I am beginning to believe so. Kisamunito has begun to run our destinies, not ourselves. Yesterday we - our Josephine and I - had our hopes, our plans, our schemes well laid. To-night they no longer exist. Before the night is much older all that Josephine has done, all that she has made you promise, will count for nothing. After that - a matter of hours, perhaps of days - will come the great fight for you and me. Until then you must know nothing, must see nothing, must ask nothing. And when the crash comes - "

"It will give Josephine to me?" cried Philip eagerly.

"I did not say that, M'sieur," corrected Jean quietly. "Out of fighting such as this strange things may happen. And where things happen there is always hope. Is that not true?"

He moved to the door and listened. Quietly he opened it, and looked out.

"The hall is clear," he whispered softly. "Go to Josephine. Tell her that she must arrange to see me within an hour. And if you care for that bit of hope I have shown you, let it happen without the knowledge of the master of Adare. From this hour Jean Jacques Croisset sacrifices his soul. Make haste, M'sieur - and use caution!"

Without a word Philip went quietly out into the hall. Behind him Jean closed and locked the door.

CHAPTER EIGHTEEN

For a few moments Philip stood without moving. Jean's return and the strange things he had said had worked like sharp wine in his blood. He was breathing quickly. He was afraid that his appearance just now would betray the mental excitement which he must hide. He drew back deeper into the shadow of the wall and waited, and while he waited he thought of Jean. It was not the old Jean that had returned this night, the Jean with his silence, his strange repression, the mysterious something that had seemed to link him with an age-old past. Out of that spirit had risen a new sort of man - the fighting man. He had seen a new fire in Jean's eyes and face; he had caught new meaning in his words, Jean was no longer the passive Jean - waiting, watching, guarding. Out in the forest something had happened to rouse in him what a word from Josephine would set flaming in the savage breasts of her dogs. And the excitement in Philip's blood was the thrill of exultation - the joy of knowing that action was close at hand, for deep in him had grown the belief that only through action could Josephine be freed for him.

Suddenly, softly, there came floating to him the low, sweet tones of the piano, and then, sweeter still, the voice of Josephine. Another moment and Miriam's voice had joined her in a song whose melody seemed to float like that of spirit-voices through the thick fog walls of Adare House. Soundlessly he moved toward the room where they were waiting for him, a deeper flush mounting into his face now. He opened the door without being heard, and looked in.

James Oliver Curwood

Josephine was at the piano. The great lamp above her head flooded her in a mellow light in which the rich masses of her hair shimmered in a glorious golden glow. His heart beat with the knowledge that she had again dressed for him to-night. Her white neck was bare. In her hair he saw for a second time a red rose. For a space he saw no one but her. Then his eyes turned for an instant to Miriam. She was standing a little back, and it seemed to him that he had never seen her so beautiful. Against the wall, in a great chair, sat the master of Adare, his bearded chin in the palm of his hand, looking at the two with a steadiness of gaze that was more than adoration. Philip entered. Still he was unheard. He stood silent until the song was finished, and it was Josephine, turning, who saw him first.

"Philip!" she cried.

Adare started, as if awakening from a dream. Josephine came to Philip, holding out both her hands, her beautiful face smiling with welcome. Even as their warm touch thrilled him he felt a sudden chill creep over him. A swift glance showed him that Adare had gone to Miriam. Instead of words of greeting, he whispered low in Josephine's ear:

"I would have come sooner, but I have been with Jean. He returned a few minutes ago. Strange things have happened, and he says that he must see you within an hour, and that your father must not know. He is in my room. You must get away without rousing suspicion."

Her fingers gripped his tightly. The soft glow in her eyes faded away. A look of fear leapt into them and her face went suddenly white. He drew her nearer, until her hands were against his breast.

"Don't look like that," he whispered. "Nothing can hurt you. Nothing in the world. See - I must do this to bring your colour back, or they will guess something is wrong!"

He bent and kissed her on the lips.

Adare's voice burst out happily:

"Good boy, Philip! Don't be bashful when we're around. That's the first time I've seen you kiss your wife!"

There was none of the white betrayal in Josephine's cheeks now. They were the colour of the rose in her hair. She had time to look up into Philip's face, and whisper with a laughing break in her voice:

"Thank you, Philip. You have saved me again."

With Philip's hand in hers she turned to her father and mother.

"Philip wants to scold me, Mon Pere," she said. "And I cannot blame him. He has seen almost nothing of me to-day."

"And I have been scolding Miriam because they have given me no chance with the baby," rumbled Adare. "I have seen him but twice to-day - the little beggar! And both times he was asleep. But I have forced them to terms, Philip. From to-morrow I am to have him as much as I please. When they want him they will find him in the big room."

Josephine led Philip to her mother, who had seated herself on one of the divans.

"I want you to talk with Philip, Mikawe," she said. "I have promised father that he should have a peep at the baby. I will bring him back very soon."

Philip seated himself beside Miriam as Adare and Josephine left the room. He noticed that her hair was dressed like Josephine's, and that in the soft depths of it was partly buried a rose.

"Do you know - I sometimes think that I am half dreaming," he said. "All this seems too wonderful to be true - you, and

Josephine, almost a thousand miles out of the world. Even flowers like that which you wear in your hair - hot-house flowers!"

There was a strange sweetness in Miriam's smile, a smile softened by something that was almost pathetic, a touch of sadness.

"That is the one thing we keep alive out of the world I used to know - roses," she said. "The first roots came from my baby-hood home, and we have grown them here for more than twenty years. Of course Josephine has shown you our little hot-house?"

"Yes." lied Philip. Then he added, finding her dear eyes resting on him steadily. "And you have never grown lonesome up here?"

"Never. I am sorry that we ever went back into that other world, even for a day. This has been paradise. We have always been happy. And you?" she asked suddenly. "Do you sometimes wish for that other world?"

"I have been out of it four years - with the exception of a short break. I never want to go back. Josephine has made my paradise, as you have made another man's."

He fancied, as she turned her face from him, that he heard a little catch in her breath. But she faced him again quickly.

"We have been happy. No woman in the world has been happier than I. And you - four years? In that time you have not heard much music. Shall I play for you?"

She rose and went to the piano without waiting for him to reply. Philip leaned back and partly closed his eyes as she began to play. The spell of music held him silent, and neither spoke until Josephine and her father returned. Philip did not catch the laughing words Adare turned to his wife. In the door

Josephine had stopped. To his surprise she was dressed in her red coat and hood, and her feet were moccasined. She made a quick little signal to him.

"I am ready, Philip," she said.

He arose, fearing that his tongue might betray him if he replied to her in words. Adare came unwittingly to his assistance.

"You'll get used to this before the winter is over, Philip," he exclaimed banteringly. "Metoosin once called Josephine 'Wapikunoo' - the White Owl, and the name has stuck ever since. I haven't known Mignonne to miss a walk on a moonlit winter night since I can remember. But I prefer my airings in the day. Eh, Miriam?"

"And there is no moon to-night," laughed his wife.

"Hush - but there is Philip!" whispered Adare loudly. "It may be that our Josephine will prefer the darker nights after this. Can you remember -"

Josephine was pulling Philip through the door, laughing back over her shoulder. As soon as they were in the hall she caught his arm excitedly.

"Let us hurry to your room," she urged. "You can dress and slip out unseen, leaving Jean and me alone. You are sure - he wants to see me - alone?"

There was a tremble in her voice now.

"Yes." They came to his door and he tapped on it lightly. Instantly it was opened. Josephine stared at Jean as she darted in.

"Jean - you have something to tell me?" she whispered, no longer hiding the fear in her face. "You must see me - alone?"

"Oui, M'selle," murmured Jean, turning to Philip. "If M'sieur Philip can arrange for us to be alone."

"I will be gone in a moment," said Philip, hastily beginning to put on heavier garments. "Lock the door, Jean. It will not do to be interrupted now."

When he was ready Josephine went to him, her eyes shining softly. Jean turned to the window.

"You - your faith in me is beautiful," she said gratefully, so low that only he could hear her. "I don't deserve it, Philip."

For a moment he pressed her hand, his face telling her more than he could trust his lips to speak. Jean heard him turn the key in the lock, and he turned quickly.

"I have thought it would be better for you to go out by the window, M'sieur."

"You are right," agreed Philip, relocking the door.

Jean raised the window. As Philip dropped himself outside the half-breed said:

"Go no farther than the edge of the forest, M'sieur. We will turn the light low and draw the curtain. When the curtain is raised again return to us as quickly as you can. Remember, M'sieur - and go no farther than the edge of the forest."

The window dropped behind him, and he turned toward the dark wall of spruce. There were six inches of fresh snow on the ground, and the clouds were again drifting out of the sky. Here and there a star shone through, but the moon was only a pallid haze beyond the gray-black thickness above. In the first shelter of the spruce and balsam Philip paused. He found himself a seat by brushing the snow from a log, and lighted his pipe. Steadily he kept his eyes on the curtained window. What was happening there now? To what was Josephine listening in these tense minutes of waiting?

Even as he stared through the darkness to that one lighter spot in the gloom he knew that the world was changing for the woman he loved. He believed Jean, and he knew Jean was now telling her the story of that day and the preceding night - the story which he had said would destroy the hopes she had built up, throw their plans into ruin, perhaps even disclose to him the secret which they had been fighting to hide. What could that story be? And what effect was it having on Josephine? The minutes passed slowly - with an oppressive slowness. Three times he lighted matches to look at his watch. Five minutes passed - ten, fifteen. He rose from the log and paced back and forth, making a beaten path in the snow. It was taking Jean a long time to tell the story!

And then, suddenly, a flood of light shot out into the night. The curtain was raised! It was Jean's signal to him, and with a wildly beating heart he responded to it.

CHAPTER NINETEEN

The window was open when Philip came to it, and Jean was waiting to give him an assisting hand. The moment he was in the room he turned to look at Josephine. She was gone. Almost angrily he whirled upon the half-breed, who had lowered the window, and was now drawing the curtain. It was with an effort that he held back the words on his lips. Jean saw that effort, and shrugged his shoulders with an appreciative gesture.

"It is partly my fault that she is not here, M'sieur," he explained. "She would have told you nothing of what has passed between us - not as much, perhaps, as I. She will see you in the morning."

"And there's damned little consolation at the present moment in that," gritted Philip, with clenched hands. "Jean - I'm ready to fight now! I feel like a rat must feel when it's cornered. I've got to jump pretty soon - in some direction - or I'll bust. It's impossible -"

Jean's hand fell softly upon his arm.

"M'sieur, you would cut off this right arm if it would give you Josephine?"

"I'd cut off my head!" exploded Philip.

"Do you remember that it was only a few hours ago that I said she could never be yours in this world?" Croisset reminded him, in the same quiet voice. "And now, when even I say there is hope, can you not make me have the confidence in you that I must have - if we win?"

Philip's face relaxed. In silence he gripped Jean's hand.

"And what I am going to tell you - a thing which Josephine would not say if she were here, is this, M'sieur," went on Jean. "Before you left us alone in this room I had a doubt. Now I have none. The great fight is coming. And in that fight all the spirits of Kisamunito must be with us. You will have fighting enough. And it will be such fighting its you will remember to the end of your days. But until the last word is said - until the last hour, you must be as you have been. I repeat that. Have you faith enough in me to believe?"

"Yes, I believe," said Philip. "It seems inconceivable, Jean - but I believe."

Jean moved to the door.

"Good-night, M'sieur," he said.

"Good-night, Jean."

For a few moments after Croisset had left him Philip stood motionless. Then he locked the door. Until he was alone he did not know what a restraint he had put upon himself. Jean's words, the mysterious developments of the evening, the half promise of the fulfilment of his one great hope - had all worked him into a white heat of unrest. He knew that he could not stay in his room, that it would be impossible for him to sleep. And he was not in a condition to rejoin Adare and his wife. He wanted to walk - to find relief in physical exertion, Of a sudden his mind was made up. He extinguished the light. Then he reopened the window, and dropped out into the night again.

He made his way once more to the edge of the forest. He did not stop this time, but plunged deeper into its gloom. Moon and stars were beginning to lighten the white waste ahead of him. He knew he could not lose himself, as he could follow his own trail back. He paused for a moment in the shelter of a spruce to fill his pipe and light it. Then he went on. Now that he was alone he tried to discover some key to all that Jean had said to him. After all, his first guess had not been so far out of the way: it was a physical force that was Josephine's deadliest menace. What was this force? How could he associate it with the baby back in Adare House? Unconsciously his mind leaped to Thoreau, the Free Trader, as a possible solution, but in the same breath he discarded that as unreasonable. Such a force as Thoreau and his gang would be dealt with by Adare himself, or the forest people. There was something more. Vainly he racked his brain for some possible enlightenment.

He walked ten minutes without noting the direction he was taking when he was brought to a standstill with a sudden shock. Not twenty paces from him he heard voices. He dodged behind a tree, and an instant later two figures hurried past him. A cry rose to his lips, but he choked it back. One of the two was Jean. The other was Josephine!

For a moment he stood staring after them, his hand clutching at the bark of the tree. A feeling that was almost physical pain swept over him as he realized the truth. Josephine had not gone to her room. He understood now. She had purposely evaded him that she might be with Jean alone in the forest. Three days before Philip would not have thought so much of this. Now it hurt. Josephine had given him her love, yet in spite of that she was placing greater confidence in the half-breed than in him. This was what hurt - at first. In the next breath his overwhelming faith in her returned to HIM. There was some tremendous reason for her being here with Jean. What was it? He stepped out from behind the tree as he stared after them.

His eyes caught the pale glow of something that he had not

seen before. It was a campfire, the illumination of it only faintly visible deeper in the forest. Toward this Josephine and Jean were hurrying. A low exclamation of excitement broke from his lips as a still greater understanding dawned upon him. His hand trembled. His breath came quickly. In that camp there waited for Josephine and Croisset those who were playing the other half of the game in which he had been given a blind man's part! He did not reason or argue with himself. He accepted the fact. And no longer with hesitation his hand fell to his automatic, and he followed swiftly after Josephine and the half-breed.

He began to see what Jean had meant. In the room he had simply prepared Josephine for this visit. It was in the forest - and not in Adare House, that the big test of the night was to come.

It was not curiosity that made him follow them now. More than ever he was determined to keep his faith with Jean and the girl, and he made up his mind to draw only near enough to give his assistance if it should become necessary. Roused by the conviction that Josephine and the half-breed were not making this mysterious tryst without imperilling themselves, he stopped as the campfire burst into full view, and examined his pistol. He saw figures about the fire. There were three, one sitting, and two standing. The fire was not more than a hundred yards ahead of him, and he saw no tent. A moment later Josephine and Jean entered the circle of fireglow, and the sitting man sprang to his feet. As Philip drew nearer he noticed that Jean stood close to his companion, and that the girl's hand was clutching his arm. He heard no word spoken, and yet he could see by the action of the man who had been sitting that he was giving the others instructions which took them away from the fire, deeper into the gloom of the forest.

Seventy yards from the fire Philip dropped breathlessly behind a cedar log and rested his arm over the top of it. In his hand was his automatic. It covered the spot of gloom into which the two men had disappeared. If anything should happen - he was ready.

In the fire-shadows he could not make out distinctly the features of the third man. He was not dressed like the others. He wore knickerbockers and high laced boots. His face was beardless. Beyond these things he could make out nothing more. The three drew close together, and only now and then did he catch the low murmur of a voice. Not once did he hear Jean. For ten minutes he crouched motionless, his eyes shifting from the strange tableau to the spot of gloom where the others were hidden. Then, suddenly, Josephine sprang back from her companions. Jean went to her side. He could hear her voice now, steady and swift - vibrant with something that thrilled him, though he could not understand a word that she was speaking. She paused, and he could see that she was tense and waiting. The other replied. His words must have been brief, for it seemed he could scarcely have spoken when Josephine turned her back upon him and walked quickly out into the forest. For another moment Jean Croisset stood close to the other. Then he followed.

Not until he knew they were safe did Philip rise from his concealment. He made his way cautiously back to Adare House, and reentered his room through the window. Half an hour later, dressed so that he revealed no evidence of his excursion in the snow, he knocked at Jean's door. The half-breed opened it. He showed some surprise when he saw his visitor.

"I thought you were in bed, M'sieur," he exclaimed. "Your room was dark."

"Sleep?" laughed Philip. "Do you think that I can sleep to-night, Jean?"

"As well as some others, perhaps," replied Jean, offering him a chair. "Will you smoke, M'sieur?"

Philip lighted a cigar, and pointed to the other's moccasined feet, wet with melting snow.

"You have been out," he said. "Why didn't you invite me to go with you?"

"It was a part of our night's business to be alone," responded Jean. "Josephine was with me. She is in her room now with the baby."

"Does Adare know you have returned?"

"Josephine has told him. He is to believe that I went out to see a trapper over on the Pipestone."

"It is strange," mused Philip, speaking half to himself. "A strange reason indeed it must be to make Josephine say these false things."

"It is like driving sharp claws into her soul," affirmed Jean.

"I believe that I know something of what happened to-night, Jean. Are we any nearer to the end - to the big fight?"

"It is coming, M'sieur. I am more than ever certain of that. The third night from this will tell us."

"And on that night -"

Philip waited expectantly.

"We will know," replied Jean in a voice which convinced him that the half-breed would say no more. Then he added: "It will not be strange if Josephine does not go with you on the sledge-drive to-morrow, M'sieur. It will also be curious if there is not some change in her, for she has been under a great strain. But make as if you did not see it. Pass your time as much as possible with the master of Adare. Let him not guess. And now I am going to ask you to let me go to bed. My head aches. It is from the blow."

"And there is nothing I can do for you, Jean?'

"Nothing, M'sieur."

At the door Philip turned.

"I have got a grip on myself now, Jean," he said. "I won't fail you. I'll do as you say. But remember, we are to have the fight at the end!"

In his room he sat up for a time and smoked. Then he went to bed. Half a dozen times during the night he awoke from a restless slumber. Twice he struck a match to look at his watch. It was still dark when he got up and dressed. From five until six he tried to read. He was delighted when Metoosin came to the door and told him that breakfast would be ready in half an hour. This gave him just time to shave.

He expected to eat alone with Adare again this morning, and his heart jumped with both surprise and joy when Josephine came out into the hall to meet him. She was very pale. Her eyes told him that she had passed a sleepless night. But she was smiling bravely, and when she offered him her hand he caught her suddenly in his arms and held her close to his breast while he kissed her lips, and then her shining hair.

"Philip!" she protested. "Philip -"

He laughed softly, and for a moment his face was close against hers.

"My brave little darling! I understand," he whispered. "I know what a night you've had. But there's nothing to fear. Nothing shall harm you. Nothing shall harm you, nothing, nothing!"

She drew away from him gently, and there was a mist in her eyes. But he had brought a bit of colour into her face. And there was a glow behind the tears. Then, her lip quivering, she caught his arm.

"Philip, the baby is sick - and I am afraid. I haven't told father. Come!"

He went with her to the room at the end of the hall. The Indian woman was crooning softly over a cradle. She fell silent as Josephine and Philip entered, and they bent over the little flushed face on the pillow. Its breath came tightly, gaspingly, and Josephine clutched Philip's hand, and her voice broke in a sob.

"Feel, Philip - its little face - the fever -"

"You must call your mother and father," he said after a moment. "Why haven't you done this before, Josephine?"

"The fever came on suddenly - within the last half hour," she whispered tensely. "And I wanted you to tell me what to do, Philip. Shall I call them - now?"

He nodded.

"Yes."

In an instant she was out of the room. A few moments later she returned, followed by Adare and his wife. Philip was startled by the look that came into Miriam's face as she fell on her knees beside the cradle. She was ghastly white. Dumbly Adare stood and gazed down on the little human mite he had grown to worship. And then there came through his beard a great broken breath that was half a sob.

Josephine lay her cheek against his arm for a moment, and said:

"You and Philip go to breakfast, Mon Pere. I am going to give the baby some of the medicine the Churchill doctor left with me. I was frightened at first. But I'm not now. Mother and I will have him out of the fever shortly."

Philip caught her glance, and took Adare by the arm. Alone they went into the breakfast-room. Adare laughed uneasily as he seated himself opposite Philip.

"I don't like to see the little beggar like that," he said, taking to shake off his own and Philip's fears with a smile. "It was Mignonne who scared me - her face. She has nursed so many sick babies that it frightened me to see her so white. I thought he might be - dying."

"Cutting teeth, mebby," volunteered Philip.

"Too young," replied Adare.

"Or a touch of indigestion, That brings fever."

"Whatever it is, Josephine will soon have him kicking and pulling my thumb again," said Adare with confidence. "Did she ever tell you about the little Indian baby she found in a tepee?"

"No."

"It was in the dead of winter. Mignonne was out with her dogs, ten miles to the south. Captain scented the thing - the Indian tepee. It was abandoned - banked high with snow - and over it was the smallpox signal. She was about to go on, but Captain made her go to the flap of the tepee. The beast knew, I guess. And Josephine - my God, I wouldn't have let her do it for ten years of my life! There had been smallpox in that tent; the smell of it was still warm. Ugh! And she looked in! And she says she heard something that was no louder than the peep of a bird. Into that death-hole she went - and brought out a baby. The parents, starving and half crazed after their sickness, had left it - thinking it was dead.

"Josephine brought it to a cabin close to home, in two weeks she had that kid out rolling in the snow. Then the mother and father heard something of what had happened, and came to us as fast as their legs could bring them. You should have seen that Indian mother's gratitude! She didn't think it so terrible to leave the baby unburied. She thought it was dead. Pasoo is the Indian father's name. Several times a year they come to see Josephine, and Pasoo brings her the choicest furs of his trap-line. And each time he says: 'Nipa tu mo-wao,' which means that some day he hopes to be able to kill for her. Nice, isn't it - to have friends who'll murder your enemies for you if you just give 'em the word?"

"One never can tell," began Philip cautiously. "A time might come when she would need friends. If such a day should happen -"

He paused, busying himself with his steak. There was a note of triumph, of exultation, in Adare's low laugh.

"Have you ever seen a fire run through a pitch-dry forest?" he asked. "That is the way word that Josephine wanted friends would sweep through a thousand square miles of this Northland. And the answer to it would be like the answer of stray wolves to the cry of the hunt-pack!"

All over Philip there surged a warm glow.

"You could not have friends like that down there, in the cities," he said.

Adare's face clouded.

"I am not a pessimist," he answered, after a moment. "It has been one of my few Commandments always to look for the bright spot, if there is one. But, down there, I have seen so many wolves, human wolves. It seems strange to me that so many people should have the same mad desire for the dollar that the wolves of the forest have for warm, red, quivering flesh. I have known a wolf-pack to kill five times what it could eat in a night, and kill again the next night, and still the next - always more than enough. They are like the Dollar Hunters -

only beasts. Among such, one cannot have solid friends - not very many who will not sell you for a price. I was afraid to trust Josephine down among them. I am glad that it was you she met, Philip. You were of the North - a foster-child, if not born there."

That day was one of gloom in Adare House. The baby's fever grew steadily worse, until in Josephine's eyes Philip read the terrible fear. He remained mostly with Adare in the big room. The lamps were lighted, and Adare had just risen from his chair, when Miriam came through the door. She was swaying, her hands reaching out gropingly, her face the gray of ash that crumbles from an ember. Adare sprung to meet her, a strange cry on his lips, and Philip was a step behind her. He heard her moaning words, and as he rushed past them into the hall he knew that she had fallen fainting into her husband's arms.

In the doorway to Josephine's room he paused. She was there, kneeling beside the little cradle, and her face as she lifted it to him was tearless, but filled with a grief that went to the quick of his soul. He did not need to look into the cradle as she rose unsteadily, clutching a hand at her heart, as if to keep it from breaking. He knew what he would see. And now he went to her and drew her close in his strong arms, whispering the pent-up passion of the things that were in his heart, until at last her arms stole up about his neck, and she sobbed on his breast like a child. How long he held her there, whispering over and over again the words that made her grief his own, he could not have told; but after a time he knew that some one else had entered the room, and he raised his eyes to meet those of John Adare. The face of the great, grizzled giant had aged five years. But his head was erect. He looked at Philip squarely. He put out his two hands, and one rested on Josephine's head, the other on Philip's shoulder.

"My children," he said gently, and in those two words were weighted the strength and consolation of the world.

He pointed to the door, motioning Philip to take Josephine

away, and then he went and stood at the crib-side, his great shoulders hunched over, his head bowed down.

Tenderly Philip led Josephine from the room. Adare had taken his wife to her room, and when they entered she was sitting in a chair, staring and speechless. And now Josephine turned to Philip, taking his face between her two hands, and her soul looking at him through a blinding mist of tears.

"My Philip," she whispered, and drew his face down and kissed him. "Go to him now. We will come - soon."

He returned to Adare like one in a dream - a dream that was grief and pain, with its one golden thread of joy. Jean was there now, and the Indian woman; and the master of Adare had the still little babe huddled up against his breast. It was some time before they could induce him to give it to Moanne. Then, suddenly, he shook himself like a great bear, and crushed Philip's shoulders in his hands.

"God knows I'm sorry for you, Boy," he cried brokenly. "It's hurt me - terribly. But YOU - it must be like the cracking of your soul. And Josephine, Mignonne, my little flower! She is with her mother?"

"Yes," replied Philip. "Come. Let us go. We can do nothing here. And Josephine and her mother will be better alone for a time."

"I understand," said Adare almost roughly, in his struggle to steady himself. "You're thinking of ME, Boy. God bless you for that. You go to Josephine and Miriam. It is your place. Jean and I will go into the big room."

Philip left them at Adare's room and went to his own, leaving the door open that he might hear Josephine if she came out into the hall. He was there to meet her when she appeared a little later. They went to Moanne. And at last all things were done, and the lights were turned low in Adare House. Philip did not take off his clothes that night, nor did Jean and Metoosin. In the early dawn they went out together to the little garden of crosses. Close to the side of Iowaka, Jean pointed out a plot.

"Josephine would say the little one will sleep best there, close to HER," he said. "She will care for it, M'sieur. She will know, and understand, and keep its little soul bright and happy in Heaven."

And there they digged. No one in Adare House heard the cautious fall of pick and spade.

With morning came a strangely clear sun. Out of the sky had gone the last haze of cloud. Jean crossed himself, and said:

"She knows - and has sent sunshine instead of storm."

Hours later it was Adare who stood over the little grave, and said words deep and strong, and quivering with emotion, and it was Jean and Metoosin who lowered the tiny casket into the frozen earth. Miriam was not there, but Josephine clung to Philip's side, and only once did her voice break in the grief she was fighting back. Philip was glad when it was over, and Adare was once more in his big room, and Josephine with her mother. He did not even want Jean's company. In his room he sat alone until supper time. He went to bed early, and strangely enough slept more soundly than he had been able to sleep for some time.

When he awoke the following morning his first thought was that this was the day of the third night. He had scarcely dressed when Adare's voice greeted him from outside the door. It was different now - filled with the old cheer and booming hopefulness, and Philip smiled as he thought how this stricken giant of the wilderness was rising out of his own grief to comfort Josephine and him. They were all at breakfast, and Philip was delighted to find Josephine looking much better than he had expected. Miriam had sunk deepest under the strain of the preceding hours. She was still white and wan. Her hands trembled. She spoke little. Tenderly Adare tried to raise her spirits.

During the rest of that day Philip saw but little of Josephine, and he made no effort to intrude himself upon her. Late in the afternoon Jean asked him if he had made friends with the dogs, and Philip told him of his experience with them. Not until nine o'clock that night did he know why the half-breed had asked.

At that hour Adare House had sunk into quiet. Miriam and her husband had gone to bed, the lights were low. For an hour Philip had listened for the footsteps which he knew he would hear to-night. At last he knew that Josephine had come out into the hall. He heard Jean's low voice, their retreating steps, and then the opening and closing of the door that let them out into the night. There was a short silence. Then the door reopened, and some one returned through the hall. The steps stopped at his own door - a knock - and a moment later he was standing face to face with Croisset.

"Throw on your coat and cap and come with me, M'sieur," he cried in a low voice. "And bring your pistol!"

Without a word Philip obeyed. By the time they stood out in the night his blood was racing in a wild anticipation. Josephine had disappeared. Jean gripped his arm.

"To-night something may happen," he said, in a voice that was as hard and cold as the blue lights of the aurora in the polar sky. "It is - possible. We may need your help. I would have asked Metoosin, but it would have made him suspicious of something - and he knows nothing. You have made friends with the dogs? You know Captain?"

"Yes!"

"Then go to them - go as fast as you can, M'sieur. And if you hear a shot to-night - or a loud cry from out there in the forest, free the dogs swiftly, Captain first, and run with them to our trail, shouting 'KILL! KILL! KILL!' with every breath you take, and don't stop so long as there is a footprint in the snow ahead of you or a human bone to pick! Do you understand, M'sieur?"

His eyes were points of flame in the gloom.

"Do you understand?"

"Yes," gasped Philip. "But - Jean -"

"If you understand - that is all," interrupted Jean, "If there is a peril in what we are doing this night the pack will be worth more to us than a dozen men. If anything happens to us they will be our avengers. Go! There is not one moment for you to lose. Remember - a shot - a single cry!"

His voice, the glitter in his eyes, told Philip this was no time for words. He turned and ran swiftly across the clearing in the direction of the dog pit, Ten minutes later he came into a gloom warm with the smell of beast. Eyes of fire glared at him. The snapping of fangs and the snarling of savage throats greeted him. One by one he called the names of the dogs he remembered - called them over and over again, advancing fearlessly among them, until he dropped upon his knees with his hand on the chain that held Captain. From there he talked to them, and their whines answered him.

Then he fell silent - listening. He could hear his own heart beat. Every fibre in his body was aquiver with excitement and a strange fear. The hand that rested on Captain's collar trembled. In the distance an owl hooted, and the first note of it sent a red-hot fire through him. Still farther away a wolf howled. Then came a silence in which he thought he could hear the rush of blood through his own throbbing veins.

With his fingers at the steel snap on Captain's collar he waited.

CHAPTER TWENTY

In the course of nearly every human life there comes an hour which stands out above all others as long as memory lasts. Such was the one in which Philip crouched in the dog pit, his hand at Captain's collar, waiting for the sound of cry or shot. So long as he lived he knew this scene could not be wiped out of his brain. As he listened, he stared about him and the drama of it burning into his soul. Some intuitive spirit seemed to have whispered to the dogs that these tense moments were heavy with tragic possibilities for them as well as the man. Out of the surrounding darkness they stared at him without a movement or a sound, every head turned toward him, forty pairs of eyes upon him like green and opal fires. They, too, were waiting and listening. They knew there was some meaning in the attitude of this man crouching at Captain's side. Their heads were up. Their ears were alert. Philip could hear them breathing. And he could feel that the muscles of Captain's splendid body were tense and rigid.

Minutes passed. The owl hooted nearer; the wolf howled again, farther away. Slowly the tremendous strain passed and Philip began to breathe easier. He figured that Josephine and the half-breed had reached last night's meeting-place. He had given them a margin of at least five minutes - and nothing had happened. His knees were cramped, and he rose to his feet, still holding Captain's chain. The tension was broken among the beasts. They moved; whimpering sounds came to him; eyes shifted uneasily in the gloom. Fully half an hour had passed when there was a sudden movement among them. The points of green and opal fire were turned from Philip, and to his ears came the clink of chains, the movement of bodies, a subdued and menacing rumble from a score of throats. Captain growled. Philip stared out into the darkness and listened.

And then a voice came, quite near:

"Ho, M'sieur Philip!"

It was Jean! Philip's hand relaxed its clutch at Captain's collar, and almost a groan of relief fell from his lips. Not until Jean's voice came to him, quiet and unexcited, did he realize under what a strain he had been.

"I am here," he said, moving slowly out of the pit.

On the edge of it, where the light shone down through an opening in the spruce tops, he found Jean. Josephine was not with him. Eagerly Philip caught the other's arm, and looked beyond him.

"Where is she?"

"Safe," replied Jean. "I left her at Adare House, and came to you. I came quickly, for I was afraid that some one might shout in the night, or fire a shot. Our business was done quickly to-night, M'sieur!"

He was looking straight into Philip's eyes, a cold, steady look that told Philip what he meant before he had spoken the words.

"Our business was done quickly!" he repeated. "And it is coming!"

"The fight?"

"Yes."

"And Josephine knows? She understands?"

"No, M'sieur. Only you and I know. Listen: To-night I knelt down in darkness in my room, and prayed that the soul of my Iowaka might come to me. I felt her near, M'sieur! It is strange - you may not believe - but some day you may understand. And we were there together for an hour, and I pleaded for her forgiveness, for the time had come when I must break my oath to save our Josephine. And I could hear her speak to me, M'sieur, as plainly as you hear that breath of wind in the tree-tops yonder. Praise the Holy Father, I heard her! And so we are going to fight the great fight, M'sieur."

Philip waited. After a moment Jean said, as quietly as if he were asking the time of day:

"Do you know whom we went out to see last night - and met again to-night?" he asked.

"I have guessed," replied Philip. His face was white and hard.

Jean nodded.

"I think you have guessed correctly, M'sieur. It was the baby's father!"

And then, in amazement, he stared at Philip. For the other had flung off his arm, and his eyes were blazing in the starlight.

"And you have had all this trouble, all this mystery, all this fear because of HIM?" he demanded. His voice rang out in a harsh laugh. "You met him last night, and again to-night, and LET HIM GO? You, Jean Croisset? The one man in the whole world I would give my life to meet - and YOU afraid of him? My God, if that is all -"

Jean interrupted him, laying a firm, quiet hand on his arm.

"What would you do, M'sieur?"

"Kill him," breathed Philip. "Kill him by inches, slowly, torturingly. And to-night, Jean. He is near. I will follow him, and do what you have been afraid to do."

"Yes, that is it, I have been afraid to kill him," replied Jean. Philip saw the starlight on the half-breed's face. And he knew, as he looked, that he had called Jean Jacques Croisset the one thing in the world that he could not be: a coward.

"I am wrong," he apologized quickly. "Jean, it is not that. I am excited, and I take back my words. It is not fear. It is something else. Why have you not killed him?"

"M'sieur, do you believe in an oath that you make to your God?"

"Yes. But not when it means the crushing of human souls. Then it is a crime."

"Ah!" Jean was facing him now, his eyes aflame. "I am a Catholic, M'sieur - one of those of the far North, who are different from the Catholics of the south, of Montreal and Quebec. Listen! To-night I have broken a part of my oath; I am breaking a part of it in telling you what I am about to say. But I am not a coward, unless it is a coward who lives too much in fear of the Great God. What is my soul compared to that in the gentle breast of our Josephine? I would sacrifice it to-night - give it to Wetikoo - lend it forever to hell if I could undo what has been done. And you ask me why I have not killed, why I have not taken the life of a beast who is unfit to breathe God's air for an hour! Does it not occur to you, M'sieur, that there must be a reason?"

"Besides the oath, yes!"

"And now, I will tell you of the game I played, and lost, M'sieur. In me alone Josephine knew that she could trust, and so it was to me that she bared her sorrow. Later word came to me that this man, the father of the baby, was following her into the North, That was after I had given my oath to Josephine. I thought he would come by the other waterway, where we met you. And so we went there, alone. I made a camp for her, and went on to meet him. My mind was made up, M'sieur. I had determined upon the sacrifice: my soul for hers. I was going to kill him. But I made a mistake. A friend I had sent around by the other waterway met me, and told me that I had missed my game. Then I returned to the camp - and you were there. You understand this far, M'sieur?"

"Yes. Go on."

"The friend I had sent brought a letter for Josephine," resumed Jean. "A runner on his way north gave it to him. It was from Le M'sieur Adare, and said they were not starting north. But they did start soon after the letter, and this same friend brought me the news that the master had passed along the westward waterway a few days behind the man I had planned to kill. Then we returned to Adare House, and you came with us. And after that - the face at the window, and the shot!"

Philip felt the half-breed's arm quiver.

"I must tell you about him or you will not understand," he went on, and there was effort in his voice now. "The man whose face you saw was my brother. Ah, you start! You understand now why I was glad you failed to kill him. He was bad, all that could be bad, M'sieur, but blood is thicker than water, and up here one does not forget those early days when childhood knows no sin. And my brother came up from the south as canoe-man for the man I wanted to kill! A few hours before you saw his face at the window I met him in the forest. He promised to leave. Then came the shot - and I understood. The man I was going to kill had sent him to assassinate the master of Adare. That is why I followed his trail that night. I knew that I would find the man I wanted not far away."

"And you found him?"

"Yes. I came upon my brother first. And I lied. I told him he had made a mistake, and killed you, that his life was not worth the quill from a porcupine's back if he remained in the country. I made him believe it was another who fought him in the forest. He fled. I am glad of that. He will never come back. Then I followed over the trail he had made to Adare House, and far back in the swamp I came upon them, waiting for him. I passed myself off as my brother, and I tricked the man I was after. We went a distance from the camp - alone - and I was choking the life from him, when the two others that were with him came upon us. He was dying, M'sieur! He was black in the face, and his tongue was out. Another second - two or three at the most - and I would have brought ruin upon every soul at Adare House. For he was dying. And if I had killed him all would have been lost!"

"That is impossible!" gasped Philip, as the half-breed paused. "If you had killed him -"

"All would have been lost," repeated Jean, in a strange, hard voice. "Listen, M'sieur. The two others leaped upon me. I fought. And then I was struck on the head, and when I came to my senses I was in the light of the campfire, and the man I had come to kill was over me. One of the other men was Thoreau, the Free Trader. He had told who I was. It was useless to lie. I told the truth - that I had come to kill him, and why. And then - in the light of that campfire, M'sieur - he proved to me what it would have meant if I had succeeded. Thoreau carried the paper. It was in an envelope, addressed to the master of Adare. They tore this open, that I might read. And in that paper, written by the man I had come to kill, was the whole terrible story, every detail - and it made me cold and sick. Perhaps you begin to understand, M'sieur. Perhaps you will see more clearly when I tell you -"

"Yes, yes," urged Philip.

"- that this man, the father of the baby, is the Lang who owns Thoreau, who owns that freebooters' hell, who owns the string of them from here to the Athabasca, and who lives in Montreal!"

Philip could only stare at Jean, who went on, his face the colour of gray ash in the starlight.

"I must tell you the rest. You must understand before the great fight comes. You know - the terrible thing happened in Montreal. And this man Lang - all the passion of hell is in his soul! He is rich. He has power up here, for he owns Thoreau and all his cutthroats. And he is not satisfied with the ruin he worked down there. He has followed Josephine. He is mad with passion - with the desire -"

"Good God, don't tell me more of that!" cried Philip. "I understand. He has followed. And Josephine is to be the price of his silence!"

"Yes, just that. He knows what it means up here for such a thing to happen. His love for her is not love. It is the passion that fills hell with its worst. He laid his plans before he came. That letter, the paper I read, M'sieur! He meant to see Josephine at once, and show it to her. There are two of those papers: one at Thoreau's place and one in Thoreau's pocket. If anything happens to Lang, one of them is to be delivered to the master of Adare by Thoreau. If I had killed him it would have gone to Le M'sieur. It is his safeguard. And there are two copies - to make the thing sure. So we cannot kill him.

"Josephine listened to all this to-night, from Lang's own lips. And she pleaded with him, M'sieur. She called upon him to think of the little child, letting him believe that it was still alive; and he laughed at her. And then, almost as I was ready to plunge my knife into his heart, she threw up her head like an angel and told him to do his worst - that she refused to pay the price. I never saw her stronger than in that moment, M'sieur - in that moment when there was no hope! I would have killed him then for the paper he had, but the other is at Thoreau's. He has gone back there. He says that unless he receives word of Josephine's surrender within a week - the crash will come, the paper will be given to the master of Adare. And now, M'sieur Philip, what do you have to say?"

"That there never was a game lost until it was played to the end," replied Philip, and he drew nearer to look straight and steadily into the half-breed's eyes. "Go on, Jean. There is something more which you have not told me. And that is the biggest thing of all. Go on!"

For a space there was a startled look in Jean's eyes. Then he shrugged his shoulders and smiled.

"Of course there is more," he said. "You have known that, M'sieur. There is one thing which you will never know - that which Josephine said you would not guess if you lived a thousand years. You must forget that there is more than I have told you, for it will do you no good to remember."

Expectancy died out of Philip's eyes.

"And yet I believe that what you are holding back from me is the key to everything."

"I have told you enough, M'sieur - enough to make you see why we must fight."

"But not how."

"That will come soon," replied Jean, a little troubled.

The men were silent. Behind them they heard the restless movement of the dogs. Out of the gloom came a wailing whine. Again Philip looked at Jean.

"Do you know, your story seems weak in places, Jean," he said. "I believe every word you have said. And yet, when you come to think of it all, the situation doesn't seem to be so terribly alarming to me after all. Why, for instance, do you fear those letters - this scoundrel Lang's confession? Kill him. Let the letter come to Adare. Cannot Josephine swear that she is innocent? Can she not have a story of her own showing how foully Lang tried to blackmail her into a crime? Would not Adare believe her word before that of a freebooter? And am I not here to swear - that the child - was mine?"

There was almost a pitying look in the half-breed's eyes.

"M'sieur, what if in that letter were named people and places: the hospital itself, the doctors, the record of birth? What if it contained all those many things by which the master of Adare might trail back easily to the truth? With those things in the letter would he not investigate? And then -" He made a despairing gesture.

"I see," said Philip. Then he added, quickly "But could we not keep the papers from Adare, Jean? Could we not watch for the messenger?"

"They are not fools, M'sieur. Such a thing would be easy - if they sent a messenger with the papers. But they have guarded against that. Le M'sieur is to be invited to Thoreau's. The letter will be given to him there."

Philip began pacing back and forth, his head bowed in thought, his hands deep in his pockets.

"They have planned it well - like very devils!" he exclaimed. "And yet - even now I see a flaw. Is Lang's threat merely a threat? Would he, after all, actually have the letter given to Adare? If these letters are his trump cards, why did he try to have him killed? Would not Adare's death rob him of his greatest power?"

"In a way, M'sieur. And yet with Le M'sieur gone, both Josephine and Miriam would be still more hopelessly in his clutches. For I know that he had planned to kill me after the master. My brother had not guessed that. And then the women would be alone. Holy Heaven, I cannot see the end of crime that might come of that! Even though they escaped him to go back to civilization, they would be still more in his power there."

Philip's face was upturned to the stars. He laughed, but there was no mirth in the laugh. And then he faced Jean again, and his eyes were filled with the merciless gleam that came into those of the wolf-beasts back in the pit.

"It is the big fight then, Jean. But, before that, just one question more. All of this trouble might have been saved if Josephine had married Lang. Why didn't she?"

For an instant every muscle in Jean's body became as taut as a bowstring. He hunched a little forward, as if about to leap upon the other, and strike him down. And then, all at once, he relaxed. His hands unclenched. And he answered calmly:

"That is the one story that will never be told, M'sieur. Come! They will wonder about us at Adare House. Let us return."

Philip fell in behind him. Not until they were close to the door of the house did Jean speak again.

"You are with me, M'sieur - to the death, if it must be?"

"Yes, to the death," replied Philip.

"Then let no sleep come to your eyes so long as Josephine is awake," went on Jean quickly. "I am going to leave Adare House to-night, M'sieur, with team and sledge. The master must believe I have gone over to see my sick friend on the Pipestone. I am going there - and farther!" His voice became a low, tense whisper. "You understand, M'sieur? We are preparing."

The two clasped hands.

"I will return late to-morrow, or to-morrow night," resumed Jean. "It may even be the next day. But I shall travel fast - without rest. And during that time you are on guard. In my room you will find an extra rifle and cartridges. Carry it when you go about. And spend as much of your time as you can with the master of Adare. Watch Josephine. I will not see her again to-night. Warn her for me. She must not go alone in the forests - not even to the dog pit."

"I understand," said Philip.

They entered the house. Twenty minutes later, from the window of his room, Philip saw a dark figure walking swiftly back toward the forest. Still later he heard the distant wail of a husky coming from the direction of the pit, and he knew that the first gun in the big fight had been fired - that Jean Jacques Croisset was off on his thrilling mission into the depths of the forests. What that mission was he had not asked him. But he had guessed. And his blood ran warm with a strange excitement.

CHAPTER TWENTY-ONE

Again there filled Philip the desire to be with Jean in the forest. The husky's wail told him that the half-breed had begun his journey. Between this hour and to-morrow night he would be threading his way swiftly over the wilderness trails on his strange mission. Philip envied him the action, the exhaustion that would follow. He envied even the dogs running in the traces. He was a living dynamo, overcharged, with every nerve in him drawn to the point that demanded the reaction of physical exertion. He knew that he could not sleep. The night would be one long and tedious wait for the dawn. And Jean had told him not to sleep as long as Josephine was awake!

Was he to take that literally? Did Jean mean that he was to watch her? He wondered if she was in bed now. At least the half-breed's admonition offered him an excuse. He would go to her room. If there was a light he would knock, and ask her if she would join him in the piano-room. He looked at his watch. It was nearly midnight. Probably she had retired.

He opened his door and entered the hall. Quietly he went to the end room. There was no light - and he heard no sound. He was standing close to it, concealed in the shadows, when his heart gave a sudden jump. Advancing toward him down the hall was a figure clad in a flowing white night-robe.

At first he did not know whether it was Josephine or Miriam. And then, as she came under one of the low-burning lamps, he saw that it was Miriam. She had turned, and was looking back toward the room where she had left her husband. Her beautiful hair was loose, and fell in lustrous masses to her hips. She was listening. And in that moment Philip heard a low, passionate sob. She turned her face toward him again, and he could see it drawn with agony. In the lamp-glow her hands were clasped at her partly bared breast. She was barefoot, and made no sound as she advanced. Philip drew himself back closer against the wall. He was sure she had not seen him. A moment later Miriam turned into the corridor that led into Adare's big room.

Philip felt that he was trembling. In Miriam's face he had seen something that had made his heart beat faster. Quietly he went to the corridor, turned, and made his way cautiously to the door of Adare's room. It was dark inside, the corridor was black. Hidden in the gloom he listened. He heard Miriam sink in one of the big chairs, and from her movement, and the sound of her sobbing, he knew that she had buried her head in her arms on the table. He listened for minutes to the grief that seemed racking her soul. Then there was silence. A moment later he heard her, and she was so close to the door that he dared not move. She passed him, and turned into the main hall. He followed again.

She paused only for an instant at the door of the room in which she and her husband slept. Then she passed on, and scarcely believing his eyes Philip saw her open the door that led out into the night!

She was full in the glow of the lamp that hung over the door now, and Philip saw her plainly. A biting gust of wind flung back her hair. He saw her bare arms; she turned, and he caught the white gleam of a naked shoulder. Before he could speak - before he could call her name, she had darted out into the night!

With a gasp of amazement he sprang after her. Her bare feet were deep in the snow when he caught her. A frightened cry broke from her lips. He picked her up in his arms as if she had been a child, and ran back into the hall with her, closing the door after them. Panting, shivering with the cold, she stared at him without speaking.

"Why were you going out there?" he whispered. "Why - like that?"

For a moment he was afraid that from her heaving bosom and quivering lips would burst forth the strange excitement which she was fighting back. Something told him that Adare must not discover them in the hall. He caught her hands. They were cold as ice.

"Go to your room," he whispered gently. "You must not let him know you were out there in the snow - like this. You - were partly asleep."

Purposely he gave her the chance to seize upon this explanation. The sobbing breath came to her lips again.

"I guess - it must have been - that," she said, drawing her hands from him. "I was going out - to - the baby. Thank you, Philip. I - I will go to my room now."

She left him, and not until her door had closed behind her did he move. Had she spoken the truth? Had she in those few moments been temporarily irresponsible because of grieving over the baby's death? Some inner consciousness answered him in the negative. It was not that. And yet - what more could there be? He remembered. Jean's words, his insistent warnings. Resolutely he moved toward Josephine's room, and knocked softly upon her door. He was surprised at the promptness with which her voice answered. When he spoke his name, and told her it was important for him to see her, she opened the door. She had unbound her hair. But she was still dressed, and Philip knew that she had been sitting alone in the darkness of her room.

She looked at him strangely and expectantly. It seemed to

Philip as if she had been waiting for news which she dreaded, and which she feared that he was bringing her.

"May I come in?" he whispered. "Or would you prefer to go into the other room?"

"You may come in, Philip," she replied, letting him take her hand. "I am still dressed. I have been so dreadfully nervous to-night that I haven't thought of going to bed. And the moon is so beautiful through my window. It has been company." Then she asked: "What have you to tell me, Philip?"

She had stepped into the light that flooded through the window. It transformed her hair into a lustrous mantle of deep gold; into her eyes it put the warm glow of the stars. He made a movement, as if to put his arms about her, but he caught himself, and a little joyous breath came to Josephine's lips. It was her room, where she slept - and he had come at a strange hour. She understood the movement, his desire to take her in his arms, and his big, clean thoughts of her as he drew a step back. It sent a flush of pleasure and still deeper trust into her cheeks.

"You have something to tell me?" she asked.

"Yes - about your mother."

Her hand had touched his arm, and he felt her start. Briefly he told what had happened. Josephine's face was so white that it startled him when he had finished.

"She said - she was going to the baby!" she breathed, as if whispering the words to herself. "And she was in her bare feet, with her hair down, and her gown open to the snow and wind! Oh my God!"

"Perhaps she was in her sleep," hurried Philip. "It might have been that, Josephine."

"No, she wasn't in her sleep," replied Josephine, meeting his eyes. "You know that, Philip. She was awake. And you have come to tell me so that I may watch her. I understand."

"She might rest easier with you - if you can arrange it," he agreed. "Your father worries over her now. It will not do to let him know this."

She nodded.

"I will bring her to my room, Philip. I will tell my father that I am nervous and cannot sleep. And I will say nothing to her of what has happened. I will go as soon as you have returned to your room."

He went to the door, and there for a moment she stood close to him, gazing up into his face. Still he did not put his hands to her. To-night - in her own room - it seemed to him something like sacrilege to touch her. And then, suddenly, she raised her two arms up through her shimmering hair to his shoulders. and held her lips to him.

"Good-night, Philip!"

He caught her to him. Her arms tightened about his shoulders. For a moment he felt the thrill of her warm lips. Then she drew back, whispering again:

"Good-night, Philip!"

The door closed softly, and he returned to his room. Again the song of life, of love, of hope that pictured but one glorious end filled his soul to overflowing. A little later and he knew that Adare's wife had gone with Josephine to her room. He went to bed. And sleep came to him now, filled with dreams in which he lived with Josephine always at his side, laughing and singing with him, and giving him her lips to kiss in their joyous paradise.

CHAPTER TWENTY-TWO

Out of these dreams he was awakened by a sound that had slowly and persistently become a part of his mental consciousness. It was a tap, tap, tap at his window. At last he sat up and listened. It was in the gray gloom of dawn. Again the sound was repeated: tap, tap, tap on the pane of glass.

He slipped out of bed, his hand seeking the automatic under his pillow. He had slept with the window partly open. Covering it with his pistol, he called:

"Who is there?"

"A runner from Jean Croisset," came back a cautious voice. "I have a written message for you, M'sieur."

He saw an arm thrust through the window, in the hand a bit of paper. He advanced cautiously until he could see the face that was peering in. It was a thin, dark, fur-hooded face, with eyes black and narrow like Jean's, a half-breed. He seized the paper, and, still watching the face and arm, lighted a lamp. Not until he had read the note did his suspicion leave him.

This is Pierre Langlois, my friend of the Pipestone. If anything should happen that you need me quickly let him come after me. You may trust him. He will put up his tepee in the thick timber close to the dog pit. We have fought together. L'Ange saved his wife from the smallpox. I am going westward. - JEAN.

Philip sprang back to the window and gripped the mittened hand that still hung over the sill.

"I'm glad to know you, Pierre! Is there no other word from Jean?"

"Only the note, Ookimow."

"You just came?"

"Aha. My dogs and sledge are back in the forest."

"Listen!" Philip turned toward the door. In the hall he heard footsteps. "Le M'sieur is awake," he said quickly to Pierre. "I will see you in the forest!"

Scarcely were the words out of his mouth when the half-breed was gone. A moment later Philip knew that it was Adare who had passed his door. He dressed and shaved himself before he left his room. He found Adare in his study. Metoosin already had a fire burning, and Adare was standing before this alone, when Philip entered. Something was lacking in Adare's greeting this morning. There was an uneasy, searching look in his eyes as he looked at Philip. They shook hands, and his hand was heavy and lifeless. His shoulders seemed to droop a little more, and his voice was unnatural when he spoke.

"You did not go to bed until quite late last night, Philip?"

"Yes, it was late, Mon Pere."

For a moment Adare was silent, his head bowed, his eyes on the floor. He did not raise his gaze when he spoke again.

"Did you hear anything - late - about midnight?" he asked. He straightened, and looked steadily into Philip's eyes. "Did you see Miriam?"

For an instant Philip felt that it was useless to attempt

concealment under the searching scrutiny of the older man's eyes. Like an inspiration came to him a thought of Josephine.

"Josephine was the last person I saw after leaving you," he said truthfully. "And she was in her room before eleven o'clock."

"It is strange, unaccountable," mused Adare. "Miriam left her bed last night while I was asleep. It must have been about midnight, for it is then that the moon shines full into our window. In returning she awakened me. And her hair was damp, there was snow on her gown! My God, she had been outdoors, almost naked! She said that she must have walked in her sleep, that she had awakened to find herself in the open door with the wind and snow beating upon her. This is the first time. I never knew her to do it before. It disturbs me."

"She is sleeping now?"

"I don't know. Josephine came a little later and said that she could not sleep. Miriam went with her."

"It must have been the baby," comforted Philip, placing a hand on Adare's arm. "We can stand it, Mon Pere. We are men. With them it is different. We must bear up under our grief. It is necessary for us to have strength for them as well as ourselves."

"Do you think it is that?" cried Adare with sudden eagerness. "If it is, I am ashamed of myself, Philip! I have been brooding too much over the strange change in Miriam. But I see now. It must have been the baby. It has been a tremendous strain. I have heard her crying when she did not know that I heard. I am ashamed of myself. And the blow has been hardest on you!"

"And Josephine," added Philip.

John Adare had thrown back his shoulders, and with a deep feeling of relief Philip saw the old light in his eyes.

"We must cheer them up," he added quickly. "I will ask Josephine if they will join us at breakfast, Mon Pere."

He closed the door behind him when he left the room, and he went at once to rouse Josephine if she was still in bed. He was agreeably surprised to find that both Miriam and Josephine were up and dressing. With this news he returned to Adare.

Three quarters of an hour later they met in the breakfast-room. It took only a glance to tell him that Josephine was making a last heroic fight. She had dressed her hair in shining coils low over her neck and cheeks this morning in an effort to hide her pallor. Miriam seemed greatly changed from the preceding night. Her eyes were clearer. A careful toilette had taken away the dark circles from under them and had added a touch of colour to her lips and cheeks. She went to Adare when the two men entered, and with a joyous rumble of approval the giant held her off at arm's length and looked at her.

"It didn't do you any harm after all," Philip heard him say. "Did you tell Mignonne of your adventure, Ma Cheri?"

He did not hear Miriam's reply, for he was looking down into Josephine's face. Her lips were smiling. She made no effort to conceal the gladness in her eyes as he bent and kissed her.

"It was a hard night, dear."

"Terrible," she whispered. "Mother told me what happened. She is stronger this morning. We must keep the truth from HIM."

"The TRUTH?"

He felt her start.

"Hush!" she breathed. "You know - you understand what I mean. Let us sit down to breakfast now."

During the hour that followed Philip was amazed at Miriam. She laughed and talked as she had not done before. The bit of artificial colour she had given to her cheeks and lips faded under the brighter flush that came into her face. He could see that Josephine was nearly as surprised as himself. John Adare was fairly boyish in his delight. The meal was finished and Philip and Adare were about to light their cigars when a commotion outside drew them all to the window that overlooked one side of the clearing. Out of the forest had come two dog-teams, their drivers shouting and cracking their long caribou-gut whips. Philip stared, conscious that Josephine's hand was clutching his arm. Neither of the shouting men was Jean.

"An Indian, and Renault the quarter-blood," grunted Adare. "Wonder what they want here in November. They should be on their trap-lines."

"Perhaps, Mon Pere, they have come to see their friends," suggested Josephine. "You know, it has been a long time since some of them have seen us. I would be disappointed if our people didn't show they were glad because of your home-coming!"

"Of course, that's it!" cried Adare. "Ho, Metoosin!" he roared, turning toward the door. "Metoosin! Paitoo ta! Wawep isewin!"

Metoosin appeared at the door.

"Build a great fire in the una kah house," commanded Adare. Feed all who come in from the forests, Metoosin. Open up tobacco and preserves, and flour and bacon. Nothing in the storeroom is too good for them. And send Jean to me! Where is he?"

"Numma tao, ookimow."

"Gone!" exclaimed Adare.

"He didn't want to disturb you last night," explained Philip. "He made an early start for the Pipestone."

"If he was an ordinary man, I'd say he was in love with one of the Langlois girls," said Adare, with a shrug of his shoulders. "Neah, Metoosin! Make them comfortable, and we will all see them later." As Metoosin went Adare turned upon the others: "Shall we all go out now?" he asked.

"Splendid!" accepted Josephine eagerly. "Come, Mikawe, we can be ready in a moment!"

She ran from the room, leading her mother by the hand. Philip and Adare followed them, and shortly the four were ready to leave the house. The una kah, or guest house, was in the edge of the timber. It was a long, low building of logs, and was always open with its accommodations to the Indians and half-breeds - men, women, and children - who came in from the forest trails. Renault and the Indian were helping Metoosin build fires when they entered. Philip thought that Renault's eyes rested upon him in a curious and searching glance even as Adare shook hands with him. He was more interested in the low words both the Indian and the blood muttered as they stood for a moment with bowed heads before Josephine and Miriam. Then Renault raised his head and spoke direct to Josephine:

"I breeng word for heem of Jan Breuil an' wewimow over on Jac' fish ma Kichi Utooskayakun," he said in a low voice. "Heem lee'l girl so seek she goin' die."

"Little Marie? She is sick - dying, you say?" cried Josephine.

"Aha. She ver' dam' seek. She burn up lak fire."

Josephine looked up at Philip.

"I knew she was sick," she said. "But I didn't think it was so bad. If she dies it will be my fault. I should have gone." She turned quickly to Renault. "When did you see her last?" she asked. "Listen! Papak-oo-moo?"

"Aha."

"It is a sickness the children have each winter," she explained, looking questioningly into Philip's eyes again. "It kills quickly when left alone. But I have medicine that will cure it. There is still time. We must go, Philip. We must!"

Her face had paled a little. She saw the gathering lines in Philip's forehead. He thought of Jean's words - the warning they carried. She pressed his arm, and her mouth was firm.

"I am going, Philip," she said softly. "Will you go with me?"

"I will, if you must go," he said. "But it is not best."

"It is best for little Marie," she retorted, and left him to tell Adare and her mother of Renault's message.

Renault stepped close to Philip. His back was to the others. He spoke in a low voice:

"I breeng good word from Jean Croisset, M'sieur. Heem say Soomin Renault good man lak Pierre Langlois, an' he fight lak devil when ask. I breeng Indian an' two team. We be in forest near dog watekan, where Pierre mak his fire an' tepee. You understand? Aha?"

"Yes - I understand," whispered Philip, "And Jean has gone on - to see others?"

"He go lak win' to Francois over on Waterfound. Francois come in one hour - two, t'ree, mebby."

Josephine and Adare approached them.

"Mignonne is turning nurse again," rumbled Adare, one of his great arms thrown affectionately about her waist. "You'll have a jolly run on a clear morning like this, Philip. But remember, if it is the smallpox I forbid her to expose herself!"

"I shall see to that, Mon Pere. When do we start, Josephine?"

"As soon as I can get ready and Metoosin brings the dogs," replied Josephine. "I am going to the house now. Will you come with me?"

It was an hour before Metoosin had brought the dogs up from the pit and they were ready to start. Philip had armed himself with a rifle and his automatic, and Josephine had packed both medicine and food in a large basket. The new snow was soft, and Metoosin had brought a toboggan instead of a sledge with runners. In the traces were Captain and five of his team-mates.

"Isn't the pack going with us?" asked Philip.

"I never take them when there is very bad sickness, like this," explained Josephine. "There is something about the nearness of death that makes them howl. I haven't been able to train that out of them."

Philip was disappointed, but he said nothing more. He tucked Josephine among the furs, cracked the long whip Metoosin had given him, and they were off, with Miriam and her husband waving their hands from the door of Adare House. They had scarcely passed out of view in the forest when with a sudden sharp command Josephine stopped the dogs. She sprang out of her furs and stood laughingly beside Philip.

"Father always insists that I ride. He says it's not good for a woman to run," she said. "But I do. I love to run. There!"

As she spoke she had thrown her outer coat on the sledge, and stood before him, straight and slim. Her hair was in a long braid.

"Now, are you ready?" she challenged.

"Good Lord, have mercy on me!" gasped Philip. "You look as if you might fly, Josephine!"

Her signal to the dogs was so low he scarcely heard it, and they sped along the white and narrow trail into which Josephine had directed them. Philip fell in behind her. It had always roused a certain sense of humour in him to see a woman run. But in Josephine he saw now the swiftness and lithesome grace of a fawn. Her head was thrown back, her mittened hands were drawn up to her breast as the forest man runs, and her shining braid danced and rippled in the early sun with each quick step she took.

Ahead of her the gray and yellow backs of the dogs rose and fell with a rhythmic movement that was almost music. Their ears aslant, their crests bristling, their bushy tails curling like plumes over their hips, they responded with almost automatic precision to the low words that fell from the lips of the girl behind them.

With each minute that passed Philip wondered how much longer Josephine could keep up the pace. They had run fully a mile and his own breath was growing shorter when the toe of his moccasined foot caught under a bit of brushwood and he plunged head foremost into the snow. When he had brushed the snow out of his eyes and ears Josephine was standing over him, laughing. The dogs were squatted on their haunches, looking back.

"My poor Philip!" she laughed, offering him an assisting hand. "We almost lost you, didn't we? It was Captain who missed you first, and he almost toppled me over the sled!"

Her face was radiant. Lips, eyes, and cheeks were glowing. Her breast rose and fell quickly.

"It was your fault!" he accused her. "I couldn't keep my eyes off you, and never thought of my feet. I shall have my revenge - here!"

He drew her into his arms, protesting. Not until he had kissed her parted, half-smiling lips did he release her.

"I'm going to ride now," she declared. "I'm not going to run the danger of being accused again."

He wrapped her again in the furs on the toboggan. It was eight miles to Jac Breuil's, and they reached his cabin in two hours. Breuil was not much more than a boy, scarcely older than the dark-eyed little French girl who was his wife, and their eyes were big with terror. With a thrill of wonder and pleasure Philip observed the swift change in them as Josephine sprang from the toboggan. Breuil was almost sobbing as he whispered to Philip:

"Oh, ze sweet Ange, M'sieur! She cam jus' in time."

Josephine was bending over little Marie's cot when they followed her and the girl mother into the cabin. In a moment she looked up with a glad smile.

"It is the same sickness, Marie," she said to the mother. "I have medicine here that will cure it. The fever isn't as bad as I thought it would be."

Noon saw a big change in the cabin. Little Marie's temperature was falling rapidly. Breuil and his wife were happy. After dinner Josephine explained again how they were to give the medicine she was leaving, and at two o'clock they left on their return journey to Adare House. The sun had disappeared hours before. Gray banks of cloud filled the sky, and it had grown much colder.

"We will reach home only a little before dark," said Philip. "You had better ride, Josephine."

He was eager to reach Adare House. By this time he felt that Jean should have returned, and he was confident that there were others of the forest people besides Pierre, Renault, and the Indian in the forest near the pit. For an hour he kept up a swift pace. Later they came to a dense cover of black spruce two miles from Adare House. They had traversed a part of this when the dogs stopped. Directly ahead of them had fallen a dead cedar, barring the trail. Philip went to the toboggan for the trail axe.

"I haven't noticed any wind, have you?" he asked. "Not enough to topple over a cedar."

He went to the tree and began cutting. Scarcely had his axe fallen half a dozen times when a scream of terror turned him about like a flash. He had only time to see that Josephine had left the sledge, and was struggling in the arms of a man. In that same instant two others had leaped upon him. He had not time to strike, to lift his axe. He went down, a pair of hands gripping at his throat. He saw a face over him, and he knew now that it was the face of the man he had seen in the firelight, the face of Lang, the Free Trader. Every atom of strength in him rose in a superhuman effort to throw off his assailants. Then came the blow. He saw the club over him, a short, thick club, in the hand of Thoreau himself. After that followed darkness and oblivion, punctuated by the CRACK, CRACK, CRACK of a revolver and the howling of dogs - sounds that grew fainter and fainter until they died away altogether, and he sank into the stillness of night.

It was almost dark when consciousness stirred Philip again. With an effort he pulled himself to his knees, and stared about him. Josephine was gone, the dogs were gone. He staggered to his feet, a moaning cry on his lips. He saw the sledge. Still in the traces lay the bodies of two of the dogs, and he knew what the pistol shots had meant. The others had been cut loose; straight out into the forest led the trails of several men; and the meaning of it all, the reality of what had happened, surged upon him in all its horror. Lang and his cutthroats had carried off Josephine. He knew by the thickening darkness that they had time to get a good start on their way to Thoreau's.

One thought filled his dizzy brain now. He must reach Jean and the camp near the pit. He staggered as he turned his face homeward. At times the trail seemed to reach up and strike him in the face. There was a blinding pain back of his eyes. A dozen times in the first mile he fell, and each time it was harder for him to regain his feet. The darkness of night grew heavier about him, and now and then he found himself crawling on his hands and knees. It was two hours before his dazed senses caught the glow of a fire ahead of him. Even then it seemed an age before he reached it. And when at last he staggered into the circle of light he saw half a dozen startled faces, and he heard the strange cry of Jean Jacques Croisset as he sprang up and caught him in his arms. Philip's strength was gone, but he still had time to tell Jean what had happened before he crumpled down into the snow.

And then he heard a voice, Jean's voice, crying fierce commands to the men about the fire; he heard excited replies, the hurry of feet, the barking of dogs. Something warm and comforting touched his lips. He struggled to bring himself back into life. He seemed to have been fighting hours before he opened his eyes. He pulled himself up, stared into the dark, livid face of Jean, the half-breed.

"The hour - has come -" he murmured.

"Yes, the hour has come, M'sieur!" cried Jean. "The swiftest teams and the swiftest runners in this part of the Northland are on the trail, and by morning the forest people will be roused from here to the Waterfound, from the Cree camp on Lobstick to the Gray Loon waterway! Drink this, M'sieur. There is no time to lose. For it is Jean Jacques Croisset who tells you that not a wolf will howl this night that does not call forth the signal to those who love our Josephine! Drink!"

CHAPTER TWENTY-THREE

Jean's thrilling words burned into Philip's consciousness like fire. They roused him from his stupor, and he began to take in deep breaths of the chill night air, and to see more clearly. The camp was empty now. The men were gone. Only Jean was with him, his face darkly flushed and his eyes burning. Philip rose slowly to his feet. There was no longer the sickening dizziness in his head, He inhaled still deeper breaths, while Jean stood a step back and watched. Far off in the forest he heard the faint barking of dogs.

"They are running like the wind!" breathed Jean. "Those are Renault's dogs. They are two miles away!"

He took Philip by the arm.

"I have made a comfortable bed for you in Pierre's tepee, M'sieur. You must lie down, and I will get your supper. You will need all of your strength soon."

"But I must know what is happening," protested Philip. "My God, I cannot lie down like a tired dog - with Josephine out there with Lang! I am ready now, Jean. I am not hungry. And the pain is gone. See - I am as steady as you!" he cried excitedly, gripping Jean's hand. "God in Heaven, who knows what may be happening out there!"

"Josephine is safe for a time, M'sieur," assured Jean. "Listen to me, Netootam! I feared this. That is why I warned you. Lang is taking her to Thoreau's. He believes that we will not dare to pursue, and that Josephine will send back word she is there of her own pleasure. Why? Because he has sworn to give Le M'sieur the confession if we make him trouble. Mon Dieu, he thinks we will not dare! and even now, Netootam, six of the fastest teams and swiftest runners within a hundred miles are gone to spread the word among the forest people that L'Ange, our Josephine, has been carried off by Thoreau and his beasts! Before dawn they will begin to gather where the forks meet, twelve miles off there toward the Devil's Nest, and to-morrow -"

Jean crossed himself.

"Our Lady forgive us, if it is a sin to take the lives of twenty such men," he said softly. "Not one will live to tell the story. And not a log of Thoreau House will stand to hold the secret which will die forever with to-morrow's end."

Philip came near to Jean now. He placed his two hands on the half-breed's shoulders, and for a moment looked at him without speaking. His face was strangely white.

"I understand - everything, Jean," he whispered huskily, and his lips seemed parched. "To-morrow, we will destroy all evidence, and kill. That is the one way. And that secret which you dread, which Josephine has told me I could not guess in a thousand years, will be buried forever. But Jean - I HAVE GUESSED IT. I KNOW! It has come to me at last, and - my God! - I understand!"

Slowly, with a look of horror in his eyes, Jean drew back from him. Philip, with bowed head, saw nothing of the struggle in the half-breed's face. When Jean spoke it was in a strange voice and low.

"M'sieur!"

Philip looked up. In the fire-glow Jean was reaching out his hand to him. In the faces of the two men was a new light, the birth of a new brotherhood. Their hands clasped. Silently they gazed into each other's eyes, while over them the beginning of storm moaned in the treetops and the clouds raced in snow-gray armies under the moon.

"Breathe no word of what may have come to you to-night," spoke Jean then. "You will swear that?"

"Yes."

"And to-morrow we fight! You see now - you understand what that fight means, M'sieur?"

"Yes. It means that Josephine -"

"Tsh! Even I must not hear what is on your lips, M'sieur! I cannot believe that you have guessed true. I do not want to know. I dare not. And now, M'sieur, will you lie down? I will go to Le M'sieur and tell him I have received word that you and Josephine are to stay at Breuil's overnight. He must not know what has happened. He must not be at the big fight to-morrow. When it is all over we will tell him that we did not want to terrify him and Miriam over Josephine. If he should be at the fight, and came hand to hand with Lang or Thoreau -"

"He must not go!" exclaimed Philip. "Hurry to him, Jean. I will boil some coffee while you are gone. Bring another rifle. They robbed me of mine, and the pistol."

Jean prepared to leave.

"I will return soon," he said. "We should start for the Forks within two hours, M'sieur. In that time you must rest."

He slipped away into the gloom in the direction of the pit. For several minutes Philip stood near the fire staring into the flames. Then he suddenly awoke into life. The thought that had come to him this night had changed his world for him.

And he wondered now if he was right. Jean had said: "I cannot believe that you have guessed true," and yet in the half-breed's face, in his horror-filled eyes, in the tense gathering of his body was revealed the fear that he HAD! But if he had made a mistake! If he had guessed wrong! The hot blood surged in his face. If he had guessed wrong - his thought would be a crime. He had made up his mind to drive the guess out of his head, and he went into the tepee to find food and coffee. When Jean returned, an hour later, supper was waiting in the heat of the fire. The half-breed had brought Philip's rifle along with his own.

"What did he say?" asked Philip, as they sat down to eat. "He had no suspicions?"

"None, M'sieur," replied Jean, a strange smile on his lips. "He was with Miriam. When I entered they were romping like two children in the music-room. Her hair was down. She was pulling his beard, and they were laughing so that at first they did not hear me when I spoke to them. Laughing, M'sieur!"

His eyes met Philip's.

"Has Josephine told you what the Indians call them?" he asked softly.

"No."

"In every tepee in these forests they speak of them as Kah Sakehewawin, 'the lovers.' Ah, M'sieur, there is one picture in my brain which I shall never forget. I first came to Adare House on a cold, bleak night, dying of hunger, and first of all I looked through a lighted window. In a great chair before the fire sat Le M'sieur, so that I could see his face and what was gathered up close in his arms. At first I thought it was a sleeping child he was holding. And then I saw the long hair streaming to the floor, and in that moment La Fleurette - beautiful as the angels I had dreamed of - raised her face and saw me at the window. And during all the years that have passed since then it has been like that, M'sieur. They have been lovers. They will be until they die."

Philip was silent. He knew that Jean was looking at him. He felt that he was reading the thoughts in his heart. A little later he drew out his watch and looked at it.

"What time is it, M'sieur?"

"Nine o'clock," replied Philip. "Why wait another hour, Jean? I am ready."

"Then we will go," replied Jean, springing to his feet. "Throw these things into the tepee, M'sieur, while I put the dogs in the traces."

They moved quickly now. Over them the gray heavens seemed to drop lower. Through the forest swept a far monotone, like the breaking of surf on a distant shore. With the wind came a thin snow, and the darkness gathered so that beyond the rim of fire-light there was a black chaos in which the form of all things was lost. It was not a night for talk. It was filled with the whisperings of storm, and to Philip those whisperings were an oppressive presage of the tragedy that lay that night ahead of them. The dogs were harnessed, five that Jean had chosen from the pack; and straight out into the pit of gloom the half-breed led them. In that darkness Philip could see nothing. But not once did Jean falter, and the dogs followed him, occasionally whining at the strangeness and unrest of the night; and close behind them came Philip. For a long time there was no sound but the tread of their feet, the scraping of the toboggan, the patter of the dogs, and the wind that bit down from out of the thick sky into the spruce tops. They had travelled an hour when they came to a place where the smothering weight of the darkness seemed to rise from about them. It was the edge of a great open, a bit of the Barren that reached down like a solitary finger from the North: treeless, shrubless, the playground of the foxes and the storm winds. Here Jean fell back beside Philip for a moment.

"You are not tiring, M'sieur?"

"I am getting stronger every mile," declared Philip. "I feel no effects of the blow now, Jean. How far did you say it was to the place where our people are to meet?"

"Eight miles. We have come four. In this darkness we could make it faster without the dogs, but they are carrying a hundred pounds of tepee, guns, and food."

He urged the dogs on in the open space. Another hour and they had come again to the edge of forest. Here they rested.

"There will be some there ahead of us," said Jean. "Renault and the other runners will have had more than four hours. They will have visited a dozen cabins on the trap-lines. Pierre reached old Kaskisoon and his Swamp Crees in two hours. They love Josephine next to their Manitou. The Indians will be there to a man!"

Philip did not reply. But his heart beat like a drum at the sureness and triumph that thrilled in the half-breed's voice. As they went on, he lost account of time in the flashing pictures that came to him of the other actors in this night's drama; of those half-dozen Paul Reveres of the wilderness speeding like shadows through the mystery of the night, of the thin-waisted, brown-faced men who were spreading the fires of vengeance from cabin to cabin and from tepee to tepee. Through his lips there came a sobbing breath of exultation, of joy. He did not tire. At times he wanted to run on ahead of Jean and the dogs. Yet he saw that no such desire seized upon Jean. Steadily - with a precision that was almost uncanny - the half-breed led the way. He did not hurry, he did not hesitate. He was like a strange spirit of the night itself, a voiceless and noiseless shadow ahead, an automaton of flesh and blood that had become more than human to Philip. In this man's guidance he lost his fear for Josephine.

At last they came to the foot of a rock ridge. Up this the dogs toiled, with Jean pulling at the lead-trace. They came to the top. There they stopped. And standing like a hewn statue, his voice breaking in a panting cry, Jean Jacques Croisett pointed down into the plain below.

Half a mile away a light stood out like a glowing star in the darkness. It was a campfire.

"It is a fire at the Forks," spoke Jean above the wind. "Mon Dieu, M'sieur - is it not something to have friends like that!"

He led the way a short distance along the face of the ridge, and then they plunged down the valley of deeper gloom. The forest was thick and low, and Philip guessed that they were passing through a swamp. When they came out of it the fire was almost in their faces. The howling of dogs greeted them. As they dashed into the light half a dozen men had risen and were facing them, their rifles in the crooks of their arms. From out of the six there strode a tall, thin, smooth-shaven man toward them, and from Jean's lips there fell words which he tried to smother.

"Mother of Heaven, it is Father George, the Missioner from Baldneck!" he gasped.

In another moment the Missioner was wringing the half-breed's mittened hand. He was a man of sixty. His face was of cadaverous thinness, and there was a feverish glow in his eyes.

"Jean Croisset!" he cried. "I was at Ladue's when Pierre came with the word. Is it true? Has the purest soul in all this world been stolen by those Godless men at Thoreau's? I cannot believe it! But if it is so, I have come to fight!"

"It is true, Father," replied Jean. "They have stolen her as the wolves of white men stole Red Fawn from her father's tepee three years ago. And to-morrow -"

"The vengeance of the Lord will descend upon them,"

interrupted the Missioner. "And this, Jean, your friend?"

"Is M'sieur Philip Darcambal, the husband of Josephine," said Jean.

As the Missioner gripped Philip's hand his thin fingers had in them the strength of steel.

"Ladue told me that she had found her man," he said. "May God bless you, my son! It was I, Father George, who baptized her years and years ago. For me she made Adare House a home from the time she was old enough to put her tiny arms about my neck and lisp my name. I was on my way to see you when night overtook me at Ladue's. I am not a fighting man, my son. God does not love their kind. But it was Christ who flung the money-changers from the temple - and so I have come to fight."

The others were close about them now, and Jean was telling of the ambush in the forest. Purple veins grew in the Missioner's forehead as he listened. There were no questions on the lips of the others. With dark, tense faces and eyes that burned with slumbering fires they heard Jean. There were the grim and silent Foutelles, father and son, from the Caribou Swamp. Tall and ghostlike in the firelight, more like spectre than man, was Janesse, a white beard falling almost to his waist, a thick marten skin cap shrouding his head, and armed with a long barrelled smooth-bore that shot powder and ball. From the fox grounds out on the Barren had come "Mad" Joe Horn behind eight huge malemutes that pulled with the strength of oxen. And with the Missioner had come Ladue, the Frenchman, who could send a bullet through the head of a running fox at two hundred yards four times out of five. Kaskisoon and his Crees had not arrived, and Philip knew that Jean was disappointed.

"I heard three days ago of a big caribou herd to the west," said Janesse in answer to the half-breed's inquiry. "It may be they have gone for meat."

They drew close about the fire, and the Foutelles dragged in a fresh birch log for the flames. "Mad" Joe Horn, with hair and beard as red as copper, hummed the Storm Song under his breath. Janesse stood with his back to the heat, facing darkness and the west. He raised a hand, and all listened. For sixty years his world had been bounded by the four walls of the forests. It was said that he could hear the padded footfall of the lynx - and so all listened while the hand was raised, though they heard nothing but the wailing of the wind, the crackling of the fire, and the unrest of the dogs in the timber behind them. For many seconds Janesse did not lower his hand; and then, still unheard by the others, there came slowly out of the gloom a file of dusky-faced, silent, shadowy forms. They were within the circle of light before Jean or his companions had moved, and at their head was Kaskisoon, the Cree: tall, slender as a spruce sapling, and with eyes that went searchingly from face to face with the uneasy glitter of an ermine's. They fell upon Jean, and with a satisfied "Ugh!" and a hunch of his shoulders he turned to his followers. There were seven. Six of them carried rifles. In the hands of the seventh was a shotgun.

After this, one by one, and two by two, there were added others to the circle of waiting men about the fire. By two o'clock there were twenty. They came faster after that. With Bernard, from the south, came Renault, who had gone to the end of his run. From the east, west, and south they continued to come - but from out of the northwest there led no trail. Off there was Thoreau's place. Pack after pack was added to the dogs in the timber. Their voices rose above and drowned all other sound. Teams strained at their leashes to get at the throats of rival teams, and from the black shelter in which they were fastened came a continuous snarling and gnashing of fangs. Over the coals of a smaller fire simmered two huge pots of coffee from which each arrival helped himself; and on long spits over the larger fire were dripping chunks of moose and caribou meat from which they cut off their own helpings.

In the early dawn there were forty who gathered about Father George to listen to the final words he had to say. He raised his hands. Then he bowed his head, and there was a strange silence. Words of prayer fell solemnly from his lips. Partly it was in Cree, partly in French, and when he had finished a deep breath ran through the ranks of those who listened to him. Then he told them, beginning with Cree, in the three languages of the wilderness, that they were to be led that day by Jean Jacques Croisset and Philip Darcambal, the husband of Josephine. Two of the Indians were to remain behind to care for the camp and dogs. Beyond that they needed no instructions.

They were ready, and Jean was about to give the word to start when there was an interruption. Out of the forest and into their midst came a figure - the form of a man who rose above them like a giant, and whose voice as it bellowed Jean's name had in it the wrath of thunder.

It was the master of Adare!

CHAPTER TWENTY-FOUR

For a moment John Adare stood like an avenging demon in the midst of the startled faces of the forest men. His shaggy hair blew out from under his gray lynx cap. His eyes were red and glaring with the lights of the hunting wolf. His deep chest rose and fell in panting breaths. Then he saw Jean and Philip, side by side. Toward them he came, as if to crush them, and Philip sprang toward him, so that he was ahead of Jean. Adare stopped. The wind rattled in his throat.

"And you came WITHOUT ME -"

His voice was a rumble, deep, tense, like the muttering vibration before an explosion. Philip's hands gripped his arms, and those arms were as hard as oak. In one hand Adare held a gun. His other fist was knotted, heavy.

"Yes, Mon Pere, we came without you," said Philip. "It is terrible. We did not want you two to suffer. We did not want you to know until it was all over, and Josephine was back in your arms. We thought it drive her mother mad. And you, Mon Pere, we wanted to save you!"

Adare's face relaxed. His arm dropped. His red eyes shifted to the faces about him, and he said, as he looked:

"It was Breuil. He said you and Josephine were not at his cabin. He came to tell Mignonne the child was so much better. I cornered Metoosin, and he told me. I have been coming fast, running."

He drew in a deep breath. Then suddenly he became like a tiger. He sprang among the men, and threw up his great arms. His voice rose more than human, fierce and savage, above the growing tumult of the dogs and the wailing of the wind.

"Ye are with me, men?"

A rumble of voice answered him.

"Then come!"

He had seen that they were ready, and he strode on ahead of them. He was leader now, and Philip saw Father George close at his side, clutching his arm, talking. In Jean's face there was a great fear. He spoke low to Philip.

"If he meets Lang, if he fights face to face with Thoreau, or if they call upon us to parley, all is lost! M'sieur, for the love of God, hold your fire for those two! We must kill them. If a parley is granted, they will come to us. We will kill them - even as they come toward us with a white flag, if we must!"

"No truce will be granted!" cried Philip.

As if John Adare himself had heard his words, he stopped and faced those behind him. They were in the shelter of the forest. In the gray gloom of dawn they were only a sea of shifting shadows.

"Men, there is to be no mercy this day!" he said, and his voice rumbled like an echo through the aisles of the forest. "We are not on the trail of men, but of beasts and murderers. The Law that is three hundred miles away has let them live in our midst. It has let them kill. It said nothing when they stole Red Fawn from her father's tepee and ravaged her to death. It has said: 'Give us proof that Thoreau killed Reville, and that his wife did not die a natural death.' We are our own law. In these forests we are masters. And yet with this brothel at our doors we are not safe, our wives and daughters are within the reach of monsters. To-day it is my daughter - her husband's wife. To-morrow it may be yours. There can be no mercy. We must kill - kill and burn! Am I right, men?"

This time it was not a murmur but a low thunder of voice that answered. Philip and Jean forged ahead to his side. Shoulder to shoulder they led the way.

From the camp at the Forks it was eighteen miles to the Devil's Nest, where hung on the edge of a chasm the log buildings that sheltered Lang and his crew. To these men of the trails those eighteen miles meant nothing. White-bearded Janesse's trapline was sixty miles long, and he covered it in two days, stripping his pelts as he went. Renault had run sixty miles with his dogs between daybreak and dusk, and "Mad" Joe Horn had come down one hundred and eighty miles from the North in five days. These were not records. They were the average. Those who followed the master of Adare were thin-legged, small-footed, narrow-waisted - but their sinews were like rawhide, and their lungs filled chests that were deep and wide.

With the break of day the wind fell, the sky cleared, and it grew colder. In silence John Adare, Jean, and Philip broke the trail. In silence followed close behind them the Missioner with his smooth-bore. In silence followed the French and half-breeds and Crees. Now and then came the sharp clink of steel as rifle barrel struck rifle barrel. Voices were low, monosyllabic; breaths were deep, the throbbing of hearts like that of engines. Here were friends who were meeting for the first time in months, yet they spoke no word of each other, of the fortunes of the "line," of wives or children. There was but one thought in their brains, pumping the blood through their veins, setting their dark faces in lines of iron, filling their eyes with the feverish fires of excitement. Yet this excitement, the tremendous passion that was working in them, found no vent in wild outcry.

It was like the deadly undertow of the maelstroms in the spring floods. It was there, unseen - silent as death. And this thought, blinding them to all else, insensating them to all emotions but that of vengeance, was thought of Josephine.

John Adare himself seemed possessed of a strange madness. He said no word to Jean or Philip. Hour after hour he strode ahead, until it seemed that tendons must snap and legs give way under the strain. Not once did he stop for rest until, hours later, they reached the summit of a ridge, and he pointed far off into the plain below. They could see the smoke rising up from the Devil's Nest. A breath like a great sigh swept through the band.

And now, silently, there slipped away behind a rock Kaskisoon and his Indians. From under his blanket-coat the chief brought forth the thing that had bulged there, a tom-tom. Philip and the waiting men heard then the low Te-dum - Te-dum - Te-dum of it, as Kaskisoon turned his face first to the east and then the west, north and then south, calling upon Iskootawapoo to come from out of the valley of Silent Men and lead them to triumph. And the waiting men were silent - deadly silent - as they listened. For they knew that the low Te-dum was the call to death. Their hands gripped harder at the barrels of their guns, and when Kaskisoon and his braves came from behind the rock they faced the smoke above the Devil's Nest, wiped their eyes to see more clearly, and followed John Adare down into the plain.

And to other ears than their own the medicine-drum had carried the Song of Death. Down in the thick spruce of the plain a man on the trail of a caribou had heard. He looked up, and on the cap of the ridge he saw. He was old in the ways and the unwritten laws of the North, and like a deer he turned and sped back unseen in the direction of the Devil's Nest. And as the avengers came down into the plain Kaskisoon chanted in a low monotone:

Our fathers - come!

Come from out of the valley.
Guide us - for to-day we fight,
And the winds whisper of death!

And those who heard did not laugh. Father George crossed himself, and muttered something that might have been a prayer. For in this hour Kaskisoon's God was very near.

CHAPTER TWENTY-FIVE

Many years before, Thoreau had named his aerie stronghold the Eagle's Nest. The brown-faced people of the trails had changed it to Devil's Nest. It was not built like the posts, on level ground and easy of access. Its northern wall rose sheer up with the wall of Eagle Chasm, with a torrent two hundred feet below that rumbled and roared like distant thunder when the spring floods came. John Adare knew that this chasm worked its purpose. Somewhere in it were the liquor caches which the police never found when they came that way on their occasional patrols. On the east and south sides of the Nest was an open, rough and rocky, filled with jagged outcrops of boulders and patches of bush; behind it the thick forest grew up to the very walls.

The forest people were three quarters of a mile from this open when they came upon the trail of the lone caribou hunter. Where he had stood and looked up at them the snow was beaten down; from that spot his back-trail began first in a cautious, crouching retreat that changed swiftly into the long running steps of a man in haste. Like a dog, Kaskisoon hovered over the warm trail. His eyes glittered, and he held out his hands, palms downward, and looked at Adare.

"The snow still crumbles in the footmarks," he said in Cree. "They are expecting us."

Adare turned to the men behind him.

"You who have brought axes cut logs with which to batter in the doors," he said. "We will not ask them to surrender. We must make them fight, so that we may have an excuse to kill them. Two logs for eight men each. And you others fill your pockets with birch bark and spruce pitch-knots. Let no man touch fire to a log until we have Josephine. Then, burn! And you, Kaskisoon, go ahead and watch what is happening!"

He was calmer now. As the men turned to obey his commands he laid a hand on Philip's shoulder.

"I told you this was coming, Boy," he said huskily. "But I didn't think it meant HER. My God, if they have harmed her -"

His breath seemed choking him.

"They dare not!" breathed Philip.

John Adare looked into the white fear of the other's face. There was no hiding of it: the same terrible dread that was in his own.

"If they should, we will kill them by inches, Philip!" he whispered. "We will cut them into bits that the moose-birds can carry away. Great God, they shall roast over fires!" He hurried toward the men who were already chopping at spruce timber. Philip looked about for Jean. He had disappeared. A hundred yards ahead of them he had caught up with Kaskisoon, and side by side the Indian and the half-breed were speeding now over the man-trail. Perhaps in the hearts of these two, of all those gathered in this hour of vengeance, there ran deepest the thirst for blood. With Kaskisoon it was the dormant instinct of centuries of forebears, roused now into fierce desire. With Jean it was necessity.

In the face of John Adare's words that there was to be no quarter, Jean still feared the possibility of a parley, a few minutes of truce, the meaning of which sent a shiver to the depths of his soul. He said nothing to the Cree. And Kaskisoon's lips were as silent as the great flakes of snow that began to fall about them now in a mantle so thick that it covered their shoulders in the space of two hundred yards. When the timber thinned out Kaskisoon picked his way with the caution of a lynx. At the edge of the clearing they crouched side by side behind a low windfall, and peered over the top.

Three hundred yards away was the Nest. The man whose trail they had followed had disappeared. And then, suddenly, the door opened, and there poured out a crowd of excited men. The lone hunter was ahead of them, talking and pointing toward the forest. Jean counted - eight, ten, eleven - and his eyes searched for Lang and Thoreau. He cursed the thick snow now. Through it he could not make them out. He had drawn back the hammer of his rifle.

At the click of it Kaskisoon moved. He looked at the half-breed. His breath came in a low monosyllable of understanding. Over the top of the windfall he poked the barrel of his gun. Then he looked again at Jean. And Jean turned. Their eyes met. They were eyes red and narrowed by the beat of storm. Jean Croisset knew what that silence meant. He might have spoken. But no word moved his lips. Unseen, his right hand made a cross over his heart. Deep in his soul he thought a prayer.

Jean looked again at the huddled group about the door. And beside him there was a terrible silence. He held his breath, his heart ceased to beat, and then there came the crashing roar of the Cree's heavy gun, and one of the group staggered out with a shriek and fell face downward in the snow. Even then Jean's finger pressed lightly on the trigger of his rifle as he tried to recognize Lang. Another moment, and half a dozen rifles were blazing in their direction. It was then that he fired. Once, twice - six times, as fast as he could pump the empty cartridges out of his gun and fresh ones into the chamber. With the sixth came again the thunderous roar of the Cree's single-loader.

"Pa, Kaskisoon!" cried Jean then. The last of Thoreau's men had darted back into the house. Three of their number they had carried in their arms. A fourth stumbled and fell across the threshold. "Pa! We have done. Quick - kistayetak!"

He darted back over their trail, followed by the Cree. There would be no truce now! It was WAR. He was glad that he had come with Kaskisoon.

Two hundred yards back in the forest they met Philip and Adare at the head of their people.

"They were coming to ambush us when we entered the clearing!" shouted Jean. "We drove them back. Four fell under our bullets. The place is still full of the devils, M'sieur!"

"It will be impossible to rush the doors," cried Philip, seeing the gathering madness in John Adare's face. "We must fight with caution, Mon Pere! We cannot throw away lives. Divide our men. Let Jean take twelve and you another twelve, and give Kaskisoon his own people. That will leave me ten to batter in the doors. You can cover the windows with your fire while we rush across the open with the one log. There is no need for two."

"Philip is right," added the Missioner in a low voice. "He is right, John. It would be madness to attempt to rush the place in a body."

Adare hesitated for a moment. His clenched hands relaxed.

"Yes, he is right," he said. "Divide the men."

Fifteen minutes later the different divisions of the little army had taken up their positions about the clearing. Philip was in the centre, with eight of the youngest and strongest of the forest men waiting for the signal to dash forward with the log. First, on his right, was Jean and his men, and two hundred yards beyond him the master of Adare, concealed in a clump of thick spruce, Kaskisoon and his braves had taken the windfalls on the left.

As yet not a man had revealed himself to Thoreau and his band. But the dogs had scented them, and they stood watchfully in front of the long log building, barking and whining.

From where he crouched Philip could see five windows. Through these would come the enemy's fire. He waited. It was Jean who was to begin, and draw the first shots. Suddenly the half-breed and his men broke from cover. They were scattered, darting low among the boulders and bush, partly protected and yet visible from the windows.

Philip drew himself head and shoulders over his log as he watched. He forgot himself in this moment when he was looking upon men running into the face of death. In another moment came the crash of rifles muffled behind log walls. He could hear the whine of bullets, the ZIP, ZIP, ZIP of them back in the spruce and cedar.

Another hundred yards beyond Jean, he saw John Adare break from his cover like a great lion, his men spreading out like a pack of wolves. Swiftly Philip turned and looked to the left. Kaskisoon and his braves were advancing upon the Nest with the elusiveness of foxes. At first he could not see them. Then, as Adare's voice boomed over the open, they rose with the suddenness of a flight of partridges, and ran swift-footed straight in the face of the windows. Thus far the game of the attackers had worked without flaw. Thoreau and his men would be forced to divide their fire,

It had taken perhaps three quarters of a minute for the first forward rush of the three parties, and during this time the fire from the windows had concentrated upon Jean and his men. Philip looked toward them again. They were in the open. He caught his breath, stared - and counted eight! Two were missing.

He turned to his own men, crouching and waiting. Eight were ready with the log. Two others were to follow close behind, prepared to take the place of the first who fell. He looked again out into the open field. There came a long clear cry from the half-breed, a shout from Adare, a screaming, animal-like response from Kaskisoon, and at those three signals the forest people fell behind rocks, bits of shrub, and upon their faces. In that same breath the crash of rifles in the open drowned the sound of those beyond the wall of the Nest. From thirty rifles a hail of bullets swept through the windows. This was Philip's cue. He rose with a sharp cry, and behind him came the eight with the battering-ram. It was two hundred yards from their cover to the building. They passed the last shelter, and struck the open on a trot. Now rose from the firing men behind rock and bush a wild and savage cheer. Philip heard John Adare roaring his encouragement. With each shot of the Crees came a piercing yell.

Yard by yard they ran on, the men panting in their excitement. Then came the screech of a bullet, and the shout on Philip's lips froze into silence. At first he thought the bullet had struck. But it had gone a little high. A second - a third - and the biting dust of a shattered rock spat into their faces. With a strange thrill Philip saw that the fire was not coming from the windows. Flashes of smoke came from low under the roof of the building. Thoreau and his men were firing through loopholes! John Adare and Jean saw this, and with loud cries they led their men fairly out into the open in an effort to draw the fire from Philip and the log- bearers. Not a shot was turned in their direction.

A leaden hail enveloped Philip and his little band. One of the log-bearers crumpled down without a moan. Instantly his place was filled. Twenty yards more and a second staggered out from the line, clutched a hand to his breast, and sank into the snow. The last man filled his place. They were only a hundred yards from the door now, but without a rock or a stump between them and death. Another of the log-bearers rolled out from the line, and Philip sprang into the vacancy. A fourth, a fifth - and with a wild cry of horror John Adare called upon Philip to drop the log.

Nothing but the bullets could stop the little band now. Seventy yards! Sixty! Only fifty more - and the man ahead of Philip fell under his feet. The remaining six staggered over him with the log. And now up from behind them came Jean Jacques Croisset and his men, firing blindly at the loopholes, and enveloping the men along the log in those last thirty yards that meant safety from the fire above. And behind him came John Adare, and from the south Kaskisoon and his Crees, a yelling, triumphant horde of avengers now at the very doors of the Devil's Nest!

Philip staggered a step aside, winded, panting, a warm trickle of blood running over his face. He heard the first thunder of the battering-ram against the door, the roaring voice of John Adare, and then a hand like ice smote his heart as he saw Jean huddled up in the snow. In an instant he was on his knees at the half-breed's side. Jean was not dead. But in his eyes was a fading light that struck Philip with terror. A wan smile crept over his lips. With his head in Philip's arm, he whispered:

"M'sieur, I am afraid I am struck through the lung. I do not know, but I am afraid." His voice was strangely steady. But in his eyes was that swiftly fading light! "If should go - you must know," he went on, and Philip bent low to hear his words above the roar of voices and the crashing of the battering-ram. "You must know - to take my place in the fight for Josephine. I think - you have guessed it. The baby was not Josephine's. IT WAS MIRIAM'S!"

"Yes, yes, Jean!" cried Philip into the fading eyes. "That was what I guessed!"

"Don't blame her - too much," struggled Jean. "She went down into a world she didn't know. Lang - trapped her. And Josephine, to save her, to save the baby, to save her father - did as Munito the White Star did to save the Cree god. You know.

You understand. Lang followed - to demand Josephine as the price of her mother. M'sieur, YOU MUST KILL HIM! GO!"

The door had fallen in with a crash, and now over the crime-darkened portals of the Devil's Nest poured the avengers, with John Adare at their head.

"Go!" gasped Jean, almost rising to his knees. "You must meet this Lang before John Adare!"

Philip sprang to his feet. The last of the forest people had poured through the door. Alone he stood - and stared. But not through the door! Two hundred yards away a man was flying along the edge of the forest, and he had come FROM BEHIND THE WALLS OF THE DEVIL'S NEST! He recognized him. It was Lang, the man he was to kill!

CHAPTER TWENTY-SIX

In a moment the flying figure of the Free Trader had disappeared. With a last glance at Jean, who was slowly sinking back into the snow, Philip dashed in pursuit. Where Lang had buried himself in the deeper forest the trees grew so thick that Philip, could not see fifty yards ahead of him. But Lang's trail was distinct - and alone. He was running swiftly. Philip had noticed that Lang had no rifle, He dropped his own now, and drew his pistol. Thus unencumbered he made swifter progress. He had expected to overtake Lang within four or five hundred yards; but minute followed minute in the mad race without another view of his enemy. He heard a few faint shouts back in the direction of the Devil's Nest, the barking of dogs, and half a dozen shots, the sounds growing fainter and fainter. And then Lang's trail led him unexpectedly into one of the foot-beaten aisles of the forest where there were the tracks of a number of men.

At this point the thick spruce formed a roof over-head that had shut out the fresh snow, and Philip lost several minutes before he found the place where Lang had left the trail to bury himself again in the unblazed forest. Half a mile farther he followed the Free Trader's trail without catching a glimpse of the man. He was at least a mile from the Devil's Nest when he heard sounds ahead of him. Beyond a clump of balsam he heard the voices of men, and then the whine of a cuffed dog. Cautiously he picked his way through the thick cover until he crouched close to the edge of a small open. In an instant it seemed as though his heart had leapt from his breast into his throat, and was choking him. Within fifty paces of him were both Lang and Thoreau. But for a moment he scarcely saw them, or the powerful team of eight huskies, harnessed and waiting. For on the sledge, a cloth bound about her mouth, her hands tied behind her, was Josephine!

At sight of her Philip did not pause to plan an attack. The one thought that leapt into his brain like fire was that Lang and Thoreau had fooled the forest people - Josephine had not been taken to the Devil's Nest, and the two were attempting to get away with her.

A cry burst from his lips as he ran from cover. Instantly the pair were facing him. Lang was still panting from his run. He held no weapons. In the crook of Thoreau's arm rested a rifle. Swift as a flash he raised it to his shoulder, the muzzle levelled at Philip's breast. Josephine had turned. From her smothered lips came a choking cry of agony. Philip had now raised his automatic. It was level with his waistline. From that position he had trained himself to fire with the deadly precision that is a part of the training of the men of the Royal Northwest Mounted. Before Thoreau's forefinger had pressed the trigger of his rifle a stream of fire shot out from the muzzle of the automatic.

Thoreau did not move. Then a shudder passed through him. His rifle dropped from his nerveless hands. Without a moan he crumpled down into the snow. Three of the five bullets that had flashed like lightning from the black-muzzled Savage had passed completely through his body. It had all happened in a space so short that Lang had not stirred. Now he found himself looking into that little engine of death. With a cry of fear he staggered back.

Philip did not fire. He felt in himself now the tigerish madness that had been in John Adare. To him Thoreau had been no more than a wolf, one of the many at Devil's Nest. Lang was different. For all things this monster was accountable. He had no desire to shoot. He wanted to reach him with his HANDS

- to choke the life from him slowly, to hear from his own blackening lips the confession that had come through Jean Croisset.

He knew that Josephine was on her feet now, that she was struggling to free her hands, but it was only in a swift glance that he saw this. In the same breath he had dropped his pistol and was at Lang's throat. They went down together. Even Thoreau, a giant in size and strength, would not have been a match for him now. Every animal passion in him was roused to its worst.

Lang's jaws shot apart, his eyes protruded, his tongue came out - the breath rattled in his throat. Then for a moment Philip's death-grip relaxed. He bent down until his lips were close to the death-filled face of his victim.

"The truth, Lang, or I'll kill you!" he whispered hoarsely.

And then he asked the question - and as he asked Josephine freed her hands. She tore the cloth from her mouth, but before she could rush forward, through Lang's mottling lips had come the choking words:

"It was Miriam's."

Again Philip's fingers sank in their death-grip in Lang's throat. Twenty seconds more and he would have fulfilled his pact with Jean. A scream from Josephine turned his eyes for an instant from his victim. Out of that same cover of balsam three men were rushing upon him. A glance told him they were not of the forest people. He had time to gain his feet before they were upon him.

It was a fight for life now, and his one hope lay in the fact that his assailants, escaping from the Nest, did not want to betray themselves by using firearms. The first man at him he struck a terrific blow that sent him reeling. A second caught his arm before he could recover himself - and then it was the hopeless struggle of one against three.

Josephine stood free. She had seen Philip drop his pistol and she sprang to the spot where it had fallen. It was buried under the snow. The four men were on the ground now, Philip under. She heard a gasping sound - and then, far away, something else: a sound that thrilled her, that sent her voice back through the forest in cry after cry.

What she heard was the wailing cry of the dog pack, her pack, following over the trail which her abductors had made in their flight from Adare House! A few steps away she saw a heavy stick in the snow. Fiercely she tore it loose, ran back to the men, and began striking blindly at those who were choking the life from Philip.

Lang had risen to his knees, clutching his throat, and now staggered toward her. She struck at him, and he caught the club. The dogs heard her cries now. Half a mile back in the forest they were coming in a gray, fierce horde. Only Josephine knew, as she struggled with Lang. Under his assailants, Philip's strength was leaving him. Iron fingers gripped at his throat. A flood of fire seemed bursting his head. Josephine's cries were drifting farther and farther away, and his face was as Lang's face had been a few moments before.

Nearer and nearer swept the pack, covering that last half mile with the speed of the wind, the huge yellow form of Hero leading the others by a body's length. They made no sound now. When they shot out of the forest into the little opening they had come so silently that even Lang did not see them. In another moment they were upon him. Josephine staggered back, her eyes big and wild with horror. She saw him go down, and then his shrieks rang out like a madman's. The others were on their feet, and not until she saw Philip lying still and white on the snow did the power of speech return to her lips. She sprang toward the dogs.

"KILL! KILL! KILL!" she cried. "Hero - KILL! NIPA HAO,

boys! Beaver - Wolf - Hero - Captain - KILL - KILL - KILL!"

As her own voice rang out, Lang's screams ceased, and then she saw Philip dragging himself to his knees. At her calls there came a sudden surge in the pack, and those who could not get at Lang leaped upon the remaining three. With a cry Josephine fell upon her knees beside Philip, clasping his head in her arms, holding him in the protection of her own breast as they looked upon the terrible scene.

For a moment more she looked, and then she dropped her face on Philip's shoulder with a ghastly cry. Still partly dazed, Philip stared. Screams such as he had never heard before came from the lips of the dying men. From screams they turned to moaning cries, and then to a horrible silence broken only by the snarling grind of the maddened dogs.

Strength returned to Philip quickly. He felt Josephine limp and lifeless in his arms, and with an effort he staggered to his feet, half carrying her. A few yards away was a small tepee in which Lang had kept her. He partly carried, partly dragged her to this, and then he returned to the dogs.

Vainly he called upon them to leave their victims. He was seeking for a club when through the balsam thicket burst John Adare and Father George at the head of a dozen men. In response to Adare's roaring voice the pack slunk off. The beaten snow was crimson. Even Adare, as he faced Philip, could find no words in his horror. Philip pointed to the tepee.

"Josephine - is there - safe," he gasped. As Adare rushed into the tepee Philip swayed up to Father George.

"I am dizzy - faint," he said. "Help me - "

He went to Lang and dropped upon his knees beside him. The man was unrecognizable. His head was almost gone. Philip thrust a hand inside his fang-torn coat - and pulled out a long envelope. It was addressed to the master of Adare. He staggered to his feet, and went to Thoreau. In his pocket he found the second envelope. Father George was close beside him as he thrust the two in his own pocket. He turned to the forest men, who stood like figures turned to stone, gazing upon the scene of the tragedy.

"Carry them - out there," said Philip, pointing into the forest. "And then - cover the blood with fresh snow."

He still clung to Father George's arm as he staggered toward a near birch.

"I feel weak - dizzy," he repeated again. "Help me - pull off some bark."

A strange, inquiring look filled the Missioner's face as he tore down a handful of bark, and at Philip's request lighted a match. In an instant the bark was a mass of flame. Into the fire he put the letters.

"It is best - to burn their letters," he said. Beyond this he gave no explanation. And Father George asked no questions.

They followed Adare into the tepee. Josephine was sobbing in her father's arms. John Adare's face was that of a man who had risen out of black despair into day.

"Thank God she has not been harmed," he said.

Philip knelt beside them, and John Adare gave Josephine into his arms. He held her close to his breast, whispering only her name - and her arms crept up about him. Adare rose and stood beside Father George.

"I will go back and attend to the wounded, Philip," he said. "Jean is one of those hurt. It isn't fatal."

He went out. Father George was about to follow when Philip motioned him back.

"Will you wait outside for a few minutes?" he asked in a low voice. "We shall need you - alone - Josephine and I."

And now when they were gone, he raised Josephine's face, and said:

"They are all gone, Josephine - Lang, Thoreau, AND THE LETTERS. Lang and Thoreau are dead, and I have burned the letters. Jean was shot. He thought he was dying, and he told me the truth that I might better protect you. Sweetheart, there is nothing more for me to know. The fight is done. And Father George is waiting - out there - to make us man and wife. No one will ever know but ourselves - and Jean. I will tell Father George that it has been your desire to have a SECOND marriage ceremony performed by him; that we want our marriage to be consecrated by a minister of the forests. Are you ready, dear? Shall I call him in?"

For a full minute she gazed steadily into his eyes, and Philip did not break the wonderful silence. And then, with a deep sigh, her head drooped to his breast. After a moment he heard her whisper:

"You may call him in, Philip. I guess - I've got to be - your wife."

And as the logs of the Devil's Nest sent up a pall of smoke that rose to the skies, Metoosin crouched shiveringly far back in the gloom of the pit, wondering if the dogs he had loosed had come to the end of the trail.

Choose from Thousands of 1stWorldLibrary Classics By

A. M. Barnard	Charles Dudley Warner	Enilor Macartney Lane
Ada Leverson	Charles Farrar Browne	Erasmus W. Jones
Adolphus William Ward	Charles Ives	Ernie Howard Pie
Aesop	Charles Kingsley	Ethel Turner
Agatha Christie	Charles Klein	Ethel Watts Mumford
Alexander Aaronsohn	Charles Amory Beach	Eugenie Foa
Alexander Kielland	Charles Hanson Towne	Eugene Wood
Alexandre Dumas	Charles Lathrop Pack	Eustace Hale Ball
Alfred Gatty	Charles Whibley	Evelyn Everett-green
Alfred Ollivant	Charles Willing Beale	Everard Cotes
Alice Duer Miller	Charlotte M. Braeme	F. H. Cheley
Alice Turner Curtis	Charlotte M. Yonge	F. J. Cross
Alice Dunbar	Charlotte Perkins Stetson	Federick Austin Ogg
Ambrose Bierce	Clair W. Hayes	Ferdinand Ossendowski
Amelia E. Barr	Clarence Day Jr.	Francis Bacon
Amory H. Bradford	Clarence E. Mulford	Francis Darwin
Andrew Lang	Clemence Housman	Frances Hodgson Burnett
Andrew McFarland Davis	Confucius	Frances Parkinson Keyes
Andy Adams	Cornelis DeWitt Wilcox	Frank Gee Patchin
Anna Sewell	Cyril Burleigh	Frank Harris
Annie Besant	D. H. Lawrence	Frank Jewett Mather
Annie Hamilton Donnell	Daniel Defoe	Frank L. Packard
Annie Payson Call	David Garnett	Frank V. Webster
Annonaymous	Dinah Craik	Frederic Stewart Isham
Anton Chekhov	Don Carlos Janes	Frederick Trevor Hill
Arnold Bennett	Donald Keyhoe	Frederick Winslow Taylor
Arthur Conan Doyle	Dorothy Kilner	Friedrich Kerst
Arthur M. Winfield	Dougan Clark	Friedrich Nietzsche
Arthur Ransome	Douglas Fairbanks	Fyodor Dostoyevsky
Atticus	E. Nesbit	G.A. Henty
B.H. Baden-Powell	E.P.Roe	G.K. Chesterton
B. M. Bower	E. Phillips Oppenheim	Gabrielle E. Jackson
Baroness Emmuska Orczy	Earl Barnes	Garrett P. Serviss
Baroness Orczy	Edgar Rice Burroughs	Gaston Leroux
Basil King	Edith Van Dyne	George A. Warren
Bayard Taylor	Edith Wharton	George Ade
Ben Macomber	Edward J. O'Biren	Geroge Bernard Shaw
Bertha Muzzy Bower	Edward S. Ellis	George Durston
Bjornstjerne Bjornson	Edwin L. Arnold	George Ebers
Booth Tarkington	Eleanor Atkins	George Eliot
Boyd Cable	Eliot Gregory	George Gissing
Bram Stoker	Elizabeth Gaskell	George MacDonald
C. Collodi	Elizabeth McCracken	George Meredith
C. E. Orr	Elizabeth Von Arnim	George Orwell
C. M. Ingleby	Ellem Key	George Sylvester Viereck
Carolyn Wells	Emerson Hough	George Tucker
Catherine Parr Traill	Emilie F. Carlen	George W. Cable
Charles A. Eastman	Emily Dickinson	George Wharton James
Charles Dickens	Enid Bagnold	Gertrude Atherton

Grace E. King
Grace Gallatin
Grant Allen
Guillermo A. Sherwell
Gulielma Zollinger
Gustav Flaubert
H. A. Cody
H. B. Irving
H.C. Bailey
H. G. Wells
H. H. Munro
H. Irving Hancock
H. Rider Haggard
H. W. C. Davis
Hamilton Wright Mabie
Hans Christian Andersen
Harold Avery
Harold McGrath
Harriet Beecher Stowe
Harry Houidini
Helent Hunt Jackson
Helen Nicolay
Hendrik Conscience
Hendy David Thoreau
Henri Barbusse
Henrik Ibsen
Henry Adams
Henry Ford
Henry Frost
Henry James
Henry Jones Ford
Henry Seton Merriman
Henry W Longfellow
Herbert A. Giles
Herbert N. Casson
Herman Hesse
Homer
Honore De Balzac
Horace Walpole
Horatio Alger Jr.
Howard Pyle
Howard R. Garis
Hugh Lofting
Hugh Walpole
Humphry Ward
Ian Maclaren
Inez Haynes Gillmore
Irving Bacheller
Israel Abrahams
Ivan Turgenev
J.G.Austin

J. Henri Fabre
J. M. Barrie
J. Macdonald Oxley
J. S. Fletcher
J. S. Knowles
J. Storer Clouston
Jack London
Jacob Abbott
James Allen
James Andrews
James Baldwin
James DeMille
James Joyce
James Lane Allen
James Lane Allen
James Oliver Curwood
James Oppenheim
James Otis
James R. Driscoll
Jane Austen
Janet Aldridge
Jens Peter Jacobsen
Jerome K. Jerome
John Burroughs
John Cournos
John F. Kennedy
John Gay
John Glasworthy
John Habberton
John Joy Bell
John Kendrick Bangs
John Milton
John Philip Sousa
Jonas Lauritz Idemil Lie
Jonathan Swift
Joseph A. Altsheler
Joseph Carey
Joseph Conrad
Joseph E. Badger Jr
Joseph Hergesheimer
Joseph Jacobs
Jules Vernes
Julian Hawthrone
Julie A Lippmann
Justin Huntly McCarthy
Kakuzo Okakura
Kenneth Grahame
Kenneth McGaffey
Kate Langley Bosher
Kate Langley Bosher
Katherine Cecil Thurston

Katherine Stokes
L. A. Abbot
L. T. Meade
L. Frank Baum
Latta Griswold
Laura Lee Hope
Laurence Housman
Lawrence Beasley
Leo Tolstoy
Leonid Andreyev
Lewis Carroll
Lewis Sperry Chafer
Lilian Bell
Lloyd Osbourne
Louis Hughes
Louis Tracy
Louisa May Alcott
Lucy Fitch Perkins
Lucy Maud Montgomery
Lydia Miller Middleton
Lyndon Orr
M. Corvus
M. H. Adams
Margaret E. Sangster
Margaret Vandercook
Margret Penrose
Maria Edgeworth
Maria Thompson Daviess
Mariano Azuela
Marion Polk Angellotti
Mark Overton
Mark Twain
Mary Austin
Mary Catherine Crowley
Mary Cole
Mary Hastings Bradley
Mary Roberts Rinehart
Mary Rowlandson
M. Wollstonecraft Shelley
Maud Lindsay
Max Beerbohm
Myra Kelly
Nathaniel Hawthrone
Nicolo Machiavelli
O. F. Walton
Oscar Wilde
Owen Johnson
P.G. Wodehouse
Paul and Mabel Thorne
Paul G. Tomlinson
Paul Severing

Percy Brebner
Peter B. Kyne
Plato
R. Derby Holmes
R. L. Stevenson
R. S. Ball
Rabindranath Tagore
Rahul Alvares
Ralph Bonehill
Ralph Henry Barbour
Ralph Victor
Ralph Waldo Emmerson
Rene Descartes
Rex Beach
Rex E. Beach
Richard Harding Davis
Richard Jefferies
Richard Le Gallienne
Robert Barr
Robert Frost
Robert Gordon Anderson
Robert L. Drake
Robert Lansing
Robert Lynd
Robert Michael Ballantyne
Robert W. Chambers
Rosa Nouchette Carey
Rudyard Kipling
Samuel B. Allison

Samuel Hopkins Adams
Sarah Bernhardt
Sarah C. Hallowell
Selma Lagerlof
Sherwood Anderson
Sigmund Freud
Standish O'Grady
Stanley Weyman
Stella Benson
Stephen Crane
Stewart Edward White
Stijn Streuvels
Swami Abhedananda
Swami Parmananda
T. S. Ackland
T. S. Arthur
The Princess Der Ling
Thomas A. Janvier
Thomas A Kempis
Thomas Anderton
Thomas Bailey Aldrich
Thomas Bulfinch
Thomas De Quincey
Thomas H. Huxley
Thomas Hardy
Thomas More
Thornton W. Burgess
U. S. Grant
Valentine Williams

Various Authors
Vaughan Kester
Victor Appleton
Virginia Woolf
Walter Camp
Walter Scott
Washington Irving
Wilbur Lawton
Wilkie Collins
Willa Cather
Willard F. Baker
William Dean Howells
William le Queux
W. Makepeace Thackeray
William W. Walter
Winston Churchill
Yei Theodora Ozaki
Yogi Ramacharaka
Young E. Allison
Zane Grey

www.ingramcontent.com/pod-product-compliance
Lightning Source LLC
Chambersburg PA
CBHW050035180626
46810CB00002B/725